RED
FLAGS

ALSO BY JN WELSH

Passion Players Series

Open Play

Red Flags

Back on Top Series by JN Welsh and Carina Press

In Tune

In Rhythm

In Harmony

Holiday Novellas

Pining Over You

Gigolo All the Way

Sea Breeze Seduction Series

Before We Say Goodbye

Stand-Alones

The Letter

RED
FLAGS

JN WELSH

 Montlake

Published by Montlake, Seattle

www.apub.com

Amazon, the Amazon logo, and Montlake are trademarks of Amazon.com, Inc., or its affiliates.

ISBN-13: 9781542034913 (paperback)
ISBN-13: 9781542034906 (digital)

Cover design by Eileen Carey
Cover photography by Wander Aguiar Photography
Cover images: © Photography-by-Stretch / Shutterstock;
© SOMKKU / Shutterstock

Printed in the United States of America

For anyone who knows how hard it is to fill hundreds of blank pages, one word at a time, and to everyone who reads them. To those who, despite the current times, still believe in love (in all its shapes and sizes) and the goodness of people. Lastly, to me, because I wrote this shiny little gem. ☺

Prologue

An award ceremony and dinner gala were the pick-me-up that Charlotte Bowman needed. Her best friend, Ayanna Crawford, was receiving a Kellinger Physical Therapy Award for her advances in physical therapy rehabilitation, and Charlotte's pride bubbled in her chest. She slid into her shouldered silver midi dress. Ayanna was Charlotte's four-leaf clover. Charlotte had been lucky to have found her in middle school because, over their decades together, they had been there for each other in ways that only true and genuine family could be. Charlotte clung to her one-of-a-kind friendship with Ayanna as a precious gift that she nourished with girls' nights, shopping outings, and loads of laughter. She'd also rabidly protected that friendship emotionally when Ayanna's father had been killed in a car accident, leaving two daughters under the care of their devastated mother. Seeing Ayanna shine made Charlotte believe not only in growth and change but in the fulfillment of one's dreams and destiny. Charlotte wanted some of that.

She sank onto the bed and pointed her feet into the strappy silver heels. The start of fall remained summerlike, with just a touch of chill in the air, and Charlotte took advantage of the weather to get in her last coat-free outfits. She stood and checked her reflection and was satisfied with the level of sexy she gave with one bare and toned arm. Her big, glistening, natural black Afro crowned her head as it always did. The heels boosted the roundness of her ass, and her D cups didn't need any help in the formfitting dress. A dark-haired Irishman popped into her head, and though she'd sworn off him, she couldn't get past the desire to know what he'd think of her when she walked into the hall in her outfit.

Eoghan O'Farrell.

Charlotte had seen the broken man transform through his rehabilitation with Ayanna to be once again the sexy womanizer Charlotte had read about online. He'd pursued Ayanna first, then Jada, Ayanna's sister. When he'd approached Charlotte at the pool a month ago, she'd hated that she'd been third in his line of pursuits, even though he'd never really met her properly or spent time with her. Still, her sharp tongue had made it clear that she expected the crème de la crème and that Eoghan neither could handle nor deserved her.

Charlotte grabbed her silver-studded clutch and a light black shawl. "His loss."

Her phone pinged, notifying her that her Lyft would be arriving in five minutes, so she made her way downstairs. Moments later she folded herself into the back seat of the car and headed to Midtown Manhattan. After tonight so many things were going to change. Ayanna was moving to Ireland part-time to be with her new boo while still traveling for her research as a physical therapist.

"What am I going to do without you here, Yaya?" she asked, mumbling to herself. Her heart hurt at the thought of being without her bestie.

Career-wise, Seam and Sole, her brand-apparel-and-footwear company, raced toward the fourth quarter. Her small but successful business had won over influencers and celebrities who wore her sportswear and some of the fashion she'd developed. Nothing, however, could beat the Heaven Heels she'd created. That shoe alone kept her company in the black and growing into other footwear using the technology Charlotte had crafted with her own hands. Her investors might have been cranky about the financials, but they couldn't deny the success. She had hopes for the new year and the new opportunities to come.

"Thank you," Charlotte said to her driver and entered the building. An attendant greeted her, then led her to a table with familiar faces, including Eoghan's sinfully gorgeous features. His tall, athletic form filled a tailored Armani suit in plum. He cleaned up too well, muting all her previous warnings about him.

Solomon, Ayanna's colleague at the institute, saw her first and rose to greet her. "Charlotte," he said, circling the round table. He clasped her shoulders and kissed her cheek. "You look lovely. Nice to see you."

Charlotte felt Eoghan's gaze from behind Solomon. "Thank you. It's always a pleasure to see you. Chloe is here too. Yaya will be so happy that you both made it," Charlotte said of Ayanna's assistant, who excitedly waved at her. Charlotte and Solomon went over to Chloe's chair, and Charlotte dipped her head down to kiss her cheek from behind. "How are you? I heard you dropped a whole human since I last saw you at the office." Charlotte stretched her hand out on Chloe's belly.

"I did. Thank you for the lovely care package you sent. I needed and used every single thing. You're sure you're not hiding your own kid? You know the needs of a mother and child."

"Just experience loving on the babies and taking care of my cousins' and friends' kids. I'm glad you're enjoying it."

"Hey, boo." Jada, Ayanna's sister, wowed in a gorgeous red mermaid gown that hugged every inch of her.

"This is perfect for you." Charlotte laughed at her little sister by another mother.

"I underwhelm in red while you are killing it in this silver ensemble. Who are you trying to catch tonight?"

"Hush," Charlotte said and then gave her attention to Ayanna's mother. "Hi, Mama Morgan."

Morgan Crawford stood to give Charlotte one of those hugs that only mothers could deliver.

"You look lovely, sweetheart. Ayanna is going to be so happy to see us all here," Morgan said.

"I'm so proud of her. This is such a big deal. Everything is going so well for her. I hope she's happy," Charlotte said.

"Charlotte," Eoghan said. Just his saying her name caused goose bumps to flare on her naked arm.

"Hey, Eoghan. How are you?" Her militant greeting was all sharp edges and boxes to keep whatever sparked between them, every time they met, contained. It must have shown on her face, because Morgan side-eyed Eoghan and then glanced back to Charlotte.

"Better now that you've arrived." His eyes appraised her from head to toe, covering her with a blanket of heat as he pulled out a chair for her next to him. She swallowed, highly frustrated with the betrayal of her body and thoughts. *We had this conversation, body. Eoghan is a no-no. Why are you doing this to me?*

Not one to make a scene on top of her weary resistance, she sat down. After sliding the chair under her, he patted her bare shoulder, and in order not to be a puddle in her seat, she erected her spine painfully straight.

"So you should be ready to get out of here soon?" she said.

"Two weeks." He confirmed the time she had left to keep her shields up.

"Are you looking forward to being home again and playing ball?"

"In a way, yes. There's still so much I haven't done here." His tongue touched the center of his upper lip as his brown eyes penetrated her so deeply she wondered if he'd seen her soul. She couldn't mistake his meaning, but she still had some strands of willpower left to deny him. All she had to do was look across the table at Jada for a splash of cold water to the face.

"I thought you'd be trying to reconnect with Jada." Charlotte couldn't resist reminding Eoghan that he'd pursued Ayanna and her younger sister before he'd directed his attentions to her.

"I told you, that day at the pool she kissed me. She just wanted to get back at Ayanna. We're all buds now," he said.

"Look, I know you think you want me, but you're out of your league. I'm known for chewing them up and spitting them out."

"I don't mind being chewed up and spat out." He charmed her with a half smile and low-lidded gaze. "Maybe it's you who can't handle me. Maybe you're scared you'll fall for me or something silly like that."

Charlotte laughed out loud, drawing glances. She pointed at Eoghan. "He's funny."

Eoghan's knee touched hers under the table, quieting her. "Laugh all you want, lass, but I know you're curious. Be a shame to miss an opportunity to try out the hardware," Eoghan said and smoothed his hand over the front of his suit.

"You drive a hard bargain, O'Farrell, but one thing you forget is that I'm not so easily swayed." She talked a good game, but as the notes of mint from his cologne mixed with his warmth, he wore her down. She'd never been so easily courted or whatever Eoghan thought he was doing. She'd had men approach her with much better game than him, but that adorable smile and dark hair that longed for her fingers to rake through it continually made her question *what if.* She was seconds away from dragging him by his gray tie to a bathroom stall and tossing away all her anti-Eoghan sentiments.

The guest of honor finally arrived. "There they are." Charlotte leaped out of her seat, her body cranked with tension that Eoghan had created. She hurried to Ayanna, who was walking in with Shane. Charlotte hugged her friend.

Ayanna pulled away from her. "You okay? You're mad tense."

Charlotte moistened her parched mouth. "I'm good," she assured her—unconvincingly, according to Ayanna's knit brows.

Charlotte witnessed her bestie scan the table of her friends and colleagues, her eyes lingering on Eoghan, and then look back at Charlotte.

"You're sure?" Ayanna asked.

5

"Yeah," Charlotte said. "Hey, Shane."

"How's it going, Charlotte?"

"You know, stirring up my usual trouble," Charlotte said and hugged the red-haired Irishman.

Shane laughed. "Just keep it legal."

Charlotte wobbled her hand from side to side. "Fifty-fifty chance of that." She added to Ayanna, "You look the fiercest tonight. Definitely best-dressed list." Charlotte pointed to the daring split on the black dress that cut close to Ayanna's hip, yet the rest of the garment covered Ayanna with a one-shouldered, asymmetrical top. "Thanks for inviting me to this shindig."

"You know you're always the first on the list," Ayanna said.

"I thought I was," Jada said.

"You both are," Ayanna said.

Ayanna's mother tentatively approached them. Ayanna and her mother had been through tough times that had destroyed their mother-daughter dynamic but now were finally reconnecting after decades of distance.

Eoghan came over to greet Shane, his phone ready to snap a photo. "Yer ma'd love to see you in this suit." He snapped a picture of the group. Charlotte, Jada, Morgan, Ayanna, and Shane all cheesed. "Now just you two," he said.

Charlotte had never thought of Eoghan as sentimental, but as small a thing as taking a picture of his best friend and his new girlfriend for Shane's mother tickled a valve in her heart, and she smiled.

After introducing Shane to everyone, Ayanna said, "Thank you all for coming. You don't know how happy it makes me to have you all here to celebrate this moment. I wouldn't be here if it wasn't for each and every one of you, and that's the truth." She choked on her words.

"You ready for this?" Shane asked.

Ayanna nodded.

Charlotte watched through blurry vision as Shane led Ayanna to her seat. Charlotte sat back down and wiped a tear that almost ruined her makeup.

"You all right then?" Eoghan asked as he covered her hand with his.

Charlotte coughed from the shock of Eoghan's touch as she swallowed her emotions.

"Mm-hmm," was all she could manage. "Thank you." She pulled her hand from his grasp even though it was the last thing she wanted to do.

The award ceremony commenced, and Charlotte snapped more photos than she had gigabytes for and cheered the loudest. Watching Shane support her friend, hugging and kissing her, filled Charlotte with inconceivable joy, and for a moment a piece of her longed to know how that felt. Then she remembered that her business and all the opportunities she had been able to take advantage of had been because she didn't have a relationship. She swatted away the annoying feelings and remembered that she was successful and had so much left still to do.

During the dinner portion she chatted with everyone at the table. Eoghan stayed close as she networked, which she found less annoying than she would have thought.

"You're good at talking to people," Eoghan noted.

"I have to be. You only get one chance to make a first impression, and I always want mine to be meaningful."

"What did you think when you first met me?"

"That you were nothing like the athlete I saw online," she said.

A touch of sadness displayed on his face. "I was different then." Eoghan popped another one of her heart valves open.

"You were going through a tough time. It's understandable. You thought your world was over. That couldn't have been easy."

"No, but I made it back with Ayanna's and Shane's help. Now I'm ripe for the pickin'."

Charlotte laughed again, a common thing when she spoke to him. "I see."

"I have two weeks left here, Charlotte, so I'm going for it," he said. "You're absolutely gorgeous, and I've not been able to keep my eyes off you."

"Eoghan," she said, not much louder than a whisper.

"Do you want to get out of here?" Eoghan asked. "This party is winding down, and I'm thinking maybe we can make our own after-hours fun. What do you think?"

Charlotte weighed the options. Eoghan would no doubt be a tasty snack, plus he'd be gone in two weeks, leaving her with little cleanup or fear of seeing him again. She saw their evening going swimmingly and at the end everything being tied up with a nice big red bow.

"I think you should get my shawl."

Charlotte Bowman tiptoed to the bathroom down the hall from Eoghan's room in Purchase House in Purchase, New York. The mansion turned rehabilitation facility had all the amenities of both. Charlotte had never thought she'd hook up with Eoghan, much less spend the night with him.

I have gots to get out of here.

In the mirror, she tried to fluff her mashed-up Afro. Her face, reflected back at her, had an afterglow that she couldn't wash off if she tried. This wasn't the worst situation she could have found herself in, but it was pretty bad. Had her best friend, Ayanna, been at Purchase House instead of at her apartment with her boo, then maybe Charlotte wouldn't have ended up here. Not that she didn't enjoy her share of hookups, but Eoghan had been off limits. Once she made a decision, she usually kept to it, yet here she was in postsexual bliss. She returned from the bathroom, gathered her things, and was about to creep out of his bedroom.

"Sneaking off, are you?" Eoghan tossed in bed, too beautiful to be ignored, his dark hair wild against the white pillow. He scratched the five-o'clock shadow on his face, which had been clean shaven last night.

Her hand instinctively went to her crotch. *Easy, girl.* If she weren't careful, she'd spend another several hours tussling with him between the sheets. She needed to go. "I have to go to work." The statement wasn't a complete lie. She did need to tinker with the prototype for the cleats she'd been developing for three years. Her best friend had told her that the design was innovative, smart, and customizable over a year ago, but Charlotte needed it to be perfect. With Seam and Sole, her brand-apparel-and-footwear company, growing slowly but steadily, she spent the weekends working on her passion project.

Eoghan slid out of bed, the deliciously creamy tone of his naked limbs fairer as compared to the heavy, slightly darker muscle between his legs. The Celtic tribal tattoo on his forearm was a focal art piece amid the light tone of skin and fabric surrounding him. The almost black hair surrounding his cock was an exact match to the loosely curled strands on his head. "Stay for a ride," he asked more than stated, approaching her.

Easy for him to say. He wasn't the one who'd landed in bed with someone who'd twice passed him over as a potential anything, like he'd done to her.

"I had fun. Thanks," she said. Charlotte clipped his chin with her index finger. His transformation from the first time she'd met him—when his overgrown facial hair had hidden his features and he'd smelled like he hadn't bathed in days, not to mention his horrible attitude—had clarified just how Ayanna had taken interest in him before his soccer injury. In two weeks, he'd head back to Ireland, and Charlotte couldn't be more relieved.

"You're sure? You won't get any more of this once I leave." His statement spoke to his messiness and his ego.

She felt one side of her lips curl into a half smile. "Very sure."

He reddened, and Charlotte was sure he thought that she was like all the other women he'd cataloged by hair color, boob size, sophistication, and looseness. She was not. She was the one who did the cataloging, and by next Tuesday, she'd be lying under another fuckboy because she needed her medicine. Eoghan O'Farrell would be a distant memory.

"So long, then, Charlotte. It's been a pleasure," he said.

"Take care, Eoghan, and have a safe trip back to Ireland." She closed the door to his room and floated down the grand staircase and past the kitchen, where she snagged a Honeycrisp apple and bit into its seasonal sweetness. She opened the house door and hesitated for a second before forcing herself to move forward. She shut the door behind her and on this episode with Eoghan.

Eoghan O'Farrell was turning over a new leaf. However, he'd never thought that he'd be so unlucky as to live in a house with Ayanna Crawford, his physical therapist, who he'd met and dated in Ireland, and not get her back into bed with him. Not to mention the disastrous visit four months ago by Ayanna's sister, Jada, who he'd been sure would end his sex drought. His ACL injury had destroyed not only his leg but apparently his mojo as well. But when he and Ayanna's best friend, Charlotte, had ended up in bed, he'd felt sure that the third time was the charm. He'd only wanted a ride, but when she'd moved against him and moaned how big and good his dick felt inside her, as well as some other lines in his ear that had driven him mad, he couldn't resist her. He'd been more than happy to keep the rounds coming, like he did drinking ale on a night out on the lash back in Ireland.

When Charlotte had ended the party an hour ago with, "I had fun. Thanks," she'd sounded just like he did when picking up a fine lass and taking her on the back seat in his car or in the back of the bar or going back to her apartment so he could make a quick exit afterward. Now here he was on the other end, wanting more and being not too gently turned down.

Thank goodness he was heading back to Ireland soon, where he'd be able to get his dick back into the full swing of things. Problem was, Charlotte wasn't so easily forgotten. Now that he'd had her, he wanted more, but she'd be in Harlem, New York, and he in Dublin, Ireland. He had more than enough on his plate without pining over a ride he'd had with a woman a plane ride away.

Fourteen days later, in his room at Purchase House, he packed his final belongings for the trip back home. Louisa, their house manager, who'd given him and his friend Shane a piece of home while they'd stayed here for his rehabilitation, met him by the stairway.

"You're off, then?" Louisa asked him as he dropped the last of his luggage at the main entrance.

"All set to be off," he said.

"I'll miss you, pet, but glad you're getting on well."

"Same here," he said. Louisa had fed him well and managed a full staff to make sure his clothes and environment were clean. If he'd needed anything to help him get well and be comfortable, she and Ayanna, his physio, had made it happen.

Louisa kissed his cheek and gave him a brief hug. "I'll be watching the games, so don't muck about. Win."

Surprised by the emotion in his chest, he felt his smile waver. "Will do, Louisa. Thanks again. For everything."

Two hours later he was buckled into a plush cream-colored seat on a private plane with matching interior.

"All set, Mr. O'Farrell?" an attendant said.

"Yes, thanks."

The attendant placed an ale can and glass on the tray before him.

"Good man," Eoghan said and settled into the overstuffed cushioning for the six-and-a-half-hour flight back to Ireland.

He'd almost forgotten what his flat looked like and missed the smells of his country, from the firing peat coming from the chimneys to the hops from the Guinness Storehouse at Saint James's Gate and even the stale seaweed smell from the muck spreader as he drove the countryside.

He looked forward to food from his ma and pints from the Paddy Bath. America, with the exception of him striking out in some way with three women he'd been attracted to, had been good to him. The journey back from his injury had been interesting, between clawing his way out of a dark place after thinking he might never play football again to touring the city in a way he hadn't done before. Ayanna had brought him back and ready to play, yet he still worried about how this next phase would play out. Training would kick things up in intensity and kick his arse for sure. If his leg gave out, how would he explain that?

Had he passed his back-to-play evaluation simply by grace? Was he really healed? The clearance allowed him to train with the lads, get himself stronger, and increase his endurance for professional play. Perhaps with his focus once again on the game, his confidence might also show up. He'd never say those feelings out loud or share that with anyone, especially his father, who'd tell him to stop being weak minded and ordinary. That he was too talented and had been paid too much to have doubts. His father'd ordered him to go out there and win games like he'd taught him to and sacrificed his life for. No, Eoghan decided. He'd never show that weakness.

He'd nearly fucked up when he had opened up about his doubts to Ayanna, but what he'd expressed to her only scratched the surface. Ayanna had given him the all clear for his injury. The rest he had to figure out himself. Soon he'd be training with his team to get back to playing on the pitch. That would have to be enough.

Chapter 1

Being robbed at gunpoint can really change the perspective of a bitch.

New York hadn't been the same since Charlotte had been mugged at gunpoint during the summer. She worked up the courage every day to open her apartment door and get outside her building. Strolling through the neighborhood, she'd always loved to patronize the shops and chop it up with people in the community, but ever since that fateful night when she'd spent hours at the police station, giving details about her assailant, her routine felt off and more like a chore. Charlotte shivered even though her winter white wool coat kept her warm. That night, she'd been so freaked out that she'd had to call her best friend, Ayanna, to pick her up from the station. Ayanna had been her anchor. Now that Ayanna seemed to only visit the States, between her work and her new relationship with Shane, Charlotte was lost without their easy chats over four-hour meals, shopping adventures, and barrels of laughter.

Luckily for Charlotte, the fall season had brought with it an opportunity for her to take the occasional drive up north to see the spectacular event of the changing leaves. The amber-and-cranberry canvas of late November was a gorgeous distraction even if none of it made her current situation an easier pill to swallow. The holidays were here, and so was the end of the financial year for Seam and Sole. Fourth quarter was always a bitch to wrap up, but this year was proving to test her in a special way. Instead of shopping on Black Friday and Cyber Monday,

Charlotte pored over documents for an important investor meeting for her sports-brand-apparel-and-footwear company.

In her home office, Charlotte logged into the virtual meeting she had scheduled with Ken and Victor, her investors for the past six years. After they began their discussion, it didn't take long for them to aim at what they thought was wrong with her company.

"It's not that we don't believe in you, Charlotte," Ken said. "It's just that we expected a higher return on investment at this point, especially based on the great exposure and reviews for all your products. We're just concerned that marketing dollars aren't being spent well and that maybe you need another employee to help streamline your business functions."

"Great exposure and reviews are what help drive sales. We're still a small company, and I'd be surprised if you found a better streamliner than Danai." Charlotte spoke of her Renaissance assistant. "I don't think that hiring anyone at this point is the solution. Seam and Sole is profitable. Year over year we hit our targets, and our trajectory is still moving in the right direction," she said, crossing her legs and straightening her pleated white winter slacks. The thick gray cable-knit turtleneck she wore did little to protect her from the chill coming from her investors.

"Yes, but they're mediocre targets," Victor said. "We'd just like to see the company do more. Enlist more celebrities for the apparel promotions. Get your shoe campaigns on major networks and sport events."

"I've done that, but those take marketing dollars that we don't currently have in our budget."

"If you want to move from a boutique sports shop, then you have to take more risks," Ken, her other investor, added.

"Risks?" Charlotte questioned. She was the queen of risk. She put everything into her company and even sacrificed her personal life, doing things like bailing on a girls' trip earlier in the year with her best friend to Ireland, to be here for Seam and Sole. She didn't dignify either Ken's or Victor's comments with further explanation.

"Thank you. I'll take all this into consideration." Sometimes she wished she could just start over without investors telling her what to do and could make her choices based on what she alone thought was best. But running a business in the big city required money, and having investors had its benefits. Still, going it alone again would give her the control she was desperate for. And what the hell did Ken mean by "boutique sports shop"? What was wrong with that anyway? Seam and Sole was an international brand for sports apparel and shoes. So she asked Ken to explain his meaning.

"I just mean that Seam and Sole can really compete if given the opportunity. Even if it gets a quarter share of the market the big companies have, it would be exponentially more successful monetarily," Ken said.

"Of course, and that's where my business plans have us heading." Charlotte pointed down to the presentation spreadsheets before her.

"Yes, but we'd like to see that happen in half the time if you want us to continue to be your investors. If not, we'll have to pull out."

"Seriously?" Charlotte asked. She'd known Victor and Ken for several years, and when they'd initially shown interest in her project, it had been a collaborative relationship.

"We have to protect our interests, Charlotte. It's not personal."

Of course it was personal. "I hear you loud and clear. Again, I'll take what you've said into consideration and discuss next steps within the month."

Charlotte ended the virtual call. *Fuckers.* She kicked off her black patent leather power pumps and closed her computer, her "leaving the office" ritual. She immediately FaceTimed her assistant, Danai Roberts, who was at Seam and Sole's main office on Fashion Avenue in Midtown.

"How did it go?"

"Not good." Charlotte ran through the highlights. "But there's a solution to this. I know there is." *And it better come quick.* Just as her investors were pushing her, she sprinted faster in the direction away

15

from them. Perhaps she, Ken, and Victor had all outworn their welcome in this relationship.

"Well, at least we still have their money for payroll." Danai winked, his model frame and long hair more appropriate for fashion week than Seam and Sole's small office in the Garment District. Charlotte loved that no matter what, Danai always wore something from Seam and Sole with every outfit and posted the look on their social media.

Charlotte returned a half smile. "True." There was that and other operational expenses. Her reserves were tight, but she could sharpen them a bit more for a catastrophe. She'd gotten a great lease for her office through a friend, and because she didn't hire in a random fashion, she had a staff of reliable, hardworking people that she paid well. The truth was that Seam and Sole was a viable company that could survive on its increasing revenue if she scaled back. Paying off her investors was another beast. "Let's get marketing together. We'll make some changes and look at costs and see if we can pacify Ken and Victor. If not . . ." She shrugged. She didn't know, but worrying Danai or the rest of her employees wasn't on her list of priorities.

"If your cleats prototype gets picked up, then maybe that can help," Danai said, reminding Charlotte of her submission to various innovative sports societies, a global reservoir for sports teams looking for the next big shoe. She had developed the cleat prototype for an Olympic hopeful in women's soccer, Oni Moore, after an injury. However, with the growth of Major League Soccer and the many stars coming out of the various leagues, Charlotte had created a design for a men's cleat as well. With all the brand recognition of the big companies, she didn't think she stood a chance at getting noticed, but hopefully, she'd get a nice nod and something that she could add to Seam and Sole's brag page on the website.

"I doubt my passion project will have any impact on this situation." She sighed. "But it was a nice thought."

"You'll think of something, 'cause you're a boss and you always do," Danai reminded her.

"I appreciate you," Charlotte said. "I'll see you in the office tomorrow. Call me if you need anything."

She hung up with Danai. The acoustically porous walls of her living space let in the sound of crickets. Charlotte paced her apartment, each step padding in search of an answer. She'd come a long way from middle and high school, and the road hadn't been paved with gold to welcome her. When she'd announced that she planned on starting her own sportswear company, she'd gotten everything from up-and-down looks used to intimidate her to flat-out mean remarks followed by snickers and personal jabs. Believing in herself took work. She'd invested in her education by studying the best, asking questions, and showing up to apprentice with craftsmen. There were many doubtful days, but she'd made it by designing the best and most useful footwear and apparel she knew how to. Today, Seam and Sole was a player in the market, yet her investors were up her ass about the trajectory of her business. She'd thought steady growth was enough while she traveled the States and the world, trying to get her brand's foot in the door. The way Ken and Victor positioned the situation, was she even a good investment anymore?

The options were limited. Sell the company and pay off her investors. Keep the company and somehow get a deal big enough to thank her investors for their support, pay them off, and go it alone. Last, get a new career. The last one stabbed her right in the stomach. Giving up wasn't something that she dabbled in when it came to going after what she wanted, especially when it came to her work. She'd had a passion for sports apparel since back in the day, when she'd always rocked the latest footwear. As a kicks collector, she'd been particularly meticulous with her collection of Jordans. When it came to heels, she'd modeled innovative pairs at her office jobs out of college, until she'd finally landed a position at a company making advances in fashionable footwear for women. Later she'd gone on to produce a working heel prototype with comfort and shock absorbency that her friend and tester could actually run in without feeling like she'd fall, get blisters, or have lower-leg soreness later in the day. The Heaven Heels were the first and still the bestseller for Seam and Sole.

She parked her pacing butt in a high chair at her kitchen counter, and with elbows on the table, she plucked at her lower lip, thinking about what her next steps should be.

She sat up as straight as her spine would allow. "Okay! You need an opportunity. Something big to hit." With soccer being an international sport, the big companies had a lot of her real estate, but her shoe was better. Maybe Danai was right. Currently, no one was knocking on her door, but maybe she just needed someone to see that even though the big companies possessed most of the market, her shoe was better.

She grabbed her laptop from her bag and opened it on the table. "Remind them you're still here." She personalized each email she sent to over one hundred people in her Rolodex. The task took her until so late in the night that *The Late Show with Stephen Colbert* played in the background, and she didn't finish until his Meanwhile segment ended. Sending the emails was a long shot, but sitting on her ass hoping and wishing for a solution to land in her lap wasn't going to get her anywhere. Tonight, when she slept, she'd pose a question to her psyche for more creative answers. Until something hit, she'd go back to Seam and Sole, assure her investors that everything was fine, and work her ass off.

Chapter 2

Eoghan had been back to training at the Dublin Rovers' facility for three weeks, and he still hadn't found his groove. He had returned to his usual workout schedule and ran the ball with the rest of the team, but he just couldn't get his feet to do what they had always done in the past—be a sure thing, run the ball, and get it into the net. With each trip and stumble, he questioned himself and his ability. By this point he should feel at home and natural on the field, shouldn't he? The truth was he performed worse than he had during his evaluation, when Ayanna and Shane had pumped him up with confidence. After that he'd assumed that the rest would fall into place and things would get back to normal. He couldn't have been more wrong.

He and his team were the defending champions in the Irish Premier League. He'd had a lot to do with the title. That was, until he'd gotten hurt, had surgery, and then gone to America to rehab with Ayanna Crawford, the best physiotherapist, if you asked him. If it had been up to his father, who thought his opinion mattered most, Eoghan would have been here in Ireland or even in Qatar, where he'd first been assigned before he'd expressed a different opinion by flipping his surgical bed, no easy feat with an injured leg, and getting a sore shoulder in addition to almost tearing his stitches from surgery. Yeah, Qatar had been a bad idea, and Ireland had been worse. He sure as hell hadn't wanted his father meddling in the day-to-day. His recovery would have been more traumatic than therapeutic.

Donal O'Farrell had been the opposite of helpful in the situation. Because his father pushed when he should step back, his bullish insertions only left Eoghan struggling and confused about his progress. No one could help him figure out how to get past this. Deep down he knew that. His body sped down the field in the simulation game, and his comradery with his team was one he had to reconnect with in his way and in his own time. His coach, Nathaniel Boyle, was one of the best he'd ever worked with, and Boyle's support for his recovery had been invaluable. Eoghan had missed running his coach's plays, even with the uncertainty of his moves. His father, on the other hand, felt as though he had the answers to all the questions and all Eoghan's problems. Back in America, his father had been unable to jump in, manipulate, change, and control situations, but now that Eoghan was often close by, staying at his parents' flat in Dublin, oul Donal was back to popping up unannounced and causing Eoghan a load of stress, especially during the shocking first few weeks of his return, which had been akin to jumping into a freezing pool after being in a scalding one.

"Don't worry, mate. It'll come," his teammate Pippin said as he jogged past him one day when Eoghan's sweaty face was scorched with frustration. He must have looked like his head was about to explode into a gory scene out of a horror flick.

"Feck off," Eoghan said to one of his best friends. Translation: *Thanks.* He kicked the grass and looked around the stadium, into the empty seats, and then into the distance above the architectural marvel of the wavy rim that hung over Aviva Stadium. Soon he'd be out on the field during game time, when tens of thousands of fans would fill the stands, night after night, not only to see the team play but also to see him play. He couldn't let them down.

His body felt good, his kit fit perfectly, and he wasn't huffing and puffing for air like his endurance was completely shot, because like clockwork he'd built that up quickly. Still, he felt like something just wasn't right. He had to get to the bottom of why the potential he could clearly see in his mind's eye and feel from head to toe slipped out of his grasp. He wiggled his toes and stretched his feet within his boots. Had they always felt like that? Was that a slight cramping feeling in his arches? Had the tightness started to move up to his shin? His calf? His knee!

When he looked at all the factors, he deduced that he'd found the problem.

The material of his white practice kit with green trim clung to his chest and thighs as he pushed himself to his limit. He knew that it would take time for him to build up the kind of stamina required for a professional football game, but that didn't stop him from pushing the envelope just to the edge. His lungs ached, and his wet hair dripped into his eyes.

"Take a break, Eoghan," Nathaniel Boyle, his coach, called to him.

"I can keep going, Gaff," Eoghan said, knowing full well that he was probably in need of rest, a towel, and a drink.

"Now," Boyle hollered, his more-blond-than-brown hair flipping in the chilly December air.

Eoghan didn't agree, but he knew better than to challenge Boyle. He simply went over to where a towel waited for him, as did an electrolyte drink to help him refuel. Whatever it was that he needed to fix, he needed to have done it a week ago. He'd already spent months away in America getting himself back from his ACL injury. The last thing he wanted to do was spend another several months getting back to where he needed to be in order to feel like a true contributor to his team. With the bane of his existence still on his feet and obviously the cause of all his troubles, he growled in frustration.

Eoghan's feet started to cramp, and he flung off the cleats, leaving them on the grass for Dodger, the kit man, to pick up. Eoghan had always been superstitious about his boots, and this time was no different, except for the fact that he was certain that his boots were responsible for his poor performance on the pitch.

"They feel off," he explained to the gaffer.

"What're you telling me for? Get a pair that doesn't," Boyle said. "You start training with the national team after winter break. Think Walsh'll go for your shite?"

"No pressure at all now," Eoghan mumbled. He looked forward to playing on the country team just as much as he'd be longing to be back in his Rovers kit.

Next came the consultation with his agent, Ronin Kelly; the kit man; and a footwear specialist. They checked his gait, his balance, his movement, and his foot measurements.

"Everything looks all right. Are you sure it just wasn't something in your boot? A pebble or dirt?" Ronin asked.

"Go chew on your pebble and a mouthful of dirt," Eoghan said. "I want out of these boots."

Ronin crossed his arms. "If you choose a different boot, you might lose your sponsorship with—"

"Fine," Eoghan said. He needed to play, and he needed better boots to do that.

"That's eight million quid," Ronin stated, and Eoghan would bet coin that his agent was testing his resolve.

Eoghan waited. If his agent thought that now was the time to have him repeat himself, he didn't know him at all.

"All right, then. I'll have a chat and see what we can do. Maybe negotiate more sportswear or something. I dunno." Ronin pulled out his phone and thumbed the screen.

"I'm sure this has been going on since I started training. The pitch feels off. My balance." Ayanna had brought him back from his injuries, and once cleared he'd had weeks of feeling good and wanting to play. He was convinced that his long-trusted shoe had lost its usefulness. If he was going to be great at football again, then he needed different boots.

His father entered the room, head high and leading with his chest, counting on his arrival to make him the focus. For the first time in a long time, Eoghan happily let Donal O'Farrell take the attention. He'd just told his agent that he was willing to give up a substantial endorsement deal with his current shoe brand to go with another company. The problem was he didn't know who that was, and he'd make yet another bet that his agent didn't know either.

"My father is not to know about the boots," Eoghan said under his breath.

"Right," Ronin said.

The kit man, Dodger, and the footwear specialist both nodded.

His father slapped his agent on the back. "Here you all are hiding. Just coming to see how Eoghan's getting on. I'm expecting to see him on the pitch after winter break."

"He's still a bit to go, but Gaff says he'll be on the pitch within the month."

"Just in time for the Harps game with the Rovers." Eoghan's competitive spirit rose to the surface. Now if only he could get his damn shoes situated.

"And the national team will be activating him to play now that he's back," his father pushed, unsatisfied with him playing only with the Rovers.

"They're aware. All in good time," Ronin soothed.

His father peered around his agent's shoulder. "What all is happening here?"

"We're just sorting some things out." His agent side-eyed him.

"Well, I've just come to collect Eoghan for supper and a pint," his father said. "What do you say, lad?"

"Sure, Da. Just give us a moment, and I'll be right out." When his father was out of the room, Eoghan looked to his team. "Find me the right boots. Fast."

◆ ◆ ◆

Later that week, Eoghan's team alerted him that they had narrowed the shoes down to five. He still hadn't felt able to drive the ball like he normally would and was anxious to correct the problem with his footwear.

"All right. Here they are." Ronin displayed a panel of footwear.

Eoghan tried on the first pair and ran across the pitch. He kicked the shoes off, opting to return barefoot. "Fucking shite."

"Not that one then?" Clive Sullivan said. His short strawberry-blond hair fell into his face. A back-office heavy from branding and marketing, Clive worked with kit selection and acquisition.

"Are you trying to ruin my career?" Eoghan asked no one in particular.

"Let's move on to the next one now," Ronin said. He crossed his arms, and though he was short, his biceps bulged his tweed jacket. Ever the smart dresser.

The next boot was better, but they took a step back with the third and fourth one.

Ronin and Clive were looking doubtful, and Dodger huffed from running down boots on the pitch. Eoghan paced in circles, his fingers digging into his hip. What if he couldn't find a boot to get him back into form?

"Last one," Ronin said. Sweat trickled to his sideburns, and worry lines creased his forehead.

"If this isn't the one . . ." Clive trailed off.

"We'll cross that bridge when we get to it," Ronin hissed.

Eoghan puffed air through his nose and, with little hope, dragged on the boots. He stood up and noticed the immediate sensation of the shoes forming around his toes, his arches, the heels, and even the tops of his feet. He jogged in place and did a few high jumps as he would when warming up, and the shocks felt completely absorbed.

"Feck, these feel fucking amazin'," he said, sounding more like he'd just slipped his shillelagh into a woman than his shoe into a boot.

"Glass slipper, is it?" Clive asked.

"These are the ones."

"There's no endorsement money with that one," Ronin said. "It's a small but established company. The shoe is customizable. We'd just need to work with them, try some options, get your input, do a few trials, and create the boot."

"I don't give a shite what we have to do. These are the ones," Eoghan repeated, in insta-love with the cleats. He never wanted to take the glove-feeling footwear off. "You've got to try these on, man."

"Pass. Here's a bit of cherry on top. The owner is a woman entrepreneur of color, which I know you want to support."

"Brilliant," Eoghan said. He might not be out in the streets protesting, but he did want to do what he could for social change here in his own country. He and his best friend Shane had grown up with their best friend Pippin, who had roots both here in Ireland and in Nigeria. Noticing the difference between Pippin's experience and their own in the countries and towns where they had played, Eoghan had quietly committed and set out to be part of the solution.

His agent handed him the details to look over when he wanted. "The company is Seam and—"

"Ronin, I don't care who it is. Spare me the details, pay them well, and get them here so I can get my boots, eh?" Eoghan knew he was being impetuous, but he'd never made a mistake based on his gut, and his gut said that these were the magical pair that would right his ship.

"Great. I'll go make all this happen. Get her here, her living quarters and office space set up, once I get her details and all meetings are had." Ronin leaned in. "Listen, the investment in your return to the game is great. Like, money-gun-at-the-strip-club great. Are you sure this is the one? Because your trial time is ending. It's time for you to be great again."

Eoghan surely understood the seriousness of the moment. He'd seen more than a few footballers lose endorsements and contracts while being fully healthy because they were unable to play as well as they had done in the past. He wasn't going to be a casualty. He put a lot of pressure on himself, and he was going to either shit a diamond or explode like a volcano. Either way he'd give it his best, and right now that depended on one factor.

"I will. Just as soon as I get my boots."

Chapter 3

Charlotte opened presents at the Bowman home in New Rochelle, New York, with a gaggle of cousins, aunts, and uncles as well as the Crawford gang, Jada and Morgan, minus Ayanna, who was spending her first Christmas in Ireland with her boyfriend, Shane. Four weeks had passed, and Charlotte still hadn't received a creative answer for Seam and Sole from her psyche—or the universe, for that matter. As her family gathered around the overly large, slightly crooked, and blinged-out Christmas tree, their voices turned up with each drink spiced with a little yuletide.

Usually, Charlotte would leave her cares at the door and enjoy her family, but today, she stressed. She had to make a decision, and she couldn't put it off for much longer. Thankfully, she had Christmas at the Bowmans' to distract her at least for a few days.

When she celebrated the holiday with her family, no matter how much work it was to cook, accommodate, and provide for extended family, she loved seeing the children grow up and reminiscing about the old days. But like any family, they were a big loving hug that suffocated at the same time.

"Where's your man?" her aunties interrogated.

"When you gonna settle down?" her cousins questioned.

"Don't wait too long now. You don't want to end up alone. Looks fade," her uncles declared.

And then there was her cousin Tanya, who had just had her second baby with her husband, Elgin. Tanya's happiness from motherhood glowed on her face, and the family, including Charlotte, tended to her every need and fawned over the children.

They eventually gathered around the dinner table to eat the extensive spread of mains and sides. Earthy herbal aromas of thyme, garlic, sage, and rosemary coming off the roasted meats perfumed the room.

"Let's bow our heads," Charlotte's father, Keith Bowman, said, and the family complied, clasping hands on either side of them as the food was blessed.

Tanya sat next to her at the dinner table. Besides the new-mother glow on her light-brown skin, she wore her hair in a stylish bun on top of her head, and her Christmas tree studs were a good choice for handsy children. The two of them had always been close, and Tanya always gave Charlotte the real deal. This time it was about motherhood. "Don't rush. If I had to do it all again, I'd travel more, go clubbing every weekend, and stay toasted," her cousin said.

Charlotte laughed. "Reckless." Hearing her cousin was like when she'd heard a bunch of *noes* for her company idea, until she'd gotten the one *yes* that had helped things take off.

"Look, someone has to be brave and speak on this. I love my husband and my kids. I wouldn't change my life, but I think you can hear how your life is going to change after you get married and have kids, but it's only until you experience it that you get it."

"Thanks, girl." Charlotte nudged Tanya with her shoulder.

"Here." Tanya handed her the baby because her cousin also knew that despite her independent-woman disposition, Charlotte loved kids and caring for them. Before she'd had her own business, she'd been the call everyone had made for babysitting. Charlotte cradled Tanya's sleeping daughter, Melody, in her arms. Charlotte looked down at the scrunched face of the warm, soft newborn, her heart falling in love with her even more.

"I'd love to see Char with a family of her own," her mother said, putting a hot pan of macaroni and cheese on a trivet at the center of the dinner table. Her long gray cornrows rested on her shoulder and contrasted with the festive red-and-green plaid holiday sweater she wore. Gabrielle Bowman's comment almost canceled out Tanya's. Just because Charlotte loved kids didn't automatically make her the best candidate for the sacrifices of motherhood.

Charlotte had watched her mom put her father's career first at the expense of her own. It wasn't like Keith Bowman had forbidden his wife to work, but it was as if her mother had made some secret pact with herself to tuck her art-dealing career behind her and do everything to support her husband. Instead of becoming just like her mom, Charlotte had decided from a young age that the only person she'd make sacrifices for was herself.

"Well, don't hold your breath. I'm running a company. Seam and Sole is my husband, and my creations are my babies." Still cradling Melody, Charlotte forked the mac and cheese with her free hand off the plate Tanya had made for her. That was the last thing her mother wanted to hear, but if Charlotte had one dominant characteristic, it was her honesty.

"Cheers to that," Jada said. Her fashionable jet-black weave had ends that looked like they'd been dipped in platinum blonde.

"What do you know about it, young lady," one of Charlotte's uncles asked.

"Nothing, and I plan to stay ignorant to it. I'm too young for all this you all are talking about." Jada worked her knife to scoop rice onto her fork before raising it to her mouth.

"Maybe we should put you at the kids' table, then," her other uncle said, prompting a wail of laughter from the table.

Jada's mouth dropped open. "I'm not *that* young."

"Then hush up and stay out of grown folks' business," Charlotte's uncle teased.

The table continued to chuckle.

"Mom?" Jada flipped her hair and shifted in her seat to face Morgan. "You just gonna let them shut me down like that?" she asked her mother, who was in the middle of serving herself another slice of honey-glazed ham.

"Yes. Own your choices, baby," Morgan said, tucking one side of her pixie cut behind her ear.

"I'm gonna own my choice to have more of this macaroni and cheese," Jada said about the bubbling, light-brown crust on the table's favorite side dish.

Charlotte could almost hear Jada's mouth salivating in anticipation. Charlotte was glad Ayanna's sister and mother were there. She missed her friend, but given that Shane had spent Thanksgiving here in the States, a holiday not celebrated in Ireland, the couple had decided to spend time with his family for Christmas this year. Charlotte understood the logic, but her heart wanted to wake up in PJs with her friend and behave like kids with the little ones, tearing open presents like they'd done for so many Christmases. Having Ayanna's family there was a consolation prize Charlotte would take any day. Another thing she was happy about was that the conversation had made its way back to the food and off Charlotte's uninhabited uterus and naked ring finger.

Later that night, exhausted from shuffling their feet to the Electric Slide and having their own little dance party, the family moved on to playing *Black Jeopardy: Holiday Edition*, which Tanya's husband, Elgin, had downloaded and projected on the TV for them to play.

"I'll take *Fix me a plate* for two hundred dollars," her father said, and Charlotte laughed so hard that her stomach felt like she'd done one of Cassey Ho's ab challenges.

"Who created this game?" she asked.

"I found it on Etsy. There are so many games. You just have to be willing to try it. They're not all great, but they nailed it with this one," Elgin said.

"It's completely ridiculous but so good," Charlotte said.

"Yo! Did you know that Elgin's name is Irish?" Tanya said randomly. "Ever since watching *You Got Served*, I thought that was a straight-up Black name."

"I love that movie, especially the beginning and the end. They can just delete the whole middle of the movie," Jada chimed in from across the room.

"You stay on some *You Got Served*," Charlotte said of Tanya's favorite movie. They used to rewind the last fifteen minutes of the movie until they knew all the dance moves.

"I used to drool over Marques Houston and Omarion. Mmm . . . ," Tanya said.

"Babe?" Elgin shook his head.

"I get to live out my fantasy with you because the main character's name is Elgin. I won the lottery." Tanya blew kisses at her husband.

"Except for the fact that I look nothing like either of the main characters." Elgin smoothed over his short black wavy hair. His creamy skin was a shade or two darker than Charlotte's rich chestnut tone.

"Anyway," Tanya continued. "His name means *high minded* or *little Ireland*."

"That's interesting." Charlotte's thoughts took on a mind of their own, and she thought about the night she'd had multiple steamy sessions with a particular Irishman.

"We should tell Yaya. That's some shit she'd love to know," Jada called over again.

"Yeah," Charlotte said, trying to tamp down the sudden heat rising in her. Eoghan was back in Ireland. There was no way to quench the thirst that dried her throat. Plus, she wasn't in the habit of wallowing in past escapades. Still, her curiosity bubbled, and she hoped he was getting on well after his rehabilitation. If she asked Ayanna, more questions would follow. She'd just have to be okay with not knowing. She buried her thoughts and again focused on her family and their conversation, only to find that Tanya had found "Pump It Up," the Joe Budden song from the last scene in the movie, and she and Jada were performing the dance moves.

"A mess," Charlotte said—that was until Tanya grabbed her, pulling Charlotte to join. Finally giving in, Charlotte said, "Remember this?" and did a horrible version of a dance sequence.

"Stop," Jada said, doubled over, her laughter interrupted by hiccups.

"Now it's a party," Elgin said as he watched their foolery.

With full bellies and filled with joy from the night, they wound down with more stories by the fire about holidays past when "the kids were young" over glasses of eggnog, mugs of hot chocolate, and glasses of wines and spirits. Before all her family left, Charlotte made her way upstairs and snuggled into the sheets and comforter of her old bed in her old room. The interrogating questions from her family had nothing on the problems she had to solve, which quickly took center stage in the theater of her mind. Satiated with joy from the evening, and her spirit lifted by her family, she hoped that the miracle of Christmas would hook her up with a solution.

The following Monday, Charlotte worried her lip as she leafed through her creative projects. Ideas from over the years covered the pages in her notebook, but there were none that she felt would give her the payoff she needed for her investors or that the company was financially ready to pursue. Danai strutted into the office of Seam and Sole with his Christmas gift the centerpiece of his outfit.

"Okay, boots," Charlotte said of Danai's hot-off-the-assembly-line pair of red over-the-knee Gucci boots, snapping her fingers in a circle around him. "I see you."

Danai, wearing a black skintight jumpsuit and tan wool coat, should have been plastered up on a billboard in an ad. He modeled the boots shamelessly. "They're nice, right?"

"Harry?" Charlotte asked of Danai's ex-boyfriend.

"I know this is a ploy to get me back, but I'm not having it. I'll take the boots, though," Danai said. "I got you a coffee and a little treat because I know you're working night and day. Mama's gotta make sure you eat."

"Ooh! Treats," Charlotte said and opened the white paper bag. "Cinnabon?"

"Call it a little pick-me-up."

"You know my heart." Charlotte cleared the area by her computer to ready her cinnamon roll for her mouth, but all the while, she couldn't take her eyes off his boots. "These are fabulous, Miss Girl," Charlotte said to him. "He really wants you back, huh?"

"He shouldn't have cheated then," Danai said and settled at his desk. "He can be sorry by his self without me, but you better believe I'm going to rock this here pair of boots."

"I hear you." Charlotte remembered the day well when Danai had been too upset to be consoled. No one liked to be cheated on, but Harry had done so publicly in the spaces that both he and Danai frequented, leaving Danai feeling not only heartbroken and ashamed but also like the butt of a horrible joke.

"What's on the docket today? I feel like operations are being held hostage until you decide what we're doing with the investors. Next year's planning is vacant. Don't tell me I need to find another job, because I can't right now," Danai said.

"First of all, that was loaded," Charlotte said. "And two, Seam and Sole is good. I haven't even checked email yet, but I have a ton of ideas I'm looking through now."

Danai looked skeptical.

"Don't give me that face. I'll figure this out," Charlotte said, even as her charged fingers turned the pages.

Charlotte's phone rang, and Danai answered it for her while she bit into the decadent, pillowy, warm pastry and sipped her coffee, barely listening to Danai on the phone.

"Please hold," Danai said and swatted at her.

"What?" Charlotte asked.

"It's a man with a lovely accent asking for you. Something about boots for a celebrity?"

"Huh?" she mumbled through a mouthful of bread and frosting.

"Sounds interesting," Danai whispered as if he hadn't placed the caller on hold.

"Are you sure it's not one of those spam calls about insurance for my car or some other ridiculous shit?"

"Sounds legit to me and definitely a call for the boss," Danai suggested.

Charlotte shrugged and picked up the line. "Charlotte Bowman."

"Greetings," a man with an Irish accent said. "Is this the same Charlotte Bowman that was plugging a boot prototype last year here in Europe?"

"Boots? No, I do athletic footwear and had been working on a women's soccer cleat," she said.

"Yes, boots. That's what we call cleats here," he said.

"Yes. That's right. My apologies," Charlotte said. She'd traveled all over Europe and knew the term well. She turned on and paid attention. "And who are you?"

"I'm Ronin Kelly, calling on behalf of one of my clients, a footballer here in Ireland. Your boots are also for men, no?" he asked.

It wasn't the first time a big corporation in her industry had come sniffing around, not to gobble the competition but to see what the young kids were doing and add to their street cred with an urban brand like Seam and Sole.

Charlotte replied, "Yes," but kept her answers simple for the time being.

"Well, I have an offer for you if you're interested."

Charlotte wanted to know more about this Ronin Kelly person but even more about his client. "Who's the client?"

"I'm inclined to reserve that information to protect my client's privacy at this point until you determine if this project is for you. I can phone in more of my colleagues to chat with you. Back-office members of the Irish national team."

Hesitancy grew at the thought of working with the Irish national team and could be summed up in one word. Eoghan. Surely, if she worked with a member of the team, she'd run into him, and she didn't know how she felt about having an ex-lover on deck.

"The contract is . . ." Ronin said the number, and Charlotte straightened. There was no way that he had said the correct number. "In dollars."

"No, in pounds."

"Oh. My. Gosh," she mouthed to Danai. Her head was spinning. Her company wasn't even worth that much, and she'd have more than enough to support Seam and Sole and pay off her investors.

"It's only fair, since your shoe will be replacing a large endorsement deal," Ronin said. "My player really wants your shoe. So there is room for negotiating if the number isn't correct, but it's best to speak with the rest of the administration. If you're interested, that is."

"I see. Yes. That would make sense," she said vacantly.

Ronin continued as her brain still ran the catch-up race. "You'll also have to move to Ireland temporarily, of course, and quickly, which hopefully won't conflict with your business operations or projects for Seam and Sole."

"I'm sure that with my team of employees and contractors, something could be worked out. I'll have to see," she said, knowing full well that this, whatever this was, had jumped to priority number one. She'd have to move to Ireland for the gig, and her best friend was spending a lot of time there these days. Could the universe have been so kind and on point with her needs?

"Will you consider it, Miss Bowman?"

Damn skippy I'll consider it! "Yes, yes, I will," she said.

"I'll be in touch later this afternoon with more necessary details and a schedule of required meetings."

"Great. Thank you."

"So . . . ?" Danai questioned, when Charlotte hung up.

"I think we're going to Ireland."

Danai leaped to his feet. "What?" He hopped around like he'd won the numbers.

Charlotte closed her watery eyes. *Thank you, universe.*

Chapter 4

Charlotte was excited for her meeting with the Irish national team members. She sat on the edge of her seat in anticipation to find out who she'd be working with. Given the time frame in which she needed to get to Ireland and work on her prototype for the player, she'd estimate that they were already behind. Nonetheless, she kept a positive state of mind and hoped she would be working with someone who had personality and shared her values like a good work ethic and timeliness.

"Greetings to you, Charlotte. Thank you for joining us today. It's a pleasure to see you again," Ronin said. They'd had two virtual meetings in which she'd finally met the man who would help change the trajectory of her life. She could tell he was short by the way he sat in his chair, but despite his height she wouldn't mess with him or encourage anyone else to. His biceps bulged through a tight black shirt that he wore informally, without a tie and with several buttons undone. She also doubted she'd be able to close both her hands around his neck even if she tried. He'd been kind and respectful when they'd spoken, and she'd come to rely on him as her anchor in the worldwide project.

"It's a pleasure to see you again, as well." Charlotte waved at his image as well as those of the other participants who filled squares on her monitor. Again, she was the only woman in the room, and she hoped that even though she was dealing with men's soccer, she wouldn't always be the only woman professional on the team.

"Let me tell you who all are joining us today." Ronin went through the list, and Charlotte made note of the people, whom she'd already researched except for one. "This is Oliver Walsh, Eoghan O'Farrell's coach for the national team; Nathaniel Boyle, Eoghan's coach for the local Dublin Rovers; and last but not least, Clive Sullivan, national team brand manager, whose responsibilities cover uniforms. Based on introductions, you've undoubtedly guessed that Eoghan is my client and will be yours now, as well. He's quite happy with your cleats, and if he could have them yesterday, he would . . ."

The man's words faded into the background like he was Charlie Brown's teacher, and all Charlotte heard was "wah-wah, wah-wah." *Eoghan?*

"Your contract is for three months, just to make sure that if the shoe requires any additional customizing, you are available to Eoghan. He's an Irish treasure, so we really want to make sure that his comeback is strong. We've lots of publicity and marketing set up for his full return."

Charlotte hemmed and hawed. "Eoghan O'Farrell."

"I know it's easy to be starstruck. He's an international star of the game. You might have heard that he recently battled an injury," Ronin said. "He's back from recovery and ready to come out blazing. He's training now but not yet ready to play, but with your boots, he will be. Right now, we want him to be as comfortable and as confident as possible. From your work with Seam and Sole and the references we've checked, we think you're someone who is able to pull this off."

"Absolutely," Charlotte forced out in the hopes that her face didn't show the universal cosmic karma that had struck twice. Once with Ayanna and now with her, and both times with Eoghan at the center. Charlotte knew more than she was at liberty to say, since her best friend had not only done Eoghan's therapy but given her the play-by-play of the dilemma of living with two men she'd assumed would stay where she'd found them. In Ireland. Charlotte and Eoghan had had their little romp, and she'd put that delightful but expired event behind her. Yaya was right. Charlotte had cursed herself.

"We hope you're excited about it, Charlotte," Oliver said. "We have a great team in the offices and on the pitch. We'll also do all we can to help you and your team have a seamless transition."

"Of course. I'm genuinely looking forward to working with the team," Charlotte said. "Has Mr. O'Farrell mentioned me or my company? I ask because Seam and Sole is a much smaller company than what I assume you're used to dealing with. For Eoghan's level of celebrity, why wouldn't he be best served with one of the conglomerates?"

Ronin's fair skin reddened enough for it to show over video conferencing. "He is struggling a bit with his current footwear and doesn't care for his current shoe. Let's put it this way: He has given up a very lucrative contract because that is how much he thinks your shoe is the one. The holy grail, if you will."

Charlotte almost laughed out loud because, one, she'd asked a question that could easily get her yanked from the contract and, two, it was funny that her passion project had been put in such a light, especially by Eoghan.

"I see," she said.

"So if everything is in order, then we're happy to move forward," Clive said.

Charlotte had most of her questions answered, and the only thing stopping her from pulling the trigger was herself. "Yes," she said at last. "Let's do it."

"Glad to hear it. Welcome to the team, Charlotte. We hope it will be a fun adventure for you."

"I'm sure it will be." Charlotte smiled at the irony. This could go well or terribly badly. She focused on the job and the contract she was about to sign. The pros outweighed the cons. Handling an ex-lover? No problem. She was taking herself and Seam and Sole to new heights, and this was an opportunity that she'd make work no matter what, and nothing and no one would stand in her way.

Charlotte adored her Harlem apartment, and though she'd miss it while away, she entrusted her spot to Ayanna's sister, Jada, who had accelerated her senior year and finished her degree in December.

"Technically, I'm a January graduate, but this gig in the city lined up pretty nicely with your plans to leave. Yaya must be flying above the clouds, knowing you're hopping over to the Irish isles."

"She screamed my ear off is what she did. I still have tinnitus." Charlotte smiled at the recollection of her conversation with Ayanna, who'd had nonstop questions that Charlotte hadn't had all the answers to.

"I'm just so happy we'll kind of be closer. I'll still be traveling, but we'll be able to do things in Dublin and in the country. I'm so freakin' psyched," Ayanna had said the day Charlotte had received the offer.

Now as Charlotte got her apartment ready for Ayanna's sister, she also started to liven with energy for her new adventure.

Jada peered into a decorative turquoise lidded jar on the side table in her bedroom. "Hey, are you taking all of these?" she asked and sprinkled a handful of condoms from her fingertips back into the jar.

"Not all of them. I'm sure they have condoms in Ireland, Jada."

Jada shrugged.

"Don't skank up my apartment," Charlotte said, walking Jada through the two-bedroom space. "I mean every word."

"Me?" Jada asked in her black skinny jeans and green midriff sweater.

"Girl, please. I know you. The cleaning service comes every Tuesday, but since you'll be here, you can keep the place clean. It's part of growing up. Keep my things as nice as you found them, or I'll have to kick you out."

"Dang, Charlotte," Jada whined. "Dead ass, that's wack AF."

"Use your words, boo."

"You're being unreasonably hard on me. I'm supposed to be embracing my independence in a fun way, by tearing up this city."

"Welcome to Chez Charlotte, where everything is off limits." Charlotte waved her hand around the earth tones and modern decor of the apartment.

Jada went to Charlotte's closet, her hand gliding over Gucci blazers, dresses by Rickie Freeman for Teri Jon, Retrofête denim, and tunics by Deeba for Wolf & Badger. "This wardrobe is dope."

"That includes my clothes," Charlotte said.

Jada dangled a pair of Bottega Veneta inkwell-and-gold high-heeled sandals. "What about—"

"And my shoes."

"That ain't even cool," Jada said.

"Nope. Or fair, or whatever other word you want to use," Charlotte said. "Every time you come here, you borrow something that I have yet to see again. Plus, I know you have clothes at your mom's house."

"I'm high-pitch irate." She sucked her teeth and rolled her eyes for good measure. "You and Yaya are just alike. No fun."

"You are going to be living in a Harlem apartment in a prime location, rent-free." Charlotte waited for Jada to retort. When she didn't, Charlotte shut down the argument with, "Yeah, that's what I thought."

Jada mimicked her, and Charlotte stifled a laugh.

No matter what Charlotte said to Jada, she knew she'd scroll through social media one day and find her sister from another mother stylin' in one of her outfits, but Charlotte prayed it wouldn't be one of the outfits she loved and that Jada would take care of it. Charlotte loved Jada as much as she loved Ayanna, and though the younger sister was a pain in Charlotte's perfect ass, she'd neither kick her out nor stay mad at her for very long.

Charlotte checked her surroundings, from her tall, floor-potted snake plant that she'd grown from a small cutting to her pops of color from the urban art that covered the wall and her cozy tan couch that was perfect for movies and popcorn with her best friend. "I think I have everything that I need."

"You sure do," Jada said, looking at the set of luggage at the door. "If you leave anything behind, I can easily mail it to you."

"Thanks." Charlotte checked her phone. "Okay, my ride is here." Charlotte hugged Jada tight. "Love you. Be good and look in on Mrs. Clements."

"I got you," Jada said. "Have fun and give Yaya real-life hugs for me when you see her."

"I will."

The driver helped her with her things, and she was on her way to the airport. After a seamless direct flight, Charlotte landed on Irish soil for the first time.

Chapter 5

Eoghan half listened to Ronin and Clive in the back office of the dressing rooms as they discussed the designer for the boots he was waiting for. That was, until the name of the company penetrated through.

"Seam and Sole, did you say?" Eoghan asked. The company name was familiar to him. Why?

"Yes, it's a company based in Harlem, New York, and owned by a woman named—"

"Charlotte Bowman." Rich deep-brown skin, gorgeous almost black curls, and a personality that soothed as much as it stung. Four months ago, he'd followed her lead and enjoyed their one night and several hours of the best sex he'd had in a long time. He'd blamed his infatuation with making her come on his lack of opportunity while in the US, which had helped ease the parting. Not to mention the fact that he'd be thousands of miles away in Ireland and back to the life he knew.

"Yeah, Charlotte Bowman," his agent said. "You know her?"

"Can't be sure." Eoghan cleared his throat. "I may have met her in New York." He hoped his face looked more relaxed than it felt and that the rapid thump of his heart was neither heard nor felt.

"She's coming here to meet you and gather some information to start her work on customizing yer boots. I've seen her designs and her technology. She's the real deal. Good on you for picking her. She has a smart prototype that will be efficient for training and give her data and feedback to adjust the boot to the perfect fitting for you."

"English."

"You get to collaborate with her on the boot. Science and style."

Eoghan's brows lifted. He wouldn't be able to just get the shoe and get on with it. By choosing the best-fit boot, he'd landed himself in a collaborative relationship with his ex-lover. "It was just one night, but . . ."

"Come again?" Ronin asked, his brows knit in curiosity.

Eoghan pursed his lips and shook his head. "When does she get here?"

"Landed this morning and should be here momentarily. Just for a bit of meet and greet."

Charlotte Bowman was in Ireland?

Eoghan brushed his hand through his hair and pulled down on his rancid jersey. "I can't meet her like this."

"You meet everyone else like this." Ronin shrugged.

"Eejit, why didn't you tell me who she was," Eoghan said.

"You said you didn't want to know names because you didn't want to be swayed. Remember?" Ronin growled. "What's the problem now? We discussed this, and you were over the moon."

Ronin was right. Charlotte was giving him an awesome shoe, one that made him feel supported like a loving embrace. She was a woman business owner of color, and he knew her to be truthful, though brutal, and best friend to his physio, who was now his best mate's girlfriend. He should still be over the moon, as his agent had reminded him, but instead, his insides felt like they did just before he got out on the pitch for a game—a mix of excitement from the thrill of competition and a little nausea. What did she expect? What did he?

His agent leaned back and studied him. "You know this bure, don't ya?"

A knock on the door sounded.

"Come in," Ronin said.

Eoghan shoved him.

"What?" Ronin mouthed.

Charlotte glided through the door, her big Afro leading the way like it always did. A turquoise-and-orange mosaic headband rimmed her head. She was accompanied by Clive, who was engaged in conversation about the stadium and how to get around.

"Oh, that was easy. I'll take that route to get to the pitch to work with the client," she said. "I'll show my assistant when he arrives."

The client?

Clive fawned over her. "If you need anything at all, just let me know." He dazzled her with his mustached smile.

"Thank you." Her full lips were lightly glossed in a pink hue, which only brought out their perfect plump shape. Today, her shimmering lids were gold, as opposed to the smoky, alluring look she'd worn the night they'd gotten together. Now, however, her long mascaraed lashes batted flirtatiously at Clive, or maybe that was just his imagination and all she'd done was blink.

Pull yourself together, man. She's just a bure.

A bure who wore a rich cobalt-blue suit with perfect press lines. If she'd traveled in this suit, not a wrinkle showed. Her shirt matched her headband, and he tore his eyes away from the deep V that only accentuated her full breasts.

Time seemed not to have changed her allure at all, and just like before, he wanted to stroke her jawline, kiss the soft spot just under her ear, and then pull her into his arms. Not only was he a sap, but he was a sap for a woman who presented an "I'm all about business" aura that made doing the delicious things he'd envisioned doing to her impossible.

"Charlotte, it's nice to finally meet you in person." Ronin shook hands with her, and she covered his hand with both of hers.

"You too, Ronin," she said.

Eoghan knew how warm and delicate her fingertips were running over his skin. He shivered. "Hello, Charlotte."

JN Welsh

"Hello, Eoghan. It's nice to see you again," she said as she stopped to stand in front of him. Her white heeled boots made her taller than her five-foot-eight height by about two inches.

"Again?" Clive asked.

Charlotte looked from Eoghan to Ronin. "Yes, we met in New York. I'm friends with Dr. Ayanna Crawford."

"Oh, really?" Ronin drawled and arched a brow.

"Good to see you again, Charlotte," Eoghan said.

"Likewise," she said. Her eyes whipped over his body before she turned to Ronin. "You look different in person." Eoghan liked the come-hither way she smiled, but preferred she'd quit directing it at Ronin.

"I get that a lot." Ronin leaned in, and Eoghan wasn't even sure his agent had a clue he'd been hooked by Charlotte and pulled into her web.

"You've gotten settled, then?" Eoghan slapped a hand on Ronin's shoulder and pushed him to Charlotte's periphery.

Her smell. He'd never forget the scent of roses and lilies mixed with grounding vanilla. Everywhere on her carried a different fragrance. Her hair smelled like tropical coconut, her skin like sun-kissed citrus, and her clothes were dusted with the florals of her perfume. Even the light scent between her legs had been different, yet they all created a symphony of drugging aromas that he couldn't resist. Obviously, his agent had also fallen prey to the unique wiles of Charlotte Bowman.

She focused on Eoghan. "Yes. Thank you." She was as nonchalant as she'd been the last time he'd been in her presence. She'd dismissed him easily as a teacher would a class for recess. Had it not been for the tiny hint of care in her eyes that fled as quickly as it had come, he might have believed her to be emotionless. He wanted to be alone with her to see what version of her he'd be working with.

"Good, good," Eoghan said and tossed Ronin a look so that he'd get the hint.

"Well, we'll leave you two to discuss Eoghan's boot," Ronin said and extended his hand to Charlotte, which she took. "See you soon."

46

"You too." Charlotte focused on Ronin like the two of them were the only ones in the room.

"Grand," Eoghan said. "Catch up with you later?"

"Bye-bye, Charlotte." Clive waved as if hesitant to leave his new-found crush.

Both men left, and finally they were alone.

Eoghan leaned against a wood panel and crossed his arms. "This is kind of interesting, isn't it? Us here together again. Who would have thought we'd even see each other again once I returned to Ireland?"

Charlotte strolled through the space. "Hmm . . . given that your best friend and my best friend are in love and so serious that the two of them should have dual citizenship in both the US and here, it was only a matter of time." With no smile for him, she shifted in her stance and crossed her arms.

"Something on your mind?" he asked.

"Did you have anything to do with me being here?" She shot straight to the point. Another characteristic he hadn't forgotten.

"I had everything to do with you being here. I needed new boots, and yours were the best ones."

"So this wasn't some ploy to get me here?"

"Ploy?" He straightened. "I don't understand your meaning." He understood very well.

"Listen, I know we hooked up and all—"

He howled with laughter, cutting her off. "You think I've been wallowing over you to the point where I orchestrated having problems with my boots, losing a major footwear sponsorship, and bringing management into the mix when they have been waiting for me to return to play for almost a year? Do you think I'm . . . um . . . what's the word now? Thirsty?"

Charlotte's lips twitched at the corner. Any man would be honored to bed Charlotte, but he had bigger things to worry about. His entire career hung in the balance, and if he couldn't get through training feeling good and able to do his job, then all the things that he'd worked for would disappear.

"So you didn't know it was me and blindly accepted my design?"

"Honestly, I didn't know or care who designed it."

"Yeah, but—"

"Your shoe fit best, Charlotte. The rest you can thank management for. They're the ones organizing all of this. All I want or need from you is your shoe."

He sounded harsh, even to himself, and her hard visage cracked slightly, but she'd come with a lot of assumptions, and the last thing he wanted was to be perceived as some lovestruck twerp. Had she been the best lover he'd had? Maybe. Who was he kidding? Fuck yes, and that was saying something, since he had catalogs of conquests on his highlight reel. However, he had to pop the fantasy bubble and her belief that he'd flown her here under some pretense.

"Okay," she responded as if unaffected.

"Why don't you have a seat?" He offered her a black cushioned chair in front of a wood desk and was relieved when she sat down.

"Would it have been so bad if I did?" he asked, sitting behind the desk, giving her the distance and space he thought she wanted.

"Yes." She leaned against his coach's desk, and he orbited her so he could continue to face her.

"Why?"

She tugged on her suit. "I don't like owing anyone any kind of debt. I just got out of that situation with my investors," she admitted. She crossed her legs, and the press lines faded slightly from the thickness of her thighs.

"What happened?" He wanted to know but wouldn't have been surprised if she shut him down.

"They wanted my company to take a different direction."

"Let me guess—you disagreed with that direction."

She nodded. "Because of this deal I was able to pay them off and start fresh. Free and clear." She puffed her chest.

"Well, Charlotte, all you owe me is a pair of boots," he said. The heaviness of her pride filled the space between them, and he imagined that being unburdened by a business relationship gone sour must have been a relief. He'd had a few of those in the past.

"That's different. You get a product; I get compensated."

The power in her statement piqued his interest. Did she see everything between them as various transactions? Had their romp in New York been completely meaningless?

"Here's the deal," she said, pulling him from the bleak tunnel he traipsed. "The process is as follows, and our deadline is tight. I need to get data, and then we have to get this shoe through the manufacturing process. You have a prototype that you can use for training, one that I had specially made, but it's just a mold and doesn't have all the precision data to accommodate your weight or absorb your shocks. This isn't a one-size-fits-all deal, so you need to contribute with feedback. As much of it as you can give me."

"Okay."

"Thanks to your management, I've been connected with the manufacturing contact that normally handles the footwear for the team. I'll be the lead contact and decision maker, building a relationship with them so they know that when we are ready to produce various versions of the shoe for you to test, we need them back as soon as possible."

"How long does it take to make a pair of boots?" He rocked back in the desk chair, briefly staring at a picture of Gaff and the owner at the championship he'd missed last year.

"Well, there's materials that need to be cut, some coming from America, Italy. Printing and stitching of the design and national team logo. Next is the assembly of the shoe, and finally quality control," she said as she ticked off each process on her slender fingers. "So depending on what kind of shoe we're making, a few days to a few weeks."

"Oh." Disappointment enveloped his words. Would that be all the time they had together?

"However, getting to that stage is weeks away. I need to test the shoe, after I get data, and improve on what new information we get from your activity. It's going to take work, and your input is valuable."

He needed this shoe. He'd be shit without it. He'd taken the intensity out of their reunion, but if she thought that she'd be in charge, she was wrong. This was his career on the line, and Charlotte was the gatekeeper between him and her innovative and customized shoe.

"I want you to know that I'll have a lot to say about this boot. It has to be perfect. I hope you understand and don't take offense to criticism, because I'll tell you now there will be lots coming."

"So long as the criticism is constructive," she said. "Don't think that you're going to be bossing me around and telling me what to do. Your profession is soccer player, and my profession is footwear-and-apparel specialist. If we stick to our individual lanes, we shouldn't have a problem."

"Agreed."

And with that one word, the two of them sealed the contract between themselves, their role, and his quest to get the boots on his feet. He'd seen master craftsmen create cleats for teams around the globe. Yet hers pushed the boundaries of innovation with their unorthodox materials and style, and his management had been very flexible with allowing him to go with a novice in their eyes. They believed in him and what he could do once he was back on the pitch. Charlotte's reputation was as much at stake as his. They would both do well to make sure that they were successful. He needed to be happy with the boot, and she needed to do her best to get him shoes he'd be happy with.

"I guess I will see you on Friday, when we'll get started?"

"Friday morning, then?"

"See you then," she said.

Unbeknownst to him, he had chosen Seam and Sole and Charlotte. He wasn't getting out of it, and she wasn't going to walk away now that she had an opportunity to take her prototype to the next level. *Let the games begin.*

Chapter 6

Charlotte's rectangular glass trophy, which she'd won two years ago for Best New Company from the Foundation of Innovative Sportswear Brands, sparkled on her desk next to a bouquet of white Christmas roses she'd gotten from the florist in her new neighborhood. Finally, she was done putting the finishing touches on her Grand Canal flat in Dublin. Winter in Ireland brought with it a chill from the water, but she'd take the midforties temps over the deep freeze that she'd normally suffer for most of January in New York. The sun flooding in from partly cloudy skies also brightened her view of the canal, and even though it wasn't perpetually green as she'd thought, there were still lush evergreens and ferns that flourished year-round.

If she wanted to function well in her new role, she needed to feel comfortable in her new space by making it her own. She'd need to be well rested to keep up with Eoghan and to be creative to work through whatever problems her client would likely have. Her at-home space was her secret weapon. That included her neighborhood. Buying flowers as well as her first pint in Ireland at Becky Morgans, the local pub, and Irish bread-and-butter pudding from the Art of Coffee in Alto Vetro helped her make the neighborhood her own. Not bad for only having been in Ireland for forty-eight hours.

Danai came out of the bedroom, where he'd been perusing the off-white walls, and into the living space. He stood by the floor-to-ceiling window wall and looked toward the canal and the barren trees in the distance, some with only a few leaves clinging to them as they headed into her first winter in Ireland.

"I see you, view. Girl, this place is nice," Danai said. "Not as nice as mine, though, but you have a better view. I really like the setup. It will work for you."

"Wait. Hold on. What do you mean, not as nice as yours?" Charlotte asked.

"You know the *community* hooks me up. National team administration gave us our locations, and my people took it to the next level."

"I want people." Charlotte crossed her arms. "Why didn't you get your community to hook me up too? I'm a fan of the level-up."

Charlotte didn't really care much about leveling up because she really liked her place. The two-bedroom was larger than her Harlem apartment but still cozy enough for her to feel like she could walk through the rooms without the sensation of being closed in. The high windows, the high ceilings, the off-white walls, and the hardwood floors were perfect canvases for the pictures and colorful urban art she'd brought with her. Once she had laid out her pink fluffy rug from home by her desk, she instantly had a boss office space similar to hers in Harlem but in view of the canal.

"I thought you would have used one of the rooms for your office, but I like this." Danai's fingers flickered over the corner of one of her cranberry-colored throw pillows on the couch. "This way, you can keep an eye on that view. I mean, you do have it in the master as well, but that is not a space for work. If you'd put your desk in there, then we would have had to have a little heart-to-heart."

Charlotte pushed her comrade. "That's not why we're here."

"Miss Ma'am, we are always here for that. You do remember that you told me about Eoghan, right?" Danai questioned. "I'm honored because I'm the only one that knows, and I'm sure Ayanna would be both happy and horrified by the news. But if you think that you and that boy are going to keep carrying on with this 'I'm the shoe designer' and 'I'm the client' bullshit, then you're out of your damn mind. I bet when you saw him, you couldn't stop staring at that man's dick. How I wish I was there."

"Danai!" Charlotte complained.

"Am I wrong?" Danai questioned with his whole face.

The truth heated Charlotte from her cheeks down to her center.

"That's what I thought."

Charlotte's affair with Eoghan was the last thing she wanted to hear or think about, much less discuss with Danai. Charlotte had her own dilemma with her New York onetime bang with Eoghan, but she had neatly packed it up and vowed not to open it until moths had eaten that situation to threads. "I'm not gonna lie. Of course I struggle with it. I'm human with real fucking feelings." But if she could at least keep up the pretenses and not sample her sloppy seconds, then it was more likely that she could do her job.

"Am I hearing this right? The incomparable Charlotte Bowman is human? With feelings?"

"Stop."

"I won't saturate a wet dish towel. You're a grown woman. I trust that you know what you're doing," Danai said. "For now."

"Look, just focus your efforts on getting me that community upgrade next time." Charlotte did her best to change the subject.

"Girl, I can't be thinking about everybody all the time. I got you next time, though," Danai said, as he gathered his teal tote bag and hooked it on his arm at the elbow.

"Okay, fam," Charlotte said, weakly holding Danai to a promise that she was pretty sure he wouldn't keep. "I'm going to be keeping an eye on this promise of yours," she teased.

"I'll see you bright and early tomorrow for day one with Eoghan. I cannot wait to meet him. This should be a treat," Danai said, thick with sarcasm.

Charlotte crossed her fingers. "Here's hoping."

"I'd like a meal next time I come here," Danai tossed behind him on the way out.

"Then you must be cooking it," Charlotte responded and heard Danai's rich laughter as the door closed.

Tomorrow, she'd need to be prepared. Tomorrow, she'd need to be ready for anything Eoghan threw at her.

Friday at the Dublin Rovers training facility, the weather rivaled a winter day in New York. The temperature wasn't as bad as the wind that whipped at them from out of the blue. Charlotte lost her scarf twice, and the cold gusts hitting Danai's long curly hair were followed with, "What the fuck?" Still, the two of them secured their equipment, setting up on field level with a table just off the checker-mowed, manicured green grass of the field. The Rovers' stadium had been easy to navigate from the first time she'd visited on arrival day. Charlotte and Danai positioned their laptops on the table to record Eoghan's data. The shadows that the gathered clouds overhead had cast against the empty stands surrounding them broke with sun, and Charlotte welcomed the bit of warmth from the rays.

As she waited for Eoghan to arrive, assistant training coaches in black-and-green tracksuits ran balls onto the field and set up various neon-yellow and bright-orange training markers and nets for the player exercises.

"Everything's all set," Danai said after double-checking the electrodes in the shoe inserts to make sure that everything communicated wirelessly. The Rovers' training facility, Charlotte had decided, was a great place to start, since the Rovers were the defending champions in the Irish Premier League. She wanted Eoghan to be in a place that she hoped made him feel good.

Eoghan arrived in his white training kit with Ronin, Clive, and Dodger, the kit man, whom Charlotte had met on her quick tour the day she'd arrived. The wind thrashed Eoghan's brown hair about, and she wanted to rake her fingers through the thick strands. It was too cold for shorts, in her opinion, but Eoghan seemed unaffected by the brisk day. That didn't stop her from enjoying the view of his strong, lean legs. She knew exactly how the dark curly hair on those legs felt against hers from the front and from behind.

She bumped into the table on her way back to Danai as the group of men made their way over to her table.

"You okay? You hit yourself pretty hard."

"I'm fine." She took great interest in her laptop, which wasn't doing much of anything at present, and bit down on the inside of her lip to keep from rubbing her throbbing thigh. "He's early. Great. I won't have to scold him for being late." She'd heard about his shenanigans at Purchase House when he'd been working with Ayanna. Thankfully, any remnants of that trifling version of him hadn't made an appearance. So far.

"Hi, Eoghan. I hope you're ready to work today," Charlotte greeted and then made introductions. "This is Danai Roberts. My colead on this project."

Danai was a gay man and proud of it. He answered to three names: *Danai*, *sir*, and *girl*. He was special, especially to Charlotte. That was one of the reasons why she took him everywhere. *Right-hand man* only touched the surface of Danai's capabilities. A fashionista with a runway walk and a genius administrator whose problem-solving skills made rocket science look dull, Danai was everything Charlotte needed. In a word, he was the fiercest.

"Danai, this is our client, Eoghan O'Farrell; his agent, Ronin; Clive, our brand manager; and Dodger, the kit man. We will be working closely with them."

"Hiya," Eoghan said, the first to extend a hand to Danai.

"Hello there," Ronin said.

"Pleasure," Clive said.

Dodger waved.

"Hello, everyone. It's a pleasure." Danai shook the hand of each person. He was taller than Charlotte and everyone else with the exception of Eoghan.

"If I'm not available, Danai is your next point of contact. Think of him as an extension of me. Please don't hesitate to approach or communicate pertinent and time-sensitive information to him. He'll know exactly what to do, including find me if need be."

"Good to know," Eoghan said.

"Mmm," Danai mumbled to her. "He can get it. He is everything a delicious treat should be."

A whip of cold air stung her cheeks, but Eoghan's evaluation quickly counteracted the brutal elements. Why in heaven's name were her reactions to him so hard to manage? She cleared her throat. "Ready to get started, Eoghan?"

"Sure," he said and jogged in place. Then took off into a jog down the way.

Charlotte's head bobbled. "What's he doing?"

"Just getting a bit of a warm-up," Ronin said.

"We need him to warm up with the data inserts as well," Charlotte said. "It's best if we get a holistic view of what his feet are doing in all aspects of play."

Clive waved him back.

Eoghan sprinted back, then did two high jumps that almost cleared Charlotte's five feet, eight inches.

Danai passed him a pair of cleats.

The distaste on Eoghan's face had Charlotte backing up. "These are my old boots." He aimed the comment right at her.

"Yes. They're fitted with electrodes that will give us some baseline data on how you are moving."

"But I don't want to be wearing the old boots," he said testily.

"I understand, but like I said. Just a baseline. We'll be right here recording."

"Why can't I just wear the new boots, and you can get your data that way?"

"Because I need to get the data from your old boots to see what's wrong, and then I can customize the prototype to make a new tester shoe for you." Did he think she liked getting under his skin? She wanted this whole exercise to run as smoothly as possible.

"Fine." He put on his cleats like she'd given him a ratty pair of old Keds to wear on his first day of high school.

"Carry on like we're not even here. We'll let you know when we need you."

Eoghan let out a hefty sigh. He might have expected his annoyance to affect her, but his bratty tactics were a mild irritation at best.

"Okay," Charlotte exclaimed without validating his negativity. "Let's do it."

Eoghan all but dragged his feet to the field.

"We'll leave you to it," Clive said, smoothing his mustache. "Again, anything you need, Charlotte, and I'm your man."

"Same goes for me. You both have us at your disposal," Ronin added, and Charlotte could have sworn she saw his biceps flex.

"Thank you both," Charlotte said before the two men departed.

"Eoghan is salty," Danai sang once Clive and Ronin were out of earshot.

"Just annoyed. Would you want to wear something that was bugging you?"

"Facts," Danai said.

Charlotte sat behind her computer that cast on dual monitors, and as Eoghan moved, the data started to record. She crossed her fingers and hoped that this first run went as painlessly as possible for both herself and Eoghan.

Not thirty minutes later and Charlotte couldn't believe her eyes or her ears. She'd thought she'd seen Eoghan at his lowest when he'd been rehabbing in New York, but this level of tantrum she'd only seen on her cousin's two-year-old after he'd been cut off from eating sugar cookies and sent to bed.

Eoghan hurled the yellow shoe across the pitch. His white shirt with green trim flew up his chest, revealing a chiseled back and well-defined abdominal muscles. The vision haunted her hands because she knew exactly what it felt like to touch him—not only there but everywhere. In addition to enjoying and silently reminiscing about the view, Charlotte thought that maybe having him perform in the old shoes with her data inserts was the worst idea next to allowing fidget spinners in schools.

"And here I thought our athletes back home behaved like toddlers," Danai said, wearing the same practice jersey Eoghan wore, over his black skinny jeans and cleat-bottomed, calf-high, heeled boots. "He is horrible."

Charlotte thought Danai's outfit was too much for day one, but he supported their client from head to toe, even with the brutal honesty.

The kit man ran to collect the cleats.

Eoghan looked visibly upset, from not moving on the field to com-pressing the ball between his hands before slamming it down on the grass, but he was about to get pissed off further by her next suggestion.

"I need you to put the shoe back on," Charlotte yelled to him on the field.

"Feeeeeeck noooooo," he shouted.

"The shoes have data inserts inside that I'm tracking." She pointed to her computer.

"I can't do anything in them. This exercise is useless," he growled, nearing the table where she sat.

Charlotte twisted her mouth to one side and analyzed him for a few seconds. "I thought you were doing fine. I mean, you're practicing so—"

"Fine? I've never been just fine. I'm team captain, for this club and the Irish national team. Fine is shite." He marched and kicked the other cleat off so hard it flew diagonally up into the air before landing a few feet from the white goal net.

"Oh, girl, no. Handle that," Danai said.

Charlotte was already heading to Eoghan. She stepped on the stiff green grass with her souped-up orange version of a pair of Seam and Sole cleats she'd worn specifically in case she had to go on the pitch. She'd seen an episode of *Ted Lasso* where Coach Lasso was ordered to get off the pitch by the kit man, who emphasized the sanctity of the pitch. She'd not only taken notes but planned ahead.

"Dodger? I'm good?" Charlotte called to the kit man and pointed to her shoes and the grass beneath her feet.

Dodger raised a thumbs-up.

What she hadn't planned on was her client's complete and utter meltdown.

Eoghan paced in a large circle, pushing back his wet dark hair. She stood still and placed both her mustard-colored-knit-gloved hands to rest on one of her hips, where the bottom of her chunky gray sweater met her Good American skinny blue jeans. The weight of the pom-pom on top of her matching hat moved to the side she leaned. She restrained herself from tapping her toe as she waited for him to calm down. His breathing dropped in tempo, and his now-linear pacing did as well.

"Do they hurt?" she asked him.

"What?" he asked.

"Do. They. Hurt?" She slowed her speech in an effort to get him to focus on her.

"No, they don't hurt. I just can't do anything in them," he replied, combing his hands through his hair.

"Clearly you're upset." She stated the obvious in case he hadn't yet realized he'd just kicked his cleats off on semiwet grass during winter. She shivered at the thought. Her digits were already numbing from cold.

"You're here to give me better boots. Have you not enough data?"

"Not yet. That's why I need you to put them back on. The longer it takes me to get the data I need, the longer it takes us to get to the next phase of tweaking the shoe. You don't want that, do you?"

He groaned.

"See, the thing is . . ." She tried to figure out how best to explain her initial findings without triggering him.

"What?" he asked when she continued to hesitate.

"You know what? It's not important."

"Speak your thoughts."

"The thing is, Eoghan, it doesn't really look like there is a problem with your current shoe. It appears to be supporting you. The shock absorption on your joints and nerves looks good and is reacting neutrally."

"Meaning?"

"Meaning there is no sign of any apparent stress or discomfort," Charlotte said.

"You think it's all in my head." The tension coming off his body snared her into its sphere, and her body stiffened.

"Don't put words in my mouth. I didn't say that."

"No, your data did," he said, air quoting "data," and his brown eyes blazed.

She inhaled a calming breath only to catch whiffs of his sweaty musk mixed with grass and winter air. "The only way for us to see what, if anything else, might be an issue is for me to get better data, so I'm going to need you to suck it up, put your shoes back on, and continue with practice."

"I don't want—" he started to complain, but she cut him off.

"Don't think about being great. Focus on making your movements as dynamic as possible. The more data I have, the more there is to analyze. Okay?" Charlotte asked.

"I'm so bad at this," she mumbled. Ayanna was so much better at coaxing her clients to get on board. Sure, Charlotte's client-facing responsibilities happened on a regular basis, but her interactions were mostly brief and with a team behind her. Not to mention she was normally brought in as a heavy to fast-forward projects. The way Eoghan shifted from foot to foot in front of her lacked confidence—in both of them.

"Trust me." She wanted to put her hand on his shoulder and pat inspiration onto him, but they'd just started working together, and with sketchy history, she didn't dare. She had years of experience in footwear and apparel and had her own company. There were many reasons he should trust her, save one. She hadn't proved to him that he'd have the shoe he wanted by the end of this process and get the result he desperately needed.

The kit man offered Eoghan the pair of cleats as if handing them to a tiger. When Eoghan didn't seem interested, the kit man looked at Charlotte.

"I'll take those, Dodger," she said, and Dodger turned over the cleats. "How 'bout it? We're doing this?"

Eoghan sighed. "I'm fucking done with these boots."

"Today is the only day you have to work with these shoes. I promise." She omitted the part where he'd have to do this with various prototypes, but he didn't need to know that right now. She held the cleats out.

"I'll give them today, and that's it." He snatched the shoes from her hand.

She smiled and then turned toward Danai, who waited as if on the edge of his seat. Charlotte held two thumbs up close to her stomach, not realizing the tension in her body until her shoulders relaxed. She hadn't lost her client on day one, and Eoghan had been willing to work with her through his disgruntled attitude.

The rest of the team and some of the staff started to make their way over. What she'd been doing with Eoghan was about to intensify given that now he'd be reacting with players during their drills.

A dark-skinned man hopped onto the field, then ran at full speed. He had a large pair of gloves tucked under his arms. His green-and-white uniform popped off the contrast of his skin. Charlotte thought Eoghan was athletic, his buddy Shane, too, but this man glided over the pitch like he was born for it. He was a specimen to measure all the sportsmen before and after him against. His long legs poetically moved under him, and immediately Charlotte recognized him as the team's goalkeeper.

"Being a baby about yer boots, are ya?" the man shouted at Eoghan. "Get on with it, man. We're waiting for you to get off yer arse and join us next month. There are plenty more fixtures for you to play." The goalkeeper clapped his hands several times, each clap getting harder and harder as if to inject fire into Eoghan.

"Who is that?" Danai asked but might as well have said, *I want that.*

"Pippin," Eoghan said, kicking his legs and jogging in place to stay warm.

Charlotte had heard about him, but they had never met.

"Introductions, please," Danai commanded more than requested. However, Pippin had already started the jog over.

Pippin braked in front of Charlotte. "Hello, deary. Pippin Adamu, at your service." Vapors from the cold resembling smoke escaped his lips. He bent into a low curtsy.

If Charlotte hadn't been so thrown by him, she would have laughed instead of the girly giggle she produced. Pippin's steel-gray eyes hypnotized her where she stood. There was gorgeous, and then there was Pippin. Charlotte could count on one hand the few times she'd found herself speechless, including this instance. Danai, too, had lost any ability to communicate beyond the caveman grunts he made in his attempts. Had Charlotte not already been with Eoghan, Pippin could easily give him a run for his money morning, afternoon, night, and even on her weekends.

"You are fine." She couldn't help herself. "I heard about you from Yaya, but dayum."

"Thanks." Pippin smiled but seemed to take the compliment in stride, like he'd heard it too many times. "I'm a better footballer." He switched gears. "I've heard loads about you."

"Really?" Charlotte dragged her eyes away from Pippin to look at Eoghan.

"He didn't hear it from me," Eoghan said, and Charlotte let the slight roll off her shoulders.

"Ayanna goes on and on about ya. Charlotte this and Charlotte that. It's a pleasure," Pippin said.

"I hope it was entertaining. We've known each other a long time, so we have a lot of history," Charlotte said.

Eoghan abruptly threw up his hands and walked off, and Charlotte couldn't help but take the action as a personal hit.

"Don't worry about Eoghan now. He's just a grumpy sod."

"Do you think his boots matter?" Charlotte asked, surprised by her own question.

"I think if it helps his confidence, it matters."

Her and Pippin's silent exchange spoke volumes. "That's what I thought."

"Dodger, pass me that wee yoke there," Pippin said and made a gesture over his face. The kit man ran over to him and handed him a towel.

"Is that how you say *towel* here?"

"You'll get used to it. Everything is *yoke*. It's just something. Anything," Pippin clarified. He stretched his body in all directions to stay warm. Charlotte wished she had on a pair of Uggs instead of her cleats and performed her own two-step to keep the circulation going in her numbing toes.

"I see," she said. "Got it."

"Can I ask ya. Are you and Eoghan still a thing?" Pippin asked, giving her face a thorough study.

"What?" Charlotte clutched her scarf. "No. Why? Did he say we were?"

"He's my best mate," Pippin said. "Not much I don't know."

"Oh, well . . . no. That's unprofessional, not to mention—"

"No need to sell it, darlin'. Your face says all I need to know." Pippin snickered, and Charlotte's imagination thrived with what she might look like in her denial.

A trail of players came onto the field, and three headed straight over to the bright, shiny New Yorkers on the field.

"Hello there. Name's Lance." The player's confidence oozed from every pore as he evaluated her with eyes as dark brown as his shaved head.

"Patrick," a shorter player said. He offered Charlotte a bright smile as he ran a hand through his light curly hair.

"Andreas." The man lunged from side to side, stretching rich brown muscular legs, and gazed up at Charlotte with narrow eyes. He wore a gray knit hat with braided yarn hanging down the sides, and the wind attacked his shoulder-length black hair.

They must have been used to introducing themselves in attendance format, because as they each raised a finger, Charlotte half expected them to say *present*. "Hi, I'm Charlotte, and this is my assistant, Danai."

"Greetings," Danai said and pawed his hand forward. Each man gave him a quick handshake.

"What's all the stuff behind ya?" Lance questioned, flicking his head at the table and equipment on top of it.

"You here from America?" Andreas asked.

"You here to fix Eoghan?" Patrick inquired.

64

The number of questions that came at Charlotte, each from a different player, flew at her like a round of bullets. They were a curious bunch for sure, but none of them seemed to be antagonistic or mean. Charlotte and her assistant were two new fixtures on the pitch, and each footballer wanted to know what she was doing there, with whom, and why. They sounded as meddlesome as any family she'd ever known, been around, or been a part of.

"I'm not here to fix anyone," Charlotte said. "I'm here to customize cleats for Eoghan. You know, boots?" Charlotte realized how silly that last bit sounded.

"Where'd you say she comes from?" Patrick asked someone behind them.

"I didn't," Eoghan said over her head, and Charlotte nearly jumped out of her cleats. She hadn't even known he was still on the pitch, much less hovering behind her.

"Harlem," Pippin explained, his eyes bouncing back and forth between her and Eoghan.

Patrick gave a low whistle. "All the way from America," he said as if making a new discovery.

"This one's the comedian," Eoghan commented.

Charlotte's head whipped from player to player.

"Of course we know what cleats are." Patrick scoffed so hard Charlotte almost apologized for the statement.

"Right, I realized that sounded silly, but anyway. I'm working on boots for Eoghan that will help him feel more comfortable on the pitch. And with any luck, help him perform better." If Eoghan didn't perform better, then surely her contract could be void and her cleat prototype obsolete before it even got going.

The group nodded.

Coach Boyle cracked an angry whistle. "Oi,'" he yelled. "This isn't a fucking tea party. Get your arses in position for drills, but not before you give me ten laps."

The group groaned and tossed accusing looks at Charlotte and Danai.

"Don't blame me or her. We didn't tell you guys to stop and interrogate us," Danai said.

"He always this brutal?" Patrick asked, and Charlotte noticed he asked most of the questions.

"You've no idea," Charlotte said, stifling a smile. In the short time that she was in Ireland, she had come to love the humor that seemed to be inherent in every Irish person she met. She kept the stereotype in perspective, like the ones people had of her race—like that all Black people could dance and sing and were good at athletics. Often true but not always. Just because the Irish sounded humorous to her when they spoke didn't necessarily mean that what they said was always funny. However, she had yet to meet an Irish person who wasn't a natural comedian, and she enjoyed those experiences.

This group of players was a crew of diverse races, ethnicities, and opinions, who, though serious about football, gave off a spirited and close-knit vibe that she wanted to be around. And then there was Eoghan, who lamented his footwear. She felt like he missed everything that was happening around them, or maybe it was just familiarity with his teammates. Still, she was new to Ireland and to the teammates around her, and most of all, she had a client who, for all his celebrity and surrounding sportsmanship, wallowed in his despair about his shoes. She didn't want his happiness on the pitch to rest in her footwear-developing hands, but somehow it felt like it did.

"I have to get on with practice. See you around, Charlotte." Pippin saluted.

"We should get back to work," Charlotte said, her anxiety trending upward. Despite the brisk outdoors, she broke into a cold sweat, and as she rubbed the back of her neck, she felt the baby hairs curl from the dampness.

"You all right, girl?" Danai asked. "You're white as a sheet."

Charlotte pursed her lips and smug mugged him. "Really?"

Danai sucked his teeth. "You know what I mean."

"O'Farrell? You need a fucking invitation? Find your arse with the team."

Eoghan continued to linger where Charlotte was as she watched the team start their laps. She gave Eoghan a nod to follow, even though her title was neither coach nor gaffer. "This data won't collect itself."

"Actually . . . ," Danai interjected.

"Shh." Charlotte pinched her hand closed, silencing Danai and simultaneously addressing Eoghan. "Be natural out there. Forget about us and just do your thing."

Eoghan offered a tight smile before heading off.

"You think you're going to be able to give him what he needs?"

Charlotte chewed on the question. "I can give the fire-breathing dragon with his shoe problems what he wants. What he needs is a different story." With that, a doom cloud headed right at her, and failure stared her right in the face.

Chapter 7

Eoghan's life woes hovered over him like the smell of turf burning. He stretched out his legs, crossed at the ankles. He pulled his beanie down farther onto his head, tightened the white plaid scarf around his neck, and shoved his hands into the pockets of his brown leather jacket. He looked out into the river Liffey despite the colorful lights outside the EPIC Museum. The wood bench ached his arse from how long he'd been fixed there like a statue that was part of the small park. His Docklands apartment building looming behind him paled in comparison to his worries about his career. He'd had a tough couple of days, and still there seemed to be no solution in sight.

Both his coaches had called him out on his play today. Basic skills that used to be second nature had seemed to just flee from him. Not only that but he was sure his father had heard about it all and would be hunting him down any minute to bombard him with questions and next steps. He needed a breather for his full head and wished he had a monotonous skill like knitting or puzzle making, painting even. Anything where he could focus on the one stitch, piece, or stroke.

On top of that, there was Charlotte. He couldn't help but be close to her, and when the lads had taken interest in her, he'd failed miserably at being neutral. She must have thought him an idiot, a pathetic gowl and a half. What a waster he'd been. Hadn't his "new leaf" turned over? Maybe he was too hard on himself. Maybe he wasn't hard enough and his father had been right all this time. He needed guidance. A hand to steer him right.

"There you are."

Surprised by the voice of his friend Shane, he jumped up. "Good man," Eoghan said and slapped hands with his best friend and pulled him into a hug. Pippin accompanied him, and both his best friends were a sight for sore eyes.

"Told you we'd find him here sulking like he's lost his dolly," Pippin said.

"All right, all right. Hold back the tears," Shane teased. His red hair had grown two inches longer since the last time Eoghan had seen him, and the strands blew in the wind like something out of a film. He patted Eoghan's back with one hand and carried a pack of beer in the other.

Pippin puckered his lips at Eoghan. "Give us a kiss, sweetheart."

Eoghan would normally playfully shove Pippin, but the emotion at seeing both his friends in his despair made him slap hands and pull his friend into a shoulder bump. He cleared his throat.

"I thought you were in Boston or some such place? What're you doing here? Ayanna with you?" Eoghan asked Shane.

Shane shook his head. "I'm back for a bit, training the new lad and working with Boyle when I can to learn the ropes. Ayanna's back in New York. She has a few clients to follow up with and work with in person, so she'll be there for a bit. I'll go in a week or two or something. We'll sort it."

"You miss her." Eoghan easily read the longing on Shane's face.

"Course he does," Pippin said. "Look at him. He's ready to board a plane tomorrow."

"It's fucking mad, isn't it?" Shane stated more than asked. "Anyway. I hear you're getting yourself ready to get back on the pitch. How's it feeling?" Shane referenced Eoghan's rehabbed leg as they all sat back down on the bench.

"It's all right. Body feels good."

Shane tossed him a beer and then handed one to Pippin.

"So what's the problem?"

"Who says there's a problem?" Eoghan cracked open his beer and took two long swigs. The cool liquid further chilled him as it slid down his throat, but it was nothing compared to the defensiveness seizing his muscles.

Pippin coughed. "I'll let you take this one, Shaney."

"So there's no problem, then?" Shane asked.

Eoghan quietly belched. "Of course there's a problem, but you don't have to point it out."

Pippin and Shane exchanged glances right over him. Shane sucked on his beer, and Pippin finally cracked open his. His friends didn't bark their opinions at him—instead they gave him the space to talk.

"It's my boots." As soon as the words came out his mouth, he felt like a dope.

"That's what Charlotte is helping you with, no?" Shane asked.

"Yeah, but it's a slow process. Now we're doing data collection," Eoghan complained.

Shane laughed at him. "Ayanna says she's good at her job, and she was a pistol when she came to the house. She's perfect for you."

"What do you mean?"

"I mean, if you thought Ayanna was tough . . ." Shane let him fill in the blanks.

"I'm aware." Charlotte had become many things to him already, and he didn't know or wasn't prepared for how else she'd impact his life.

"So." Shane studied him. "Did you shift?"

Eoghan could have gasped. "No. We've not made out. Why would you ask me that?"

"Because you've slept with her," Shane said.

"You should see your face, man," Pippin laughed. "I've seen it before." He pointed at Shane.

"What's that supposed to mean?" Eoghan looked back and forth between his friends.

Shane chuckled.

"Never mind, eejits," Eoghan said. "Oi," he directed at Shane. "Does Ayanna know?"

"They're best friends. Of course she knows, but Charlotte's chosen to keep it to herself. So Ayanna's waiting her out."

He should be happy that Charlotte didn't kiss and tell, but the news toyed with him. Did she think so little of him that he wasn't even worth gossiping about with her best friend?

"Now don't go getting into your thoughts and feelings about it," Shane said. "You have enough on your plate with football, don't you?"

"Fuck off." He did have enough on his plate, but no matter how hard he tried, Charlotte still piled on a portion of flirty eyes and a perfect arse. When he'd seen the lads surround her, he'd tried to walk away, wanted to leave her to the salivating wolves, but he couldn't. He'd gone all soft for her and had needed to protect her.

"Your best course is to work with Charlotte, get the best boot if that's the problem, and start getting after your training. Time's passing, and neither Boyle nor Walsh'll stand for much more of your whining and moaning about your shoes."

"I know it," Eoghan huffed.

"So, um . . . how's your father been with all this?" Shane asked.

"The usual," Eoghan said, though he'd been successful at avoiding him in large doses and hadn't really needed to go head-to-head with his da. "He doesn't know about Charlotte or the sponsorship."

"He's going to eat the head off ya," Pippin said.

"And then meddle more soon after," Eoghan said.

"Oul Donal's not an easy one." Pippin gulped down half his beer.

"He means well," Shane said.

Eoghan stared at a long water taxi passing down the river and thought it apropos that as the boat passed, so too had his opportunities to stand up to his father. He had his doubts that his father would actually listen to him even if Eoghan tried.

"Talk to him," Shane urged.

"Donal is not like Conor," Eoghan said, referring to Shane's father. "There's no talking to him. He's truly Father Knows Best."

"One day you will," Shane said and then hissed. "Feck! It's Baltic out here. My dick's about to freeze up." He jumped up and moved about to warm up.

Pippin followed with his own dramatic dance to ward off the cold. "I'm all for the heart-to-heart, but I'm with Shaney."

"It was nice and peaceful until you two showed up." Eoghan stood, and they headed toward the street to Eoghan's flat, where they'd finish the rest of the beers.

"I can help," Shane said, blowing into one fisted hand while the other carried the beers. "With the training."

"You came to America with me," Eoghan stated. "I thank you for that, but I'll sort it on my own."

"Feck off, you." Shane shoved him. "We've helped each other all these years. Me, you, and Pippin. The MAKin' crew. Take your little pity monologue and shove it up your bollocks," Shane said. "Me, Pip, the lads . . . we'll get you back. You'll get you back."

Eoghan nodded, not realizing how much he'd needed the pep talk. "Thanks for showing up."

"Thank your bollocks," Pippin said.

Eoghan smiled. "Love to you too, sweetheart."

Chapter 8

Charlotte still hadn't yet gotten her jet-lagged life together, even though she had been in Ireland for two weeks. She still yawned most of the day and found herself wide awake in the middle of the night. Even with a dose of melatonin to help her body get the time zones square, she was on the struggle bus. Her challenging sleep schedule didn't stop her from working, even if it did feel like she was burning the candle at both ends.

She reminded herself to meticulously review the data she'd collected and triple-check the measurements for Eoghan's tester. Sure, his presence complicated things, like how the heat from his body after working out on the field drew her body nearer. Or the way he whipped his sweaty hair out of his face. And how he rested his foot on the soccer ball as he listened to his coaches—the pose giving her a full view of his muscular thigh and lean calf. She wet her lips with her tongue at the thought.

She blinked herself back to the task at hand. "I'm a warrior, a professional." She wouldn't let their history dominate her job. While evaluating her prototype, she made sure to work with her vendors to secure the memory foam material for the different versions of Eoghan's shoe. She adopted the Apple technique and never got all her supplies from the same place so that no one could figure out her design. It was a good technique and motivated her to finally see her vision for the shoe come to fruition.

The hour was late back in New York, but Charlotte had yet to talk to her mom. Her days with Eoghan were stressful, especially with his cranky disposition about his footwear. She could use a little of her mom's soothing voice. She called home.

"Hey, honey." Gabrielle Bowman's cheerful greeting warmed Charlotte like an embrace. "How's it going over there? You settling in?"

Eoghan had lost his damn mind. Despite that, his image haunted her upon waking and when she closed her eyes before bed. She was under crunch time to produce cleats for him, and if the shoe failed, he'd fail, and she didn't want him to fail, because even if she denied it to herself, the universe knew she cared about him and his success. If they both were unsuccessful, then this opportunity would blow up in her fucking face. Charlotte didn't know how to respond, so she kept it simple.

"Things are fine, and I'm settling in okay."

"Hmm. So what's wrong?" her mother asked, and Charlotte shouldn't have expected anything less from her mom than for her to read her vocal cords.

My client is a pill. "Nothing. I might be jet lagged. Danai and I have only been here for a few weeks, and we're still trying to catch up energy-wise. How are you doing?"

"No different from the last time you called. Your father is going on a golfing trip with his club, and I'm going to see Whitney's new grandbaby girl. She is so excited. That makes three," her mother said, with all the unsaid implications. Charlotte's aunt Whitney had three grandchildren, and Gabrielle Bowman had none.

"That's great, Mom."

"Yeah. I can't wait to have my own someday. Maybe Whitney's luck will rub off on me."

"You have another daughter you banking that on?" Charlotte's question wasn't one of bravery. It just slipped out. She envisioned her mother pressing the heel of her hand against her forehead and shaking her crown of gray braids at the comment.

"Don't say that, Charlotte," her mother scolded. "You love kids. I know you want to have your own someday soon. I know you do."

"Maybe. It depends, Mom. You know how important my career is." Charlotte had seen her mother sacrifice her dreams and, for a long time, her passions in support of her father's engineering career, over and over. It had taught Charlotte one thing, and that was to put herself first, enjoy her men on the side, and never regret giving anything up.

"Yes, I know. You and Ayanna make me so proud with all you've both accomplished. You're in Ireland working for a big sports team. I couldn't have ever imagined that for you, baby," her mother said. "I just don't want either of you to miss out on having a family of your own."

Ayanna, her best friend and Gabrielle Bowman's daughter from another mother, hadn't been spared Charlotte's mother's hounding. Charlotte wished that her mother's pride didn't come with a caveat, but after a tough day, she'd take it.

"Be honest. How was your day?" her mother inquired again.

"Shitty," Charlotte blurted.

"All right, now we're getting somewhere," her mother said.

Charlotte storyboarded her interaction with Eoghan in three acts. Meeting, altercation, and then blowup.

"This is a new client. Do what you always do. Get to the heart of the matter," her mom reminded her. "The blowup isn't personal."

Charlotte wasn't so sure. According to Eoghan, he only needed or wanted her shoe. Given that they'd been fuck buddies, how was she to know what was personal from what wasn't?

Her mom continued. "Once you know what's at stake for him, you can work toward relieving that worry for him and the team. And while you're at it, show 'em who's the boss, dear."

Charlotte's mother would have made a great businesswoman. Along with being an accomplished art dealer, she was an intuitive force and used her skills to make a beautiful home rich with masks from Malawi, Tracht clothing from Munich, clay bowls and fabrics from Paraguay, and furniture from Paris. For Charlotte and her father, Gabrielle Bowman ran her home with organizational skills that rivaled the best in the business. Museums and art societies called her for her creativity, knowledge, and experience, as well as contacting her with countless offers for director and board positions. All of which her mother refused. Charlotte loved her father, but her dad's less exciting and less lucrative profession always came first, and that setup stumped Charlotte to the point that the confusion turned to motivation. She'd internalized the fact that her mother was always sacrificing so many opportunities for him. After seeing that all her life, she made sure that she did the opposite of what her mother did.

However, in this case, though the circumstances weren't quite what her mother presumed, Charlotte had to get to the core of Eoghan's neuroticism about his cleats. Sure, they'd had a brilliant bone months ago, and their attraction was still on a high setting, but they were adults, actively adulting, and she wouldn't be here, in Dublin, if he hated her product. "You're right, Mom. There is more going on here for him personally," Charlotte said.

"And I suspect for you too. You didn't take this contract to sit around and buff your toenails, dear. You've got to work for the success you went there to get."

"Okay, pep talk," Charlotte said, snapping her fingers.

Her mother's yawn came through her laugh. "Well, I'm only up this late to talk to you."

"Give Dad my best."

"I will, baby."

Charlotte ended the call with her mom and looked at her design. With failure staring her in the face, she reverted to the philosophy that helped her survive. *Get what you want and get out.*

Chapter 9

Charlotte blinked her dry, heavy eyes open. She had to be on point today more than any other day if she was going to get anywhere with Eoghan. When he'd asked her to lunch to further discuss her design, she'd been floored. They'd barely gotten through the preliminary data-collection process. Eoghan had shunned her questionnaire, and the practice session with the data inserts had been an absolute nightmare. As he was her client, she should be welcoming a meeting to find out more about his needs. However, the thought of time alone with Eoghan had her tummy doing backflips and forward tumbles. He'd given up a sponsorship for her shoe. If things didn't work out like he wanted, surely he'd give her the boot for another boot.

Aviva Stadium was nothing like the training facility for the Rovers. The stadium was a gigantic piece of art, and she'd had to ask for directions several times to get to where she needed to be. The towering glass rim gave the feeling of movement with its wave design. Today, before meeting Eoghan, Charlotte walked the perimeter of the pitch and looked out at fifty thousand empty seats. Her lungs constricted and her heart thumped in her chest at the thought of them being filled with hollering fans.

"Yikes," she said, shivering.

She headed inside, winding through doors and past corridors to wait outside the locker room for Eoghan. As players made their way out, each regarded her like some sort of novelty. Some of the men grunted acknowledgment of her presence, nodded, or ignored her altogether as they made their way past her, the smell of postpractice funk mixed with steam from showers and postdressing cologne. She shouldn't have been surprised by their reaction given the fact that they didn't know her or why she was hanging around. She was neither a girlfriend, wife, publicist, nor journalist. All of whom were handled in something of an assembly line of interactions. She might have insider access, but she was more of an outsider than the people waiting. It wasn't a novel place for her to be or feel but not the most fun either.

Three familiar faces passed her on their way out and immediately brightened her mood. Lance, Patrick, and Pippin were the only known quantities here at Aviva, since they were also national team players.

"Charlotte, nice to see you. How're ya gettin' on?" Pippin asked.

"Hi," Charlotte said, her loneliness dissipating with his greeting. "I'm doing okay."

"Waiting for Eoghan?" Patrick, ever the inquisitor, asked.

"Yeah," she said. "He's in there, right?"

"Don't worry yourself. He'll be out in short order," Patrick added with what Charlotte could only define as formality.

"Next time you have to come out with us," Lance said. "And your assistant, of course."

"I don't know if that's a good idea," she said in an attempt to keep to her side of the professional line.

"We'll take that as a yes," Lance said. "Till next time."

"Mr. Celebrity," Pippin mouthed to her about Lance, and she stifled a laugh. "Take care, Charlotte," he said, and they all moseyed along.

Eoghan finally came out. A five-o'clock shadow painted his face, but his shape-up was on point, and his partly dry hair was neatly combed to the side. Today, he smelled like what Charlotte thought a mint julep might.

Lord help me.

He screeched to a halt as if surprised to see her there. "You're here."

"Hello to you too." She didn't expect cartwheels or a choreographed dance, but a simple hello would have sufficed.

"No. Sorry. Hello," he said, recovering. "It's just that we never . . . I didn't expect to see anyone just outside the dressing rooms."

"You're not the only one," she said. "Well, here I am. Thought we could chat on our walk to lunch as well."

"Walk?" he asked.

"Yeah. You know, that activity where you put one foot in front of the other," she said, deadpan.

It took a moment for the joke to land on him, but it did, and he chuckled, a sound that was a bit goofy, cute, and sexy, all at the same time. If she weren't as smart as she was, it would have had an impact on her.

"No walking, except to my car." Unlike many of the men coming out of the locker room in tracksuits, jeans, or other casual wear, Eoghan wore a gray sweater and black-and-gray knit scarf tied in a simple loop around his neck and tailored black trousers.

"Oh." She swallowed, drooling over how well he dressed. "I, uh . . .don't have a ton of time. I thought we could just grab a bite."

"Charlotte, I've just been through hours of practice, which you can imagine is pretty intense. I need a proper meal. If this isn't a good time—"

"No," she said. "I can flex. I'll just send a note to Danai to expect me later." She pulled out her phone and thumbed the update in a text to her assistant. "See—all done. Now, where are we going?"

"Madigan's Kitchen," he said. He looked too dressy to be coming out of practice. His leather jacket hung on his arm, and a workout bag rested on his shoulder.

"Lead the way," she said but walked toward the double doors. He stopped her.

"Why don't you go first. Outside there's a black Infiniti and my driver, Garrett. Hop in and I'll follow," he said.

"Seems elaborate."

"Yeah, well, unless you want to be bombarded with questions and flashing lights, it's probably a better way."

Charlotte heard the symphony of press more than saw it. "No thanks." She'd seen the way that the rabid media attacked athletes for a quote or response to plays, rival players, or their careers. This was just practice, yet she didn't want to be connected to the mayhem of walking out with a star athlete. All she wanted to do was get the information she needed for his shoe. "All right. I'll go and wait for you."

Charlotte slipped out unnoticed, which she thanked her lucky stars for because the press and the people around were salivating for responses. Outside she none too quickly found the Infiniti. Perhaps the driver usually waited to see Eoghan before he drove up. She knocked on the window. The man barely pressed the automatic button and rolled the tinted window down only several inches to cover her with questioning eyes.

"Hi. Eoghan sent me. He asked me to wait for him in the car," she said.

"Yeah, tell me another tale, darlin'," he said. "Off with you."

"No, seriously," Charlotte said, understanding that the man didn't know her and thus why she would be trying to get into his car.

"And why would he do that?"

"Because I'm working with him. Give him a call. That's the only reason I'd be knocking on your window, Garrett. That's your name, right?" she asked, trying to build trust with the driver.

"I've fallen for that before." He gave her an up-and-down look. "Run along, now." He rolled the window back up.

Charlotte scoffed and gasped. "What the fuck?" She could understand why his driver might think that she was some woman trying to make her way into Eoghan's car to surprise him into something scandalous, but she wasn't *the one* . . .

She leaned against the car, and the automatic click of the window sounded again.

"Off the car," Garrett called.

She paced in her pumps. Did she look like some big-hair-don't-care trollop? She wore a Givenchy suit and Calvin Klein blouse and Dolce overcoat. Was that who Eoghan normally entertained? She folded her arms across her chest, feeling cheap, like that one time she'd thought she'd been dating this handsome lawyer and he'd ushered her out the door after she'd shared his bed and her heart with him.

Eoghan walked toward her and the car, his arms and shoulders questioning. "Why aren't you sitting inside? It's Baltic." He looked down at her pumps. "And more comfortable."

"Your driver wouldn't let me in," she said, her voice shaky with more vulnerability than she intended. The slight by his driver took on a life of its own and morphed into her self-conscious feelings of being other, not accepted for who she was. A Black woman business owner and not something to be used and discarded.

Eoghan reddened. "This is . . . Jesus, Mary, and Joseph. I'm sorry, Charlotte. I should have texted him to make sure. This is my fault. There are a lot of people, not just women, who try to find entry any way they can. It's not an excuse, just an explanation."

He put an arm around her, and she slid out of it. He might have wanted to comfort her, but puffy dark clouds stormed her headspace. She couldn't speak.

Eoghan marched over to the driver's seat. "Oi. She's with me, ya melter."

"Boss? I didn't know." Garrett scrambled out of the car and approached her. "Beggin' your pardon. Genuinely, miss."

She rolled her neck, and the knots in her shoulders stretched every neck muscle to its snapping point. She cleared her throat. "We should get going. I have to get back."

Garrett went to open the door for her, but Eoghan shooed him away, grumbling his disapproval. "I've got it," he said and held the door open for her to slide into the back seat. "We're going to Madigan's."

"Got it, boss." Garrett fumbled with the keys and started the ignition.

Eoghan was right. Inside the car was warmer and more comfortable. She rubbed her hands together to take the chill out of her fingers.

"You all right?" he asked.

"Mmm-hmm," she lied. "Thanks."

They drove in silence for a bit. Her taking her time to neutralize, him waiting, and the sound of the moving car their only company.

"You said you had a lot on your mind about the boot design," Eoghan said softly.

"Yeah." She turned her body toward him. Talking about work, she could do. "One of the things that might be a minor issue is your big toe. I realize the memory foam material has to be just right for you to feel the ball as well as protect your feet. You're going to have to practice in them all the time. Even before the design is on them, because you have to get used to the fit. Unfortunately, this is not a put-on-and-go situation. I mean, it is, but you'll have to break them in, and that might take a little longer than it would with all the other cleats you've worn."

"I see. How long are we talking? Is it still within the time frame you mentioned before?"

"So far, yes. I asked you quite a bit on the questionnaire, thanks for filling it out by the way, but now that you've been able to test the cleats out, how do they feel? These microadjustments are really important, so don't hold back."

"Well, because my big toe extends a bit past my other toes, I need a bit more accommodation there without losing the perfect snugness I feel with the other toes."

They arrived at Madigan's, and this time Garrett opened the door for her and Eoghan. They walked down a cobblestone street on Crown Alley. The inside was much nicer than the outside, and the aroma of sautéed onions, garlic, and roasted meat made her stomach take on a life of its own. Inside was classic wood paneling and a massive carved dark-wood bar.

"Good afternoon, Mr. O'Farrell. Your table is waiting."

"Thank you, Roisin," Eoghan said. "Please." He escorted Charlotte in the direction of the waitress. He held the chair out for her, and she sat as he slid the chair under her.

"Thank you," she said, looking up at him, his fragrance hovering over her like warm mist. She blinked and reminded herself that she was too smart and experienced to fall for someone like Eoghan, no matter how good he smelled or how gentlemanly he behaved.

"You're welcome." He seated himself. Seltzer and warm bread were immediately brought over. The yeasty yumminess of the baked goods whipped at her nose.

"Would you like a glass of wine or a beer, Charlotte?" Eoghan asked.

"The seltzer is fine. I have to get back to work and don't want to be sluggish."

"Okay." He tilted the basket of bread her way. "Guinness bread," he said, pointing to a brown bread.

"Shut your mouth," she said.

"No joke." His smile dared her to deny herself.

Their waitress hung around.

"What would you like, Charlotte?" he asked. "This is my usual, so they normally bring it right out. They have a lot of options, so get whatever you want."

"What's your usual?"

"Steamed mussels, duck-liver crème and dips for the breads, gratin of prawns, and lime-dressed salad," he said.

"I'll have what he's having," she said to Roisin, "but can I also have the soft, warm risotto, if you'll share it with me?" The last part she asked of Eoghan.

"Yes, but that's just the starter." The inviting tone made her want to eat with him for the rest of her life.

"Uhh, okay," Charlotte said, confused by how fast and far her thoughts had traveled. She ordered the pork shoulder and roasted seasonal veggies, and he ordered the duck confit with steamed veggies. Roisin took their order, then made herself scarce.

He rubbed his belly. "My stomach thinks my throat's been cut," Eoghan said.

She chuckled with a mixture of amusement and horror. "What?"

"Just means I'm hungry." He smiled.

"Man, these sayings get me every time." She shook her head.

"We aim to please."

"You work out really hard. I can see why you'd be hungry," she said. "This meal is going to put me to sleep. I didn't realize we were having 'linner.' You know, lunch and dinner?"

He laughed that sweet laugh that always found its way to the center of her chest.

"I thought I wouldn't see you smile again today." Eoghan poured her a glass of seltzer and some for himself while she tore into the bread. "I'm really sorry about what happened with Garrett. I know he is too. He'll find a way to make up for it. I can only imagine how that made you feel."

"I know people make mistakes based on their experience, but no matter how many times it happens, being made to feel less than will never be easy," she said. "For anyone, I suppose."

"It won't happen again, Charlotte. Not on my watch. I promise you that," he said.

She nodded and knifed butter on her bread. The flavor of stout and fennel popped on her tongue, and her mouth watered for more. "Mmm. It's like a fennel butter," she said, chewing the dense bread.

One corner of Eoghan's mouth curled upward as he watched her. "Wait till you taste the food."

"Do you come here often?" she asked.

"At least once, sometimes twice a week. They feed me well, and I'm not bothered much, if at all." He smiled at her.

Charlotte hadn't had much to eat that morning, and when the fragrances of the place made her mouth spring like a fountain, she knew she was hungrier than she'd realized. "Thanks for suggesting this."

"No worries. It's good to talk on a full stomach," he said.

"Is that an Irish saying?"

"Dunno. Just sounded right."

He was something special. She'd seen him be a jerk football player to her friend and then seen him humbled on his way back from injury. He'd been a womanizer to her friend's little sister, but then with her, he'd been one of the most generous lovers she'd experienced, even for a bone-and-bounce. Now he charmed her too easily, and she wondered if he even knew he was doing it.

"You're different." She fiddled with the place setting before her and then took a sip of water.

"Different how?" he asked.

"From when I first met you. You know, at Purchase House that first day with Yaya."

He reddened through his creamy skin and groaned. "Don't remind me. I was pretty horrible back then. Torn up."

"Yeah. I mean, you had a few struggles. Then there was that whole situation with Jada. I mean, you were going at the ladies pretty hard."

"Is that how you still see me? Think of me as this aimless man whore?" he asked as he untied his scarf and put it on the back of the chair.

She was taken aback by his seriousness. "Honestly?"

"I'd expect nothing less," he said, giving her all his attention.

"I don't know yet. Since I've been here, you've been open to collaborating on your cleats, but you throw tantrums like Danai throws shade."

"Tantrums?"

"Yes." She said what she meant and didn't back down.

"What you call tantrums, I call strong disagreements." He fluttered one brow.

She laughed. "I'm being serious."

"I know. Go on."

She hesitated. She didn't want her honesty to create a barrier between them as partners on his cleats or in any other way that might matter to her, but she couldn't lie to him. "I guess I'm still figuring out who you are rather than who you want me to see."

He tilted his head and shrugged. "I guess that's fair since I've been doing the same with you."

She scoffed. "Me?"

"Think you're the only one trying to figure things out?"

"I'm an open book," she said, unsure of the truth in her statement. Wasn't she?

"You're sure about that?" he asked.

Their food came, and Eoghan dug in.

After a few chews of her own food while grappling with the feelings swirling in her, she used her work as a crutch and asked, "So you said you had all these ideas?"

"Yeah, I need to feel the ball. One thing about the foam is that it feels great, like my foot is having a spa treatment, but I need to feel the ball."

"So you're saying that you need it to be thinner?" she asked, spooning risotto into her mouth and enjoying the velvety, buttery feel and the explosion of herbs.

"Maybe?" He forked his prawn gratin and shoved the food into his face. "Is that the only option, to make it thinner?"

"I think so."

"Won't that ruin the whole reason why I like the boot in the first place?"

"Not necessarily. The vamp is where you're striking for power. The insole is absorbing the shock. What we can try is making the vamp thin enough for you to feel the ball. The trick is keeping the comfy feel."

"You can do that?"

"Of course I can. It won't be easy. It'll be tricky, but we'll do a few iterations until we get it right."

"Not condescending at all," he said.

"Oh. Is that what my face is saying?" she asked.

He gave her that look that, without words, expressed an *obviously* vibe. His expression gentled, and his eyes lowered from her eyes to her lips.

She licked her bottom lip, her tongue betraying her as it lingered. "Anyway, we can make these kinds of microadjustments with the insert. What else were you thinking? We want to get it right, so don't hesitate."

They continued to eat their food.

"How're you getting on? You like your flat?" he asked. "Are we Irish growing on you yet?"

"I'm doing okay. Yaya hasn't been here, so it's just been me and Danai figuring out things. I miss her. I wish she was here." Charlotte scooped more creamy rice on her spoon. She hoped she didn't sound like some wayward tourist.

"It's got to be tough leaving home to go someplace new for a bit. I've visited New York, but going there for rehab was different," he said.

"Actually, I think I'm more relaxed here." She chewed on her lip, not sure how much she wanted to bring up. "After I'd gotten mugged, my home and community took on a menacing feeling I couldn't shake. On top of that, my best friend was in another country. Maybe I needed the change."

"What happened? I remember when Shane and Ayanna went to your aid, but that's as much as I know."

She spun her spoon in her food.

"You don't have to—"

"No," Charlotte interjected. "I always take the long way home when I can. I love walking the neighborhood, even at night. My mother used to say that the more people see you, and you greet them, the more angels you have looking out for you."

"Mmm. That's a good saying."

"It wasn't that late, maybe nine or something, and literally out of the blue this man grabbed me from behind on an empty street. It was a coward move. I struggled, and when I wouldn't quit, he pulled out a gun and aimed it right here." She pointed to her face. "'Gimme what you got,' he yelled at me, and I was frozen, and the only thing that came to mind was a western I'd seen where the narration said, 'staring down the barrel of a gun.' That's all. Isn't that the silliest thing you've ever heard?" she asked him.

"You were scared. Your mind gave you what you could handle," Eoghan said, leaning toward her.

"He took my bag, everything in it, and ran off. When I came out of what I can only believe was shock, I went straight to the police." She tried to eat, but her appetite had waned. "I couldn't stop shaking." She fisted and released her hands. "That's when I called Yaya to come."

He quietly observed her, and she waited for him to speak, but he didn't.

"My flat is really nice," she hurried to say.

He reached across the table for her hands and gathered them in his, rubbing them and stroking them. The sympathy in his eyes made her want to weep, and she blinked several times.

"I'm sorry that happened to you, Charlotte."

She gulped down the thick emotion in her throat.

"We'll have to remedy that," he said.

"What? My flat?" she asked, confused.

"No, you dope," he teased. "We have to get you out and about. Fill you with the joy of the Irish isles. See the scenes."

"Oh, I didn't tell you to make you feel bad for me." That he might pity her made her feel worse.

"I don't feel bad for you. I feel irresponsible. You're my best mate's wan's best girlfriend. It's my duty to help you get acquainted with our fair country." He puffed his chest, and that made her smile.

"Okay, but not until we make progress with your boots. That's priority," she reminded him.

He rolled his eyes so dramatically that she snorted.

"Fine, then." He leaned in. "But when you're ready, Charlotte, I'm at your service."

A flash of heat caused her to cross her legs under the table.

The waitress returned, breaking the connection between them with a chef's knife.

Eoghan cleared his throat, and she fixed the napkin on her lap. This was how it had started, a glance here, a flirt there, and then she'd been in bed with him.

"No," she said out loud, once the waitress was out of earshot. "I know that look."

"I know that look too." He sat back in his chair, his whole body one big, warm, enticingly gooey cookie she wanted to sink her teeth into, savor, and swallow.

"The answer is still no."

"You don't think about what happened between us, ever?" he asked.

"No," she lied, and he called her on it.

"Then what are you saying no to, Char?"

Eoghan was the only one outside of her family to call her by her nickname.

"I . . . see, what I mean is . . . we just need to keep that back in New York."

"I think about you." He slapped his hand on the table as if he were playing cards. "Prawns?" he offered as if it were the natural flow of conversation, with the exception of the devilish smirk on his face.

"Behave yourself, Mr. O'Farrell."

"Charlotte," he sighed, "both you and I know that's the last thing either of us wants."

Her heart banged in her chest, and she was ravenous as she dipped into his plate of prawns. If she fanned herself, his effect on her would be too obvious, so she opted to stuff her face until she felt neutral again.

Three prawns and one thick buttered slice of Guinness bread later, she finally spoke. "I really need to get back. This was good. I got what I needed from you."

"I got what I needed as well," he said. He called for the check and wrapped up the bill. As they left the restaurant, she couldn't help but feel that this meeting with Eoghan had started a countdown she hadn't intended to trip.

After dinner, Garrett drove to her flat, passing through Sandymount and Grafton Street, full of upscale boutiques and shops; the lush parks of Saint Stephen's Green; and the art and historic buildings on O'Connell Street.

"I haven't seen these parts yet. Isn't that crazy. I've been here for three weeks, almost a month," she said. "That's so unlike me. I know so much about this place from researching when Yaya and I were supposed to come for our girls' trip, yet I haven't really been out." She shook her head.

"You will. We've plenty of time," Eoghan assured her.

They arrived at her Grand Canal apartment building, and she gathered her bag to jump out, leaving behind the heat and enticing fragrance of Eoghan O'Farrell.

"Can I come up and see?" he asked.

She gasped. "Absolutely not."

"What? Don't think you have the willpower to resist me?" he teased. She hated that he might be right. She could easily control herself, couldn't she?

"Okay, but just for a minute. I have to work on your prototype." She hoped that the mention of his shoe would keep them both in check.

"I just want to see that your accommodations are up to par, Charlotte. No funny business," he promised.

They took the elevator up to the fifth floor, and she unlocked her apartment with her phone. Eoghan entered, and as she moved in behind him, she marveled at how large he looked in her space. Like with most athletes, his superhuman figure quickly became the focal point. He'd left his jacket in the car, and his GQ gray sweater and black slacks against the backdrop of the floor-to-ceiling window created the perfect image for a cover. Moreover, he commanded her space like he belonged there, which didn't piss her off but relaxed her in a way she hadn't yet felt in the apartment. Her pulse quickened, and she inhaled deeply to keep her head screwed on.

"It's all right," he said. His version of *it's nice*. "I can picture you here," he said, "dancing with your glass of wine like that first night we snogged."

"No comment." She remembered every minute of the first time his lips had touched hers. That had just been the start. Even she hadn't been prepared for the electricity that had ignited between them, and soon her back had been against the wall with him inside her, and she'd never wanted it to end.

"You remember very well, I think," he said.

She hung out by the window, while he strolled over to her desk, peering at the organized chaos of her work. Then down the corridor he went and stopped outside the master bedroom.

"Just making note," he said.

She rolled her eyes so hard her sockets hurt. "I don't know what for," she said and turned back to the window. The overcast sky darkened with the early setting sun, and the lights from the building had begun to take center stage.

She heard his footsteps as he approached and pressed his body against her from behind. He waited as if letting her get used to the feel of him again before he slid his arms around her. The view of the building lights shimmering off the canal reminded her of Manhattan at night, when the city skyline was aglow. She sighed, leaning back against him. She missed the warmth of a lover's body. She missed his body.

"Eoghan," she whispered. "You said no funny business."

He turned her to him, and she learned just how soft and inviting his sweater felt under her palms as she rested them on his chest.

"And I meant it, Char. This isn't funny or about business." He leaned in, encouraging her to meet him halfway.

"There's so many reasons why we shouldn't," she said, and before any more words were spoken, she pressed her lips to his. Sparks flying had nothing on the power of the cosmic storm that swirled between them. He moaned, opening his mouth to receive her seeking tongue. She needed him more than she ever wanted to admit to herself. How did he get inside her so easily? Why did she let him?

His hands crept under and up her blouse, and the feel of his large hands covering her breasts made her buckle against him. He leaned her against her desk, her furry rug beneath her feet.

Her cute doorbell chimed in several harmonic melodies, and she could have taken the hard end of a broomstick to it. Eoghan apparently didn't hear it.

"Eoghan," she called.

"Yes, love."

"It's the door," she gasped, choking on desire. "We have to stop."

"Now?" he asked in disbelief. He raked his hands through his hair, his pelvis pressed against her and unwilling to move. "No, lass," he said in utter disappointment.

"It's Danai. He's here to work. I need you to go," she said and gently pushed him away. He'd already started to stiffen up, and disappointment sank her shoulders at the unfinished business.

He leaned back to look at her with flushed cheeks and arousal in his low-lidded gaze. He stepped back, and she fixed her rumpled clothing.

"Coming," she said. She made sure that he was ready before opening the door.

Danai stood leaning against the frame. "I was wondering when you were going to let me in. I mean, I was out there for a minute. What're you . . ." Danai's eyes landed on Eoghan behind her, and Charlotte pursed her lips as if urging Danai to not make a comment or ask a question about the optics.

Danai did a poor job of hiding a very large and very assuming smile on his face. "I didn't realize you had company."

"Eoghan and I were going over the shoe," Charlotte said.

"Hiya, Danai," Eoghan said without a shred of shame.

"He was just leaving." She craned her neck to encourage Eoghan to support her statement.

"Yeah," he said. "Thank you, Charlotte. I'll see you both at practice." He passed her, his hand none-too-discreetly grazing her ass. Her body called for him, but he continued through the door.

She saw Danai, on his way in, quietly gasp and clutch his pearls, too excited for the door to close for the gossip.

"I don't want to talk about it," Charlotte said before Danai could ask.

"Girl, you better tell me something before my head pops."

"We just made a mistake."

"A mistake? Okay, that's why your blouse is out of your pants and your lipstick is literally all over your face. Not to mention that perfectly coiffed Afro is lopsided."

Charlotte went to the mirror, and true to Danai's words, she looked ruined.

"I knew that 'I'm not here for that' shit wasn't gonna last. You like that man. Admit it and have your fun. Who knows, maybe it'll turn out to be more than that?"

"Not another word," Charlotte said.

"But—"

"Nah-uh." Charlotte shook her head. She and Eoghan had just opened a can of worms, and she had a feeling that there would be no stuffing the wiggly things back inside.

Chapter 10

Charlotte's phone jolted her awake. She'd finally fallen asleep two hours ago because she'd tossed and turned most of the night replaying her kiss with Eoghan. She could kick herself for letting him come up to her apartment.

"Hello?" Charlotte coughed and cleared sleep from her throat.

"Glad you're up," Eoghan said. "They're not right. They need to be smaller and shorter or just forget about it and do a slip-on."

Charlotte blinked several times and sat up. "What?" she asked. She racked her cloudy brain as she tried to figure out why the sun hadn't come up yet, why he'd called at this hour, and what on earth he was talking about.

"The laces on my boots. They're not right. So I was thinking—"

Charlotte stared at the phone, the noise of Eoghan's voice filling her quiet space like a sound at an annoying frequency. "Are you for real right now?" *Who the fuck calls anyone at almost four in the morning about shoelaces?*

"Yes. The clock is ticking on manufacturing, and I'm not sure if the shoe should have laces or just be a slip-on after this last test."

"Oh. You're for real?" She was at his mercy. "Dude . . . listen, you can't be calling me at four in the morning, talking about your shoelaces not being right. You sound crazy, and worse than that, you started my day off on a shitty note."

"You said I can call you anytime. Your rules," he said.

"Yes, but I didn't literally mean anytime. Who does that?"

"Then you should have been more specific," he said.

"Why are you even up?" she asked.

"We have training. Unlike you Americans and your flexible work hours, us footballers have practice, and we'll get fined for not being there, on time, and ready to give it our all."

"What does me being American have to do with it?" she asked.

Silence.

"That's what I thought."

"Are you just waking up?" Eoghan asked.

"Mmm." She stretched deeper into her pillows, closing her eyes. "I don't have to be up for another three hours."

"So you're in bed, then?" he asked. His already robust tone dropped to a sexy octave.

"No, I'm not." She tossed the covers off. Talking to him in bed was dangerous business, and she took their conversation to safer territory.

"Look who's getting in her beauty rest. Wish we could all be so lucky to sleep in."

"I didn't choose to be a footballer," she said. "Might I add, getting up at seven is a very reasonable wake-up time." She got out of bed and shrugged into her robe. She padded her feet to the kitchen to start her coffee machine. "So you're saying you don't like the laces?"

"Not at all, just that they're not right. I need them to be smaller."

She tightened the robe around herself. The cooler temperatures from a nearby window permeated the apartment despite the heat. "That's not a ridiculous request, but don't you think that you could have waited for us to connect after practice?"

"No. I wanted to help you get your creative juices flowing," he said. She couldn't miss the humor in his voice.

She sat at the counter in the kitchen. "Don't you worry about my creative juices. Thank you for your insight, but really, don't call me again unless the sun is fully out and people are on their way to lunch."

"Well, then maybe we should have lunch again?" he suggested. "Or dinner?"

"Is this an excuse to take me out?" she asked and immediately realized the error of her question. For someone trying to keep things business, the flirt in her busted out.

"Do I need an excuse?" he asked, then immediately backpedaled. "You don't have to answer—"

"No."

Silence. The crack of dawn wasn't within their usual seducing hours, and maybe that was why she was more malleable to the suggestion that he wanted to see her again, outside of their work.

"Noted."

She smiled into the phone. "I'll see you when you get here." Lord help her, her ship was barely staying afloat.

Later that morning, after Charlotte and Danai arrived at the stadium, three men were up in the stands to watch her work with Eoghan, including Clive, the brand manager. At least they appeared to be watching her, but she quickly noted that she and Danai weren't the main event at Aviva Stadium and paid the men with Clive no attention. For all she knew, they could be grass experts in suits.

However, two other visitors arrived, and she didn't have to guess who the pair entering the stadium was because, in some way, they both looked like her client. Ayanna had told her about Eoghan's parents. She hadn't classified either Grace or Donal O'Farrell as bad or good, just opinionated and less flexible than Shane's parents.

The woman, who must be Grace, hurried to Eoghan and after a kiss and quick hug said, "Here you go, pet. I know you love eating with the boys, but you need more home-cooked meals now that you're back on the pitch." She then turned to someone passing, who Charlotte believed assisted one of the assistant coaches. "Have someone run this to a fridge somewhere and make sure Eoghan gets this before he leaves today." The wind lightly blew her dark hair, which was tinted with a bit of red that covered her grays.

"Yes, madam."

Charlotte looked on. *That shit really works in celebrity world?* She often gave her employees or contractors instructions, but nothing so personal or presumptuous as asking any random joe to run food to a fridge. Her interest in the family gathering grew, and Charlotte found herself drifting closer to Eoghan and his family.

"Mam, you didn't have to do that," Eoghan complained. "I could have come and picked it up or something."

"Me and your da wanted to see you out here. It's been so long since we've had a chance to watch you play. It seems as though practice is our only way to see you these days," Grace said and moved in for another kiss from Eoghan, who obliged with a peck on the cheek. "How are you, pet?"

"Good. Working through it." Eoghan eyed his father as if he'd given the wrong answer. Damn, Charlotte thought, his aura and posture changed from a man in charge to a grown-up child in seconds.

"You need to get on so you can get back out there, son." Though his father's words started out robust and then tapered into something softer, Charlotte couldn't deny the pressure of one line. "Who's this?" he asked with his hands stuffed in the pockets of his open blue shearling coat, which moved with the gesture.

"This is Charlotte Bowman. She's helping me figure some things out. Her assistant is setting up over there," Eoghan said. "Charlotte, this is my father, Donal, and my ma, Grace."

"Nice to meet you both." She couldn't help but notice how Eoghan trimmed and carved the details about her. She stroked her chin at his intentionally cryptic response. If she hadn't been so struck by Donal's resemblance to his son, she might have had a quip ready.

National team coach Oliver Walsh ran over to them. "Sorry, Gaff," the real gaffer said to Donal. "We need to let Eoghan finish with Miss Bowman before practice. Gonna have to ask you to take a seat in the stands."

Charlotte had conflicting feelings about Walsh directing Eoghan's parents off the field. She wanted to get more information about Eoghan's father, who clearly inserted himself in the minutiae of Eoghan's athletic career.

Danai strutted over as if to the beat of Wu-Tang Clan's "Triumph." He didn't need music or even to open his mouth for all eyes to be on him. Charlotte couldn't help but smile.

"Okay, I have everything set up. All we need Eoghan to do is do what he does, and we'll see how his body responds with the prototype."

"Round two on shoe data collection, here we go. You cool to get started?" Charlotte asked Eoghan, whose eyes kept wandering to the area in the stands where his parents sat.

"Yeah." He gave her a brief smile that lacked joy. Sure, collecting more data through shoe trials wasn't a party, but shouldn't his parents' presence uplift him?

"Make Mama proud." She winked at him, and that seemed to relax him a bit.

She went over to where Danai had set them up.

"You know something?" Danai questioned. "I think I like them all. They're like scrumptious little white and milk chocolate morsels."

"Who are you talking about?" Charlotte literally looked around for candy.

"The players, girl. Haven't you heard a word I said? I like that little Lance one. He's not gay and not even my type, but I make him wonder. You know?"

Charlotte laughed as she watched the speed and velocity of Eoghan's movement. He kicked the ball into a goal.

"Oh shit! Did you see that?" Charlotte questioned Danai, who was about to go in deep about Lance. "His impact with the ball is in the red."

"Yeah, he kicks hard, girl," Danai said and nonchalantly scribbled down some notes.

Charlotte gave Danai one of her smug mugs. "You've seen this before?" she asked.

"So have you. You just weren't looking at those numbers. Your exact words were, 'We'll focus on impact later—right now I just need to get an overview of how his shoe is doing,'" Danai said, doing his best Charlotte voice.

"You're funny," Charlotte said, her eyes pinned to the screen. "His foot is literally a weapon. That's why when these players get hurt by another player, it's bad."

Danai nodded.

"What are you doing there?" a male voice said from over Charlotte's shoulder. She immediately recognized Donal's firm voice.

"Hello," Charlotte said, craning her neck. Not only did Donal come into view, but the men who she'd seen in the stands had made their way behind her setup.

"Hiya, Charlotte," Clive said, waving energetically.

"Hi there, Clive." Charlotte suddenly moved into better-than-her-best mode.

"Do you have the design of the shoe handy?"

"Yes, of course," she said, and without her even asking, Danai handed Eoghan's shoe design to Clive, who then passed it to the other men in casual suits and wool coats.

"Don't mind us. Carry on."

"I asked what you're doing there," Donal said again.

She'd all but forgotten about Eoghan's father. *I'm working* was what Charlotte wanted to say in response to Donal's rude interrogation, but she kept her cool and decided that giving a contentious response would do neither her nor Eoghan's father any good.

"I'm collecting data from Eoghan's shoe activity on the field."

"Shoe activity? You mean his boots."

"Yes, sir," Charlotte said, because her parents had raised her with manners, and if a person was older than her by any significant amount, then they were a sir or ma'am. "His shoe is collecting information. There are tiny electrodes recording how fast he's going, the impact of the ground on his body, and whether or not the shoe is protecting him."

"Protecting him? I don't understand any of it," he said.

Charlotte pointed to the various graphs on the screen. "See, this is velocity. This is impact," she explained. "When Eoghan moves, we can see the intensity and frequencies. Based on this, adjustments can be made to his cleats to work better for him. This is a great tool to use so we get it right."

"Sounds like a bunch of tech foolishness to me."

Charlotte twisted her body toward him. She knew Donal wasn't an unintelligent man, especially when she met judgment in his eyes. She could have told this man anything. He didn't approve of her role in his son's career, and that was the bottom line.

"What he needs to do is train and train hard. That's what has always gotten him through," Donal said, not only dismissing her expertise but also proving to her that yes, he could be more anti.

"Obviously, he's training hard, and that's not getting him any-where," her assistant mumbled.

"What was that?" Donal asked.

Charlotte jumped in. "I can explain more to you after we're done here, but I really do need to focus on what's happening." She didn't need to put on the headphones attached to listen to anything but some music, but she did to avoid more questioning from Donal.

"So you're just going to leave me out here with no headphones?" Danai side-eyed her so hard that Charlotte had to stop herself from busting a gut.

"You're doing great, Eoghan," Charlotte yelled and clapped above her head. If she was the only one out there cheering him on and wishing for his best, she'd make sure he heard her loud and clear.

After his workout for Charlotte, the last thing Eoghan wanted to do was drag himself to where his father waited, and he found himself hurrying over to Charlotte. He dropped the black-and-white football he carried onto the grass, placed his foot on top, and stretched. He wished the release he got on his shin and calf also worked his tight shoulders.

"How was that?" he asked.

"We got a good amount of data. Maybe in the beginning you were pandering to the shoe because you knew we were collecting data, but now what we're getting is more natural. Authentic," she said.

"Good, good," Eoghan said vacantly.

"Hey, do you know who those people are with Clive?" she asked him and pointed.

He felt his brows lift. "Those are the big bosses. The owner and a council member. They come on the field every once in a while to see how things are going or watch from the screens in their offices."

"Hmm." Charlotte squinted her eyes in their direction. "They asked to see your shoe design."

He took a deep inhale and hoped that the organization wasn't displeased. He should connect with his agent to get the word on the street. As if he didn't have enough on his plate, his father bolted over. "Shite." Before he allowed his father to speak, Eoghan asked, "Where's Mam?"

"She'll wait in the car," his father said.

His mother often pulled that move for two reasons: one, to allow his father to boss him without intervening and, two, so his father would hurry up bossing him if he knew she was waiting.

"Oi," his father continued. "What's all this about working together on this and collaborating with that? Sounds like this woman's in charge of you."

There his father went. Shooting his mouth off about a situation he had little information on and ruining the process. "She's working on my boots."

"So she told me herself. What about someone Irish to do the job right?" Donal was in stellar form, which mortified Eoghan on Charlotte's behalf.

"Her shoe was the best, and she's loads of experience, Da," Eoghan said and glanced at Charlotte, who obviously bit her lip and crossed her arms over her chest, likely to avoid giving it back to oul Donal as good as she got.

"Says you," Donal said.

"Let's take this inside. Excuse us." Eoghan hated leaving Charlotte like this, but he'd rather spare her his father's opinions and absorb the man's wrath alone.

Eoghan took his father to the empty conference room that was available. Charlotte and Danai sometimes met in there after practice, but right now he needed to get his father alone and defuse his charge.

"This is the malarkey you've been hiding these few weeks past." His father had been digging his nose into what he and his agent were up to, and Eoghan had clearly instructed Ronin, Clive, and Dodger to keep it from his father.

"I wasn't hiding," he lied.

"Yes, you were, and from both yer ma and me. I see right through your fibs."

Eoghan fisted his hands. "Da, this isn't an issue you need to involve yourself in."

"You're my son. I took you to the games, paid for the camps, flew you to meet agents and all the different clubs sniffing about for you. It is an issue I'll involve myself in, thank you very much."

Eoghan loved his father, but he kept sticking his nose where it didn't belong. Donal had done everything to help get Eoghan to this level, but now that he was in the league, he trusted the people around him. With his father breathing down his neck, whether it was about his playing, his endorsements, his practice, or his future, Eoghan did his best to avoid catastrophes due to his father's interference.

"Do you think you made a good choice with the shoe?" Donal asked. "You didn't even tell me you were having trouble with your boots. To just throw away an endorsement like that. You should have consulted me." Apparently, his father knew more than he'd been letting on.

Eoghan sighed. "There was nothing to consult with or about. They're my boots."

"And you lost money because of it. I raised you better'n that." His father used the one thing against him that he hated the most. Shame.

"I have other contracts, and there will be more."

"You're sure about that?" his father inquired, throwing another log onto an already raging fire of doubt. "How you've been playing hasn't exactly been to the level you were before that injury they sent you to America to fix. I told you, you should have stayed right here at home to get your leg back."

This was what his father did: nitpicked at everything until he got what he wanted or until Eoghan was so tired of all the negativity that he'd fold.

"Getting rehabbed by Ayanna in America was the best thing that ever happened to me, Da, and you know it." Not only had his time in America helped him rehab, but it was through that connection that he'd met Charlotte, and now she'd designed a shoe that he hoped would help him play better. "I really don't want to get into this at the moment, Da," he said.

"Hold on there—" His father grabbed his shoulder. Something Eoghan hated. When he'd been a child, the move had hurt his small, lanky body, but now that he was an adult, it was an annoying attempt to make him feel small.

A knock sounded on the door. Eoghan shrugged out of his father's grip just as Charlotte entered. Her eyes slid between him and his father.

"Hi," she said. "I'm not interrupting, am I?" she asked. "Danai and I need to head out."

"Not at all." Eoghan's smile pulled at his cheeks. He was sure the tension showed on his face.

"Here's the shoe lady herself," his father said.

"If by 'shoe lady' you mean that I own a footwear-and-apparel company and have currently been contracted to work on a cleat for Eoghan, then yes."

Eoghan took that as his cue to back her up. "Charlotte is a professional, Da, just like I told you. She is experienced, and her prototype was the best one I tried."

"You could have asked me for my opinion. I might have had a better option for you," his father said.

"Should I go?" Charlotte asked, her feet already pointing in the opposite direction. "Yes, I should go."

Eoghan reached for her wrist. "Please stay," he said, his words softer than the ones he'd shared with his father. "You might have information to share."

His father's eyes zeroed in on their hand connection, but Charlotte didn't pull away, and Eoghan didn't let her go until she glided past him.

"Okay," she said simply and shifted her body to one side, both her hands resting on her hips. This was her fighting stance, and the words that would come out of her mouth next were her jabs and punches.

"Charlotte is the best option for me," Eoghan said.

"Says you, but I have yet to see any progress in your playing." His father fanned the air. "A shoe is supposed to fix that? I need you to show up, son. Get on the field and dominate like you used to. We've worked too hard to let anyone ruin that."

"That sounds encouraging," Charlotte mumbled. "Perhaps he just needs you to support him."

"What was that, girl?" Donal barked his question.

Charlotte rose to her full height, which was taller than his father's, her posture as erect as the steeple on Saint George's Church. "Maybe he just needs you to support him," Charlotte enunciated slowly.

"And you know my son better'n me now?"

"I know his feet better than anyone, including him. So in that area, I'm the chief," Charlotte said. "I'd be happy to answer any quest—"

"I don't need you to answer any questions, deary. I just want my son to have everything he needs to play his sport. So long as yer doin' yer job—"

"Then I think we're done here. Absolute joy to meet you," Charlotte said. "Eoghan? A word."

Eoghan followed Charlotte as she walked out the door.

"Yaya told me he was a tough cat, but damn."

"He's my da," was all Eoghan could say.

"You okay? Sounds like he'd been at it before I arrived."

He shrugged. "No different than any other time."

She studied him. "He's a parent, but that doesn't mean he knows everything about you, especially if it makes you feel bad. You're a grown-ass man. It's okay to remind him every once in a while."

"He's done a lot for me. I'm here because of him."

"I'm sure, but you're also here because of you, your talent, and your drive to be a great player. He can't play the game for you. So do whatever you need to do in order to be your best on the field. That includes wearing a brilliant shoe by yours truly."

He laughed then, and she seemed to relax with him.

"Is the conference over, or do I need to come back? Make an appointment?" Donal, who had not quite reached them, asked.

Charlotte's jaw dropped and stayed ajar for a worrying length of time. "Wow," she finally mouthed. "I'm serious, though. I can stay, protect you from the big, bad wolf."

That she spoke of protecting him moved him in a way he neither had expected nor was prepared to feel. "No." He sounded like a vise had clamped his lungs. "Go. I'll catch up with you later about what you found in practice." He wanted to kiss her, and by the way she lingered, she wanted to kiss him too. If there was a bright side to her coming in while his father had berated him, it was this moment with her.

"Later," she said and left.

"What are you doing, son?" Donal asked. "You're making all the wrong decisions here."

"They're mine to make," Eoghan said with newfound confidence.

"I don't think—"

"Mam's waiting for you, Da," Eoghan said and walked his father out.

Chapter 11

Charlotte checked her phone, certain that she'd read the elapsed time incorrectly. She'd been on hold for twenty minutes, waiting for James, head of manufacturing. The project was approaching its third round, and she didn't know why getting Eoghan's new tester was taking so long.

"I'll have to call you back. He's still in a meeting," Shaun, the assistant, said into her ear, and again Charlotte got the runaround.

She sighed.

According to Clive, James at the manufacturing factory was a bit of a melter, which she'd come to understand meant a nuisance, but when it came to meeting the needs of the club, James was a reliable point of contact. She'd never had to go up the chain to get things done, because she *was* the chain. However, she felt like a newbie on the block getting played.

"Please make sure that you do. It's important that I get what I need with better turnover time than this."

"Will do, madam," Shaun said.

Charlotte had shown up to the factory several times and sent emails to document her attempts, yet James remained elusive. "See, this is why I get heated," she said to Danai, who had been communicating with their team in New York to maintain Seam and Sole's business operations.

"I know you've already been down there, but they need to know that you're the boss. Roll some heads, sis," Danai suggested.

"Trust me, I want to, but things are different here."

"Different how? Business is business. If they want money, they have to deliver the product."

"I'll work it out." Charlotte had learned her lesson when she'd visited different parts of the world where bullying the American way didn't work. She was still figuring out when to put her foot down and when to have a little more patience, but the latter was certainly running low.

"Okay, but if getting Eoghan's tester for round three is a problem, he won't be able to play in the shoe we've been working on."

"Thanks for that." Charlotte frowned.

"You're welcome, baby," Danai said.

They wrapped up their day at the stadium by reviewing her data and uploading it to yet another email to the manufacturer for Eoghan's tester prototype. Charlotte couldn't wait to get to her flat and plop down on the couch after a long day. On the way out, they passed Clive's office, the clear glass giving a view to passersby. Clive saw her and popped out of his office. His strawberry-blond hair and mustache nicely complemented his pressed heather-gray shirt, charcoal slacks, and polished brown shoes. It was different wear from the few times they'd met. He was in office mode for sure. However, the speed at which he approached made her wonder if he was going to stop or run into her.

"Hey, Clive," she said, sure her eyes were bugging out. "You scared the shit out of me."

"Hey, Charlotte. Sorry 'bout that. I often take things at a bit of a giddyap," he said. "Glad I caught you. Spare me a few minutes for a chat, if you have the time?"

Charlotte quickly glanced down at the watch on her wrist. "Yes, of course," she said and then turned her attention to Danai. "Meet you downstairs, and we'll walk back together."

"Got it, boss." Danai left, and Charlotte followed Clive into his office and sat in a chocolate-brown cushioned chair across from him.

"How are things going with James?" Clive asked. "Hopefully well."

Her body hit the backrest. "They're okay," Charlotte said, hit by the inquiry. Her quick response lacked acting skills.

Clive's brows furrowed. "You aren't having any trouble, are you? If you are, it's no problem for me to step in."

That was the last thing Charlotte wanted. She ran a whole company, and when things like this happened, she took care of it. She didn't want Clive or anyone thinking that she couldn't handle a vendor. "No, no, no. Everything is fine," she said. "I will definitely let you know if that changes."

"All right, then," Clive said, twitching his mustache. "I don't have a lot of time, so I'll get right to it."

"Okay." Her body slipped into "oh shit, I'm in trouble" posture, but she kept her poker face steady.

"What do you know about the signature boots for the club?" he asked.

Not the turn of conversation she'd expected. "Signature boot?"

"Yes. The national team has three different sets of cleats, one that they always perform in at home, one for away fixtures, and then a signature boot that they can wear during special periods in the season. The latter one is based on their personalities."

"I've seen some sports teams in the States have a signature shoe. It's really cool," she said.

"We've been watching you and your work with Eoghan. You know how much I appreciate what you've been doing, but the bosses are wowed by the design of the shoe. Tell me, would you be at all interested in designing this year's signature cleats?"

"For the national team?" she asked.

"Yes," he said.

Holy shit! By the dry feel in her mouth, she must have been catching flies. She moistened the thing up enough to speak. "But isn't that reserved for someone from Ireland? Like a national treasure artist? It would seem more patriotic, which I know that team is. I'm American." Charlotte might have been prepared to hear many things when she'd stepped into his office, but this wasn't one of them.

"You're right, but management wants to take a new approach and follow Eoghan's lead by trying out new talent."

"Eoghan?" Charlotte asked.

"Yes. When he takes on a venture, he and his agent try to be part of the solution and support our ever-changing population by choosing to work with the best entrepreneurs, no matter the sex or color. It made Eoghan very happy that the boot he ended up choosing fit the parameters of the social change he's interested in."

Charlotte was floored. Eoghan continued to surprise her at every turn.

"Additionally," Clive continued, and Charlotte wasn't sure she could take much more, "the players as a collective have seen some of your designs for Eoghan, and you quickly became the prime candidate. They want a better shoe than their Portugal rivals. Additionally, management wanted to give the design a new edge. We'd still use the artist for the element, but you have the shoe, which just like Eoghan's would be on international display, in a big way."

She tried to catch up from the great news she'd learned about Eoghan, because she needed to pay attention to the here and now with Clive. She couldn't pass this up. Her prototype had first been picked up by their celebrity player, and now her design would spread to the rest of the team. She wondered what thoughts they'd all have. She thought more about the creativity of the new project than about the tasks she'd need to juggle.

"This is for the World Cup. There is no grander stage."

She squirmed in her chair, excitement in her bones. How had she gotten so lucky? "Yes. Of course, yes."

"Good work, Charlotte, and congratulations to you," Clive said.

"Thank you."

"I'll deliver the news up the channels. Someone will firm things up within the week, and you can start working with the team shortly after. Do you have any questions for me?"

"No. I mean, not right now, but I'm sure once the shock has worn off, I'll have tons." The nerves had already started to bubble inside her like butterflies congregating around their favorite flower.

With a project like this, she'd be able to not only wrap up any loose business ends and really reclaim Seam and Sole but also reorganize the company for the consulting business she wanted to do. She had to revise her goals because, here in Ireland, she'd met every last one.

Charlotte floated to where Danai waited for her near the exit.

"What was that all about? They're done, and we're heading back to New York?" Danai asked with a mixture of hopefulness and sadness.

"It's worse than that," Charlotte said in her most serious tone as they left the building and stepped into the frigid February air.

"No . . . ," Danai groaned. "Hit me with it."

"Unfortunately, they want us to design the signature cleats for the Irish national team."

"The one where you work with the individual players?"

"Yes."

"Oh my Lord," Danai exclaimed. "Trick, this is great news. How dare you scare me like that?"

"I couldn't resist," Charlotte said. "You stay an easy target."

Danai groaned. "This is absolutely amazing. Now we get to see just how big all their feet are and compare the swag with the size."

"Gutterized," Charlotte said, shaking her head and laughing.

"Me?" Danai asked. "I'm not the one smashing my client."

"First of all, there is no smashing, and there will be none," Charlotte said, trying to convince herself as much as her assistant.

"Yet," Danai corrected.

"So wrong."

"And also, so very right."

"You know that's not what I meant."

"I know that boy is skipping through that big forehead of yours."

Charlotte covered her forehead with her hand. "My forehead is not even that big."

"Remember when we talked about feelings? Would it be so bad to let that boy into your heart a little bit?" Danai asked.

The problem was that Eoghan had found his way into her thoughts since before she'd touched down in Ireland. Once they'd kissed and been seconds from taking it further before Danai had interrupted, Charlotte couldn't get him out of her mind, and as a result her business exterior thickened. That was, until his bullying father had made her want to protect him like she did the Crawfords.

"Oooh, you are overthinking." Danai pinkie pointed at her. "I can see it."

"Can we just get back to the great deal we just landed," Charlotte said, her skin hot under her coat despite the cold.

Danai flipped on a dime. "This is greatness, queen. We will definitely need to celebrate."

"Not till it's finalized."

"We have to tell somebody." Danai sounded desperate.

"It'll be finalized within the week."

"So that doesn't mean we have to wait in sharing the good news, do we? I mean, you can't give me great news and expect me to cork it like a bottle of Black Girl Magic brut sparkling wine. It has been mentioned." Danai, beside himself with the thought of being silenced to secrecy, slowed his walk and sulked.

"I know, but it's important for us to not jump the gun here. When the papers are inked with my signature, then you can tell the world. Till then, I'mma need you to keep it zipped." Charlotte gestured over her mouth.

"Fine, fine," he said, then got back to business. "By the way, while you were in with Clive, James's assistant called back."

"And?" Charlotte asked.

"The prototype for Eoghan's cleats is ready for approval. All you need to do is authorize it, and they can start manufacturing. He should be able to play with it in three weeks."

"Three weeks? But I thought the ETA on that shoe was two weeks tops. The marketing team are doing a whole spread for him in the papers, billboards, the lot."

"I know, and he won't be back until Monday," Danai said.

"Damn, can I have one celebration without a crisis on the other end of it for once?" Charlotte asked. "And who takes weekends off in this business?"

"Huh . . . we don't," Danai said. "We stay on the grind."

Charlotte shook her head, her frustration stuck in her chest like a pill in need of liquid to wash it down.

A gust of frigid wind, fragrant with peat and wood from burning stoves, knocked Charlotte off her path like manufacturing threatened to do, but Danai reached out and dragged her back.

"Let's hurry up. It's balls out here," Danai said.

That made Charlotte laugh despite the bad news. "It's Baltic," she corrected.

"To each his, her, or their own," Danai said and put his arm around her.

Charlotte didn't know how she was going to manage her time with all the balls that were being thrown her way. She had to somehow get Eoghan's shoe on time, work on the signature shoe, and avoid getting drawn back into her ex-lover's spell. They were coming at her hard and fast. She'd just have to do her best to keep them all in the air.

Chapter 12

Eoghan wanted to personally congratulate Charlotte on being selected to work with the players on their signature shoes. Now that it was official, both Clive and Ronin had let him know, since he'd been the one who'd picked Charlotte to come to Ireland to work on his shoe. His motivation to see her had less to do with his shoe than it did with this woman's innate ability to make him feel things he tried not to.

The day when he'd first seen her apartment, she'd shut him down at lunch and when he'd asked to come up. Yet her body had called him to her, and he still hadn't forgotten the feel of her curves as he'd pulled her into his arms. She'd hung on to him like he'd been her lifeline to this reality, and he'd been more than willing to drown and succumb to wave after wave of desire.

He made his way down to the conference room, only to pop in on a lively scene within the tan walls. Charlotte sat behind a large similarly colored desk with Pippin and Lance sitting in the chairs before her. Patrick and a few other players, some standing and others sitting on the edge of a nearby also-tan table, huddled around Charlotte, laughing like captivated children being read a story by their favorite librarian. She was the brightest element in the room, in a pumpkin-colored wool turtleneck dress that hugged her arms, her shoulders, her breasts. The room was hot with the lads' excited bodies and more cologne than he'd normally have to endure from them in the dressing rooms. Most of all, they were in his place by her.

"I want mine to have a flashy gold seal," Lance said, his speech and shoe idea very characteristic of his Mr. Celebrity persona. Loud and harsh.

"I'd like mine in orange. Like your pretty dress. That's my color," Pippin said, ever smooth as he pointed to Charlotte.

"I'll make a note of that," she said, pushing her chair back against the wall and giving him and everyone a view of her full body as she crossed her legs.

Was she purposely trying to rile him and the lads up? Though her dress went down to the calf, the seductive cross-over slit showed enough of her enticing legs, even with her brown suede knee-high boots.

"It would be cool if I could test out the cushioning," Patrick said, insulting Eoghan.

The hell he would. That was Eoghan's cushioning. Until it was done for him, it was off limits.

Danai typed furiously as well as recording the session on his tablet.

"What's all this?" Eoghan asked.

"We're giving Charlotte ideas for our boots. We can have elastic or laces. And the flag unites us, but management agreed that we could have a specialty design so long as it didn't clash or overshadow the patriotic colors."

"That right?" Eoghan said vapidly, his tracksuit tightening around the collar.

"You here to give your suggestions on your signature boot too?" Pippin winked at him.

Eoghan rolled his eyes the way Charlotte would when his melter tendencies, or anyone's really, got to her.

"The design is perfect, mate," Lance noted, sounding like Eoghan in his old days. "The ladies are going to love it."

"Now that I've seen a game in person and how you all pound the pitch, it is helping me fine-tune the shoe," Charlotte said. "I know that not all of you will be changing to my shoe. Some of the team will be designing their own, which is also kind of cool, but I'm happy that you all love the design and the extra touches we can make to really personalize a pair for you."

"We can continue this discussion when we go out," Patrick said.

"Go out?" Eoghan asked, not realizing he'd made his way closest to Charlotte.

"We're taking Charlotte and Danai to the Paddy Bath. You know, where all our great ideas happen," Pippin said. "Get on it, man."

Eoghan frowned. "Anyone gonna tell me we were going out?"

Everyone looked at Eoghan.

"Check your phone," Pippin tossed out, then turned his attention back to Charlotte. "On us, love. Our way of giving you a real welcome to the team."

"That's sweet of you guys." She glanced over at him as if to check in with him. She didn't need his permission or his approval, but he wished she'd show him that she at least wanted him there. He'd thought after they'd kissed that maybe things might soften tremendously between them, but the needle had only moved slightly.

"You know something? Charlotte hasn't really been out on the lash much," Danai said.

"What?" Eoghan asked. "I didn't know you wanted to."

She stared at him for a few seconds too long, like she was evaluating an enigma. "It's cool. It's not your responsibility."

Even his comrades recognized the shade.

"It is," Eoghan said. "Ayanna would have my throat, and then Shane."

"Chill, Eoghan. It's not that deep." Charlotte busied herself with a few papers on her desk, and Eoghan couldn't shake the feeling that it actually was that deep.

"I've been to Dublin Castle, the George to meet my people," Danai said. "I even did a few stops on the red bus. I even rented a bike and rode to Trinity College to do some research on something for the New York crew. My people got me, but Miss Charlotte here likes to work till three in the morning."

"Oh, that will not do, Charlotte. Definitely, you're coming out with us," Patrick said. "Let's go."

Was that why she'd sounded so groggy when he'd woken her up to talk about his boots last week? She'd just gotten to bed. He rubbed his face. When they'd gone out to eat, she hadn't been drinking, because she'd perceived their lunch as just business, but he'd dressed smarter for her. Had she not noticed? Hadn't he been thoughtful enough? Hadn't he communicated with her that he was glad she was here? They'd even had a moment, and things had certainly warmed up between them. Had he imagined it all?

"Yes, let's go," Charlotte said. As they all piled through the door, she turned to Eoghan. "You coming?"

Eoghan checked his phone like he did before he got on the move. He was part of a group text with Pippin and Shane.

"Of course I'm coming." He grabbed his jacket and read the texts as he followed everyone out.

Shane: Ayanna is back. Wants to surprise Charlotte.

Pippin: Nice one.

Shane: Get her to the Paddy Bath

Pippin: Done

Shane: Eoghan, you dope. Grace us with a response

Pippin: He's too busy daydreaming about snogging Charlotte.
He's in a terrible state.

Pippin added a GIF of a child crying and rolling on the floor with the words *terrible state* on the bottom.

Eoghan peered over at Pippin, who watched him react to each text, then responded.

Eoghan: We'll get her to the bar. Heading there now.

"You'll ride with me," Eoghan said to Charlotte.

"Okay, Grumpy Smurf," she said.

Her slag took a little bite out of his shortcomings, but he vowed that he'd do better by her.

◆ ◆ ◆

A month and a half ago, Charlotte had been poring over Seam and Sole's papers, trying to figure out how to appease her investors. Not only had January brought with it an opportunity for her cutting-edge footwear design to be part of a national campaign featuring Eoghan, but she'd also be creating a signature shoe for players on the Irish national team. She didn't know what the odds were, but she was happy to be favored.

Now, two weeks into February, the contracts with the team were tight, and she was able to start communicating with the rest of the team about what they wanted for their signature shoe. She looked forward to talking at the Paddy Bath further with the eclectic bunch.

The car ride with Eoghan had consisted of two questions: "Are you excited to go out?" and "Here we are. You have everything you need?" Charlotte had answered yes to both. She left her coat in the car since the bar was close and the bulky garment would only be a hassle to store.

Her coat was the least of her worries. She didn't know what was wrong with Eoghan. He wasn't normally this tight lipped. She tried to shrug it off as they met up with the rest of the group and headed into the bar.

When she entered the Paddy Bath with the team, the scents of energetic bodies and beer stung her nose. She welcomed the warmth and the tavern-style vibe. With a detailed blackboard drink menu in colorful chalk overhead as well as some items written on the glass in neon dry-erase marker, the place made her feel like a regular even though she'd just arrived. She'd expected the patrons to freak out from seeing a group of players from the national team in one place, yet they enjoyed their pints, cocktails, and food quite unaffected.

Charlotte hadn't been out in so long that she'd almost forgotten how to act in a social setting. She vowed that she'd get her ass out and enjoy Dublin and the rest of Ireland from now on. Moving farther into the bar, she spotted a frantically waving figure, and her spirits rose tenfold.

"Surprise!" Ayanna said. She was wearing a shimmering purple off-the-shoulder top and jeans and holding on to the velour waist of Shane's tracksuit.

"Yaya," Charlotte yelled, ran to her friend, and hugged Ayanna tight, spinning her around with her. "Bitch, you didn't tell me you were back."

"I got back last night. Was so tired I crashed for most of the day, but I wanted to celebrate your contract with you. Shane helped me get you out so I could surprise you. You're not mad that we didn't get a one-on-one?"

"No! I'm just so happy to see you. I miss you so much," Charlotte said, then lifted her hand up to Shane for a high five. "What's up, Big Red? It's been a minute."

Shane turned a shade of red that Charlotte had never seen. She checked in with Ayanna for support. "He okay?"

119

Ayanna nodded but also blushed through her golden-brown skin. "We're going to have to find you another nickname for him. That one's reserved," she said.

Charlotte busted out laughing. "Understood," she said. "Chill, Shane. We're all adults here."

As if on cue, Lance stood up on the chair and started a chant that the bar responded to in unison. Charlotte nearly covered her head from the shouts streaming over it.

"Most of us, anyway." She pointed at Lance.

"We don't call him Mr. Celebrity for nothing," Eoghan said.

"Liam," Ayanna called to a handsome bartender, whose shoulder-length blond hair was swinging with him. "This is Charlotte," Ayanna said and pointed.

"*The* Charlotte?" Liam said. "Your best bud from America?"

"The one and only," Charlotte said.

"Heard loads about you. Glad you've finally made it to our country. How long have you been here so far?"

"About a month," Charlotte said.

"And you've just now made it to the bar?" Liam asked.

Shane and Ayanna looked at Eoghan, and she hoped they didn't blame him. They'd both been busy since she'd arrived. He'd been stressed about his playing and his boots, and she'd been stressed managing him, his boots, and the manufacturer.

"I'm glad to be here now. It wouldn't have been the same without Yaya." Charlotte hugged Ayanna.

"And me," Danai interjected.

Ayanna hugged the tall pouting man. "We'd never leave you out, Danai," Ayanna said. "This feels like we're in New York but better."

"Yes!" Danai exclaimed.

Eoghan squeezed his way closer to her. "What are you drinking, Charlotte?"

Her body turned on, leaning toward him without her permission. "What do you suggest?"

"For you? A Harp." Eoghan's brown eyes searched her face as if reading her beer profile. "It'll keep you on your feet."

Had it not been for Ayanna, Charlotte wouldn't know that when Eoghan teased her or slagged her, like many Irish men, he was flirting. "Okay, thanks."

Eoghan slid his way through to the bar and called the order to Liam.

Ayanna gave her a mischievous nod. "So you'll be here longer now that you're doing the signature shoe. Does that mean that you're going to stay through the season to see the team play?" Ayanna's hopeful cheese warmed Charlotte's heart.

"What? Girl, I don't know. I have to see where the wind takes me. I mean, who knows what opportunities will come my way after something like this."

"Back to New York?" Ayanna asked.

"I don't want to plan too far ahead. That's how I was able to come here. That and the universe," Charlotte said.

"It would be nice if you stayed," Ayanna hinted.

"Bitch, you're never here," Charlotte said, hooking her arm around Ayanna's neck.

"Real facts, but I will be. My schedule is finally tapering down. We'll be able to do so much together."

"You two plan on settling down here in Ireland?" Charlotte jutted her head at Shane, who gave them space to do their girlfriends thing.

"We haven't decided." Ayanna gazed lovingly at Shane. "But we'll definitely be spending more time together in one place."

"You are so whipped," Charlotte mumbled as Eoghan returned.

"Here you are," Eoghan said.

"Thank you." Charlotte took the pint from him. His fingertips grazed hers and sent a chill through her that was cooler than the glass he held.

"Just think about it," Ayanna said.

"Think about what?" Eoghan asked.

"I'm trying to get Charlotte to think about staying here in Ireland a little longer." Ayanna nudged her friend's shoulder.

"Sounds like a good idea to me," Eoghan said. "Maybe we can change your mind."

Charlotte wasn't shocked that he agreed, just that he agreed so quickly and publicly. "I don't know," she whined. Why did Yaya put her on the spot like that?

"I'm glad the lads have taken to you," Eoghan said, clinking his pint glass with hers. "Cheers."

"Cheers," she returned. "Are you really okay with that?"

"Course." He looked taken aback. "Why wouldn't I be?"

"You didn't seem very excited when they asked me out."

He shoved his hands into his pockets. "Because I wanted to take you out. To celebrate with you. I hadn't been checking my phone. It was only just before we left that I read the texts about the surprise for ya. I guess I felt like they'd beaten me to it. I should've been the one. All for the best in the end. I'm no good with secrets. Might've given the surprise away."

She stared at him for a minute.

"Don't go getting sentimental. I know you're far from home and that your friend isn't here often. Thought I'd do my duty."

"Your duty."

He blushed. "You know what I mean, Charlotte. I want you to feel okay, here. At home."

That really threw her for a loop. He'd mentioned doing better, but with his practice and her project, she had little time to really relax and take advantage of the country she was visiting.

"You guys seem like a family. It's sweet."

"Yes, a dysfunctional one."

They laughed together.

Lance again started to loudly shout, but this time he sang a song, and Pippin joined him. All Charlotte could get out of it was "the craic was ninety in the Isle of Man."

"It's the name of the song," Eoghan said and tried to teach her the words as he sang. He put his arm around her, the vibrations of his chest stronger than that of the shouting bar. She mumbled until the refrain, when she sang the title of the song. She looked over at Yaya, who was singing every word.

This bitch is Irish now. Charlotte laughed as her bestie held her man and they sang the song together. Soon Charlotte got most of the repeating verses and chorus. She held Eoghan by the waist only because many of the patrons held on to each other and belted out the bar anthem. As they sang, he stared down at her, and she couldn't deny how adorable he was when he wanted to be and how much she liked him close to her. The song ended, and the normal music in the bar resumed with "Waiting for Tonight" by Jennifer Lopez, which was an odd mix, but she let that one go. She and Eoghan separated as Pippin headed toward them with stress lines on his face.

"Incoming," Pippin said to Eoghan.

Charlotte could tell something was up. She just didn't know what.

A raven-haired woman on a mission beelined toward Eoghan.

"Oh no," Eoghan groaned.

While Charlotte's eyes ping-ponged between Eoghan and the dark-haired woman, Eoghan's eyes ping-ponged between her and the woman.

"Channing, what a surprise," Eoghan said.

They'd just started having the craic, but with Channing's arrival, it was minus craic altogether.

"You." Channing pointed at Charlotte, whose friends had gathered, as Channing had made a very loud and raucous entrance. "You're with this tart now?" Channing asked Eoghan but kept a steady eye on her.

Charlotte did a double take. "Who is she talking about?" she asked Danai and Ayanna.

"I don't know, because you are not the one," Danai said.

Ayanna, normally not confrontational, took on her tough New York exterior.

"Here I am enjoying my little Harp and the company of good friends, so why is this woman coming for me?" Charlotte asked her friends, yet she kept her eyes on Channing. She had been in Ireland a hot second. Not even long enough to scratch her ass, much less make enemies.

"Yer back for more punishment then, Chan," Pippin said.

"It's Channing," the woman corrected.

"I see not much has changed there," Pippin mumbled to Shane, who exchanged glances with Eoghan. Charlotte knew that "handle that" look and hoped Eoghan heeded the call before the New Yorkers in the building did.

"Shut yer bake," Channing snarled at Pippin.

"No need for insults, darling. Yer showing your arse," Pippin said.

"Let's everyone calm down," Eoghan said.

"I can't believe you're here," Channing said. "And with her."

Charlotte sighed at the annoyance. First, she was mistaken for one of Eoghan's groupies, and now one territorially approached her. It wasn't surprising based on his track record in New York. While he'd been injured and in his pity party, he'd made sure that he'd baked in a little intimate fun for himself. It irked her, but who was she to judge when if they were back in New York, he'd easily bump into several of her conquests? Maybe even two in one day. The thing was, she didn't want the altercation to turn into a fight, which this woman looked ready to initiate, but she was ready for one if Channing took it to that level.

"Eoghan?" Ayanna said, shouldering her way in front of Charlotte. "I highly suggest you sort your business with Channing."

"What are you going to do? Take your earrings off?" the woman said. The stereotype gave Charlotte chills.

"See, that's what too much TV will get you. Looking foolish in a bar, making statements you know nothing about," Charlotte said.

Danai on the other hand gasped and patted his chest. "Nah-uh. Someone needs to snatch this trick."

Charlotte's assistant had taken the words out of her mouth. Her representative. Nearby onlookers who were in earshot and view of the situation stared at Channing's reddening face and agitated movements with wonder, while Charlotte viewed her with condescension because the way she was behaving only made her look thirsty as fuck. Charlotte almost felt sorry for her. Charlotte shifted her stance into that "I'll wait while you find your life" pose that commanded attention. Both she and Yaya had learned that people often had *angry Black woman* on the tips of their tongues, so their approach was to become a blank slate to display everyone else's wild behavior.

"You left for America without a word. Then you come back and don't even phone me. Now I find you with . . . this . . ." She didn't even identify Charlotte as human. Channing added in an additional comment, one that Charlotte didn't understand, but from just the look on her face and the expressions of the patrons in the bar who overheard, it was straight-up nasty.

"Enough," Eoghan growled. "You kiss yer ma with that gob, do ya?"

This might not have been about Charlotte, but Channing's verbal assault was more than she was willing to take. In her mind she might have beaten Little Miss Long Legs' ass, but they had levels to go before they reached that point. For her part, anyway.

Charlotte slid both her arms around Eoghan's waist from behind. "Who are you?" she asked, shelling out a microaggression of her own. The move was an antagonizing one, but one thing she wasn't used to doing was taking anything lying down.

Eoghan tensed at her touch but didn't move out of her grip. He let her hold him.

Channing lunged for her, but Eoghan tucked Charlotte farther behind himself.

"Whoa! Careful, girl. You don't want to hurt yourself," Charlotte said, but deep inside she prayed that this woman wouldn't touch her, because once that match was lit, she'd regress to middle school, when she'd protected Yaya and Jada after their father had died. They'd been children taking care of themselves and gotten picked on by bullies about everything from their clothes and hair to their quiet, introspective moments and emotional outbursts. Charlotte had made it her mission to protect them physically when necessary.

Channing's frustrated tears started to flow.

"Now, now. There's no need for that." Eoghan, like many men when confronted with a crying woman, was befuddled by the waterworks.

Charlotte felt bad for Channing despite her antics, and all accusatory glares went to Eoghan.

"Don't cry now. Come and let's have a chat," Eoghan said and ushered Channing away.

"What the fuck is this shit," Danai whispered in her ear. "Is this man's dick that magical?"

Yes, it is.

"I mean, Little Miss Thing had a full meltdown," Ayanna added.

I can understand. Even though Charlotte couldn't fully relate to Channing, she understood rejection. It was one of the main reasons why she'd often been the first to reject her lovers—to save herself the trouble of nursing her confidence back. If she stayed ahead of that, she'd be fine. However, Eoghan, though she'd sworn off him, still had a pull on her that she couldn't quite shake.

"It's kind of sad. I mean, I'm pro expressing your feelings, but that's next level." Charlotte wondered what Eoghan and Channing were doing. Was she trying to convince him to have a last ride? Was he letting her kiss him?

Chill. He's not yours.

"It's not a big deal," Lance said. "Channing knows you have his attention. The ladies have a hard time letting go sometimes. Eoghan'll right it."

"There are fleets of them," Patrick said, and Shane shoved him.

Charlotte's already intense frown gave her a headache. If that was supposed to make her feel better, it didn't.

"Not helpful, eejit," Shane said.

"Next round is on me," Andreas shouted.

The bar cheered, and good humor seemed to circulate once again.

"And the round after that is on me." Danai shrugged and danced to the music playing. This time a Banx & Ranx edit of "Slow Motion" by Kevin Lyttle played.

More cheers erupted.

The song was a joyful banger, and Charlotte moved her body to shake off some of the negative energy. "I love us." Charlotte hugged Danai and Yaya and even extended her hug to Shane and Pippin.

A round of shots materialized, and though Charlotte indulged in that round, she passed on the next. Liam on his iPhone kept the tunes coming with "ABCDEFU" by Gayle, which surprisingly felt fitting for the situation. Charlotte peered over at Liam, who pointed at her with a bright smile. She gave him a high thumbs-up and bounced with her friends and the players.

"Shake it, Patrick," Charlotte said, while Danai somehow sandwiched Lance with Andreas, and Charlotte and Ayanna laughed so hard that they couldn't move. Fun was again the main course, and it felt good.

Eoghan returned and headed straight for her.

"I'm sorry about that, Charlotte. It's nothing to do with you. Channing's just going through some things," he said.

Channing emerged a while later and mumbled an apology to her. Now pushed to the outskirts, the woman appeared sullen.

"It's cool," Charlotte said. "Come drink with us and tell me all about Eoghan."

"Come again?" Danai asked, apparently overwhelmed by Charlotte's turn of cheek.

"You're kind, especially for how I treated you, but I'm off," Channing said.

"You don't have to go." Charlotte couldn't believe the words coming out of her mouth.

"Maybe another time." Channing left the bar, and the thick tension in the air dissipated almost as quickly as it had come.

"Will she be all right?" Charlotte asked Eoghan.

"She's just a little put out. She'll be okay," Eoghan promised. "One of the lads will make sure she gets into a car okay."

Charlotte nodded.

"This is too much maturity for me," Danai said and went to sprinkle his Funfetti elsewhere.

Charlotte really hoped never to buck up on Channing again but agreed with Danai's comment nonetheless.

Ayanna and Shane had also broken off, leaving her once again with Eoghan.

Eoghan moved like he was caged in his own skin. He raked his hand through his hair and, though he wasn't dancing, hopped from foot to foot.

"You okay?" Charlotte asked.

"It's I who should be asking you," he said.

With no quip or comment in her arsenal, she shrugged.

"You wanna get out of here?" he asked her.

After what had just happened, she'd be a damn fool to go anywhere with him. "Sure."

Damn if she wasn't a full-on fool.

Chapter 13

Eoghan drove Charlotte to her place even though the walk wasn't very far. The drive hadn't been long enough for her to enjoy the heat, but regardless, she welcomed the shelter from the cold.

"You can park in my space. I don't have a car, so . . . ," she said and let him fill in the blank with the many options: . . . *so you don't have to park on the street* . . . *so you can come up* . . . *so you can stay over.*

"Thanks," he said.

On their elevator ride up, she pondered the many questions she had for him about what had happened at the bar. She'd heard from Ayanna about Eileen, Shane's ex-girlfriend, and how it all had gone down with Eoghan. Thankfully, the two best friends had mended things. However, whether it was past, present, or future, Eoghan proved to be hard for women to get over. She had questions.

Deciding that nothing could squelch the attraction between them or change where she knew they'd inevitably end up once in her apartment, she opened fire.

"What was all that about with Channing at the bar?" she asked.

He scratched the hair on his chin. "You want to talk about that now?"

"Yup," she said, admiring how sexy he looked in his black-and-gray Givenchy tracksuit, the hot style among many of the players, including Eoghan. He really should be wearing a hat.

"We hung out a few times before I got injured," he said. "Over a year now. It was a casual thing for me. I guess it wasn't so casual for her. I didn't know until now."

"Had you seen her before tonight?"

He shook his head.

"I see."

"She's a nice girl, but maybe I wasn't clear enough about what went on between us two," he added.

Given Charlotte's history with men, he most definitely hadn't been clear about his and Channing's status. "Yeah, she was definitely hurt."

"That's not what I wanted."

"You seem tore up about it. I'm glad," Charlotte said.

Eoghan frowned and turned to stare at her, his shoulder leaning on the back of the elevator as it stopped on her floor. "You're glad?"

"Yup. It makes you less of a dick," she said and exited the elevator as it opened.

He followed her. "That what you were thinking about me this whole time? That I'm a dick?" he asked.

"Kind of, but you continue to shine through."

He rubbed his face and sighed.

"All I'm saying," she said as they walked to her door, "is that even your booty calls need to know when the tie is cut. You know what I mean?" Charlotte remembered the look on Channing's face after Eoghan had spoken to her. In the past Charlotte had probably worn the same expression, whether in public or in private.

He stuttered and sputtered to find words.

"I'm not judging you." How could she when she had her own lineup back in New York? "I'm just saying it's the best and most honest way to break things off."

"Is that what you did with me that night after the gala?" he asked.

"No. First of all, we only fucked that one time at Purchase House. So there wasn't anything to break off," she politely corrected him. "Still, when I left that day, was I clear?" she questioned rhetorically.

"Crystal."

Charlotte smiled as she opened the door to her apartment.

They flopped out of their shoes on their way in, and in the dark of her apartment, the view of the canal and the bright lights from the museum set the stage.

"I still can't believe this view," he said. "It's almost better'n mine."

"It's gorgeous," she said.

Eoghan started singing "Only Girl (In the World)" by Rihanna as he danced toward her. He changed the perspective of the lyrics. "I want to make you feel like you're the only girl in the world."

Charlotte doubled over in stitches from his off-key, on-key version of the song. "So smooth." She made her way to the bathroom to wash her hands and face, buzzed off his humor. Eoghan followed her, filling the doorframe.

"What're ya doin' there?" he asked. His large form made the bathroom feel ten times smaller, and there was no getting away from the manly intoxication of his fragrance.

"I'm just cleaning up a bit." Being in the bar singing and drinking and all the pollutants of the day had gone right to her skin.

As she cleansed her face, his arms circled her waist from behind, startling her, and she peeked between the soapsuds.

"Eoghan? What are you doing?" she asked.

"I'm washing up a bit too," he said and soaped his hands.

With each movement his hard body pressed against her back, his arms squeezed her sides, and he kissed her neck from one side to the other and back again. She bent to rinse her face and felt the impression of his firm arousal.

A sigh escaped her.

"I like cleaning up with you," he mumbled against her ear, his teeth capturing the lobe and giving it a gentle tug. His tongue followed.

"Me too." She turned within his arms, and though they were both still wet, she hooked her arms around his neck and brought his face to hers. His supportive arms encircled her, and she moaned into his open, hot mouth. Her tongue darted in search of his, and once they met, they toyed and wrestled as the ignited passion between them popped.

Eoghan spread the easy-access slit on her Amur merino-wool dress and gathered it up to her waist as she maneuvered herself to wiggle out of her tights. She shivered under the touch of his cooler hand, sliding between her legs to her center, where his finger delivered marvelous touches that drove her up the wall.

"Eoghy," she cried.

"You haven't called me that since New York."

"I slipped," she said, her mouth lurching in hunger for his.

"You slipped," he teased and playfully bit her bottom lip.

"Uh-huh," she said.

"Say it again," he commanded.

She shook her head.

He licked her lips but avoided her desperate attempt to kiss him, and he intensified his torturous touches between her legs. When his fingers found entry and slid against her insides, all while his thumb caressed her sensitive button, she whimpered his name.

"Oh shit, Eoghy," she moaned, and his mouth crashed onto hers, smothering her cries and devouring her mouth, her tongue, her soul. Her legs opened wider as her hips circled to try to control the pressure on her clit, but by the devilish glint in his brown eyes, he'd milk this and her for as long as possible.

She undid the tie on his tracksuit pants and pushed them down his strong legs, unwrapping him like the gift he was. After pushing the material down, she stopped to unzip his jacket and pushed it over his defined shoulders.

"This is new," she said. The tribal tattoo that had only covered his forearm four months ago was a full and gorgeous sleeve now. She ran her hand over his skin. "This is beautiful," she said, more about the lean muscle of his arm than the ink work.

He shrugged the jacket off the rest of the way and held her by the waist. "Thank you, but my tattoo is the last thing I want to talk about, Charlotte," he said and took her mouth again.

"Agreed," she said. Her mouth left his, and as her open-mouthed kisses trailed down his chest and over each strong bump of his abs, she savored the hint of bergamot from his soap and a sweet floral from the cologne on his clothes. He approved each of her caresses with deep grunts and moans that vibrated his torso.

She sacrificed her own pleasure and continued down to her knees, dragging his pants and boxer briefs down with her to his ankles. Her excitement to reunite with his dick was off any chart in her memory bank. He was ready for her mouth, and when she took him inside, he gripped one edge of the sink, while the other hand rested on her head, where his fingers glided into her Afro and massaged her scalp. Though he was a rough footballer, she loved his gentle ways when they had sex.

"Fuck, lass," he moaned, and his hips jerked.

Her hands caressed his hips and went around to his ass, which clenched as her mouth sucked and glided on his shaft.

"Condom," he choked out. "In my pocket."

She pulled his stiff muscle out of her mouth with a loud smack. "I got you," she said and retrieved the contraception from the pocket of his suit. She quickly fitted him with it.

"C'mere to me," he said, pulling her up to him.

She yanked her turtleneck dress over her head while Eoghan undid the front clasp on her bra. She shrugged out of it and then jumped up onto Eoghan, her legs wrapping around his waist. He held her easily, and though they were in the small bathroom, the confined space didn't dampen either of their need.

"Let me take you to bed," he said.

"No. Here." She could feel him between her legs, hardening, growing. She missed his feel, and even the small jaunt to her bedroom would be too long. "Now."

Eoghan reached between her legs for his cock and rubbed the tip against her with excruciatingly slow circles over her clit. She frantically sought something to hold on to. A nearby towel rack was the only option, and she reached for it, curling her fingers around the slim silver rod just as Eoghan sank into her.

She flinched and bucked as if darted by a tranquilizer, and her body both weakened and awakened for the ride Eoghan was about to give her. He kissed at her neck, nibbling with his lips and teeth up and around her ear. Her hand crooked around his neck, her fingers sliding slightly from the layer of his sweat.

"You good?" she asked.

"Better than." He roughly captured her lips, and her mouth pressed against his with equal fervency. Both his hands cupped her ass, and he massaged her cheeks, simultaneously manipulating her and moving to drive deeper into her.

"Fuck, Eoghan. Do you always have to be so damn good?" she asked, and he laughed.

"I can be bad if you want me to." His head dipped down to her breasts, and he sucked her skin loudly, kissing her in between nibbles until his hot mouth covered her nipple, biting the taut, swollen bud. The nerve shock scattered through her body, and she felt it all the way down to her clit. She let the towel rod go to greedily slide her fingers between herself and Eoghan to rub herself. Eoghan, with his mouth still devouring her titties, glanced down at her activity, moaning his approval.

He made eye contact with her, which only intensified every caress. She licked her lips and could only imagine how clearly her desire displayed on her face as the pressure between his thrusts and her self-pleasure built her up. She moved wildly, chasing ecstasy and oblivious to the insecurity of their embrace.

"I'm coming," she squealed.

"Me too." He pummeled into her but waited for her, squeezing his eyes shut. "Come, love."

His encouragement meant everything to her in that moment, and she exploded. His eruption tumbled out, and in a symphony of moans and shouts, they clung to each other, writhing against one another.

It all happened too fast for two people enthralled in heavenly bliss. Her hand slipped from his sweating neck, and with nothing else to hold her up except Eoghan's grip on her waist, she fell back fast and hard. She heard Eoghan shout her name, and then he faded to black.

BLACK WOMAN FOUND NAKED AND DEAD IN BATHTUB
WITH PREMIER FOOTBALLER.

Eoghan could see the headlines now. He wouldn't give a shit if only he knew Charlotte was all right. She'd hit her head hard enough to be unresponsive, and in a panic he called 999. Ayanna would kill him if he hurt her friend. Much less killed her. Regardless of his possible fate, all he wanted was for Charlotte to be okay. He loved her stank attitude, loved her commitment to working with him and the team, loved fucking her, loved . . .

Shane and Ayanna arrived at the hospital soon after he got there.

"What happened? Is she all right? How'd she get hurt?" Ayanna pummeled him with questions, all of which he did not want to or couldn't answer.

"We were at her place, and she hit her head in the bathroom." Eoghan purposely kept it vague. Less detail for the rags.

Shane studied him, and after Eoghan conveyed some voiceless information, it was clear Shane knew exactly what he and Charlotte had been up to in the bathroom. "You all right, then?" Shane asked.

Eoghan shrugged his response, unable to stay still. He was far from okay.

"She'll be all right, mate," Shane said.

Ayanna had been the first one Eoghan had called after the ambulance. It was late, but he'd known that Ayanna was the family Charlotte would want in an event like this.

The doctor came out to give them a quick summary. "She's fine, just a little foggy with maybe a little bit of temporary short-term memory loss."

"How short?" Ayanna asked.

"Not long. It's all normal with a little inflammation, but she's gotten some medicine. Once the swelling goes down, she'll be right as rain."

Eoghan had never hated the stupid saying more than right now. This was more than he could take, and before he knew it, he was heading toward the exit.

Shane noticed first. "Hold on. Where're you off to?"

"I just need to go." He choked on the stinging smell of antiseptic, and the white walls closed in on him.

Shane grabbed his arm. "Charlotte is laid up, and you're going to blow her off? That's too low even for you."

Eoghan yanked himself free and staggered away from the cryptic beeps of equipment toward the exit. "I'm going. Now."

Outside the hospital, he walked and walked, his limbs fighting to stay tight and resistant to the deep, cool breaths he chugged. How could he have been that careless? That Charlotte had gotten hurt, and on his watch, fucked with him in a way he'd never experienced before. He picked up the pace to outrun what had happened and his fear. Fuck! She'd scared the hell out of him when she'd lain unnaturally slumped and unmoving in the bathtub. He squeezed his eyes with his fingers to eradicate the image. He started to run, but he couldn't outrun his feelings. Charlotte meant more to him than he'd realized, and the thought of her hurt or worse unraveled him. When he'd left the hospital exit, he hadn't known where he'd go—he'd just needed air that wasn't soaked with the consequences of what he'd done. He looked around. All he'd done was run circles around the building. He couldn't leave her. He needed her to be okay. Fuck, he needed her.

When he made his way back to Charlotte's hospital room, Shane stood there with arms crossed as nurses in white and blue uniforms and doctors with stethoscopes around their necks passed them by. At least now Shane didn't blur in his vision and walls kept their shape.

"Don't lecture me, now. I just needed a moment," he said.

"She's waiting for you," Shane said.

Eoghan nodded and entered the room. Her vibrancy was only slightly dulled by the injury. A white sheet covered her, and a pillow had been tucked behind her head.

"I see you dragged your sorry ass back in here," Charlotte said as he made his way toward her. "You left. That was real fucking mature, you asshole. I wouldn't even be in the situation if I wasn't fucking you in the bath—"

Eoghan cupped her face, which looked small in his hands, and descended on her to capture her lips. He needed to feel her warmth and to reassure her that though he'd misstepped, he was with her. "I'm sorry. I freaked out for a moment. I shouldn't have left and won't do it ever again."

"You better not," Charlotte commanded and then looked over his shoulder, and an intense blush powdered her rich deep-brown skin.

He followed her gaze to see Ayanna, her waist held by his best friend. Ayanna brimmed with happiness as if her smile might stretch off her face. "Looks like you're in good hands. We're gonna head out."

When the friends left, Eoghan was glad to be alone with Charlotte.

"This wasn't how I wanted tonight to go," he said.

"It got off to a pretty intense start," she said.

"Didn't expect it to end with you here," he said. He pecked her lips, remembering how beautifully tortured she'd looked as he'd pleasured her.

"Come on, Eoghan. You have to admit it was fun."

"Until it wasn't." His face ached from frowning.

"I'm okay, you know," she assured him and touched his face.

"I should have held you better," he said.

"Don't blame yourself. This is biology's fault." She smiled. "They're keeping me overnight, which is ridiculous."

"It's precautionary," he said.

"You don't have to stay. I'm fine," she said. "Plus, I think you're not allowed to."

"I'm staying," he said and pulled up a chair close to the bed. "Get some rest. I'm right here."

◆ ◆ ◆

The next day in Charlotte's apartment, Eoghan hovered over her like she was made of glass and would drop from a blood clot in her brain at any moment. Of course, that was ridiculous, he reminded himself, but he couldn't help but worry about her. He'd been so high off her that he'd failed to support her and keep her safe during such an intimate moment between them.

"Eoghan," Charlotte called.

He peered down at her sitting figure on the couch in her apartment. A frown was etched on her face.

"Sorry, what was that?" he asked.

She sighed. "Are you staying tonight?"

He had wanted nothing more for the past few weeks than for her to invite him to stay the night with her. Why now? "No. You should rest your noggin." He did a poor job of being funny, but Charlotte's well-being was no laughing matter.

"You're never going to touch me again, are you?" she asked, snuggling into the cushion.

"Just not tonight." He laughed, moving closer to her. "I don't have that kind of willpower."

"I told you it wasn't your fault, Eoghan, and I meant it. We both were in deep, and I am in perfect health. The doctor even said so."

He stroked her chin. "You're a horny little nymph, aren't you?"

"Did you just call me a nymph?" She laughed. "I'm dead. I have never been called that. It sounds wild."

She was so fucking cute, even when she slagged him. "That's why your head is as big as your 'fro." He patted her hair.

They teased each other back and forth, and it felt nice to forget about how he'd nearly killed her.

"The only way to get over what happened is for us to do it again," she said.

"What?" He backed up to the other side of her apartment.

"Yeah. You have to fuck me in the bathroom again. This time we have to be successful."

"We were successful." He winked. They'd both achieved stellar orgasms that night, and he'd never forget coming inside her any more than he'd forget dropping her in the bathtub.

"You know what I mean," she said, standing up.

He didn't bother to instruct her to sit down, because the only time she followed his instructions was when they were intimate. "That's not going to happen."

"We'll see." She sauntered over to him and ran her fingertips over his shoulder and down the front of his chest.

"Sex affects your blood pressure." He inhaled sharply at the mischief in her eyes as her hands moved over his abdomen and down to his belly button with no sign of stopping. "You can get a bad headache and . . ." His pelvis moved forward instinctively, and knowing where this would head if they didn't stop it, he grabbed her hands with his own. "Charlotte, please," he begged. "Just give me a few days for the trauma to ease up."

"Fucking me is traumatizing, now?" She crossed her arms.

"Woman." He kissed her good and firm, claiming her, marking her, before he pulled away. "Soon," he said, struggling to let her go.

She giggled. "We'll see."

Chapter 14

Charlotte sat in the stands as Eoghan was about to play with the Dublin Rovers, wearing one of the test shoes she had for him. She was still waiting for the manufacturing of his third-round boots, the most important in their series, but James wouldn't be back until tomorrow, and she'd be at the factory bright and early to demand answers.

If Charlotte kept her head down and did her work, she might just be able to convince herself that Eoghan wasn't setting up a bought-and-paid-for cottage inside her heart. Maybe it was just the beauty of Ireland, the thrill of being abroad, or the work she did that had sparked her creativity and entrepreneurial spirit again. Maybe it wasn't Eoghan.

Her psyche rejected the probability.

"Hiya."

Charlotte turned her head in the direction of the voice to find Clive Sullivan from the national team at the game. "Hey, Clive. What are you doing here at the Tallaght Stadium? Shouldn't you be at Aviva?" Charlotte asked.

"I'm here to see Eoghan play. I'm not scouting or anything too intense. They are behind me a little further out, but lots of people want to see if their national treasure is up to the task of winning games again," he said.

"Great," Charlotte said.

"That reminds me. I heard you got hurt the other day. You all right?" he asked.

Charlotte blushed at the thought of the details surrounding her minor injury. "Yes, thank you for asking. It was minor, but I'm healing."

"Good, good."

"Eoghan's form looks well." Charlotte brought the conversation back to her client. "The shoe has most of the adjustments."

"Most?" Clive asked.

Charlotte could have kicked herself in the face for opening up the door to this line of questioning. "Yeah, we're waiting for his last tester shoe before we finalize the design."

"Ah, okay," Clive said. "That'll be here soon, I'm sure."

"Yes," Charlotte said, but she had her doubts.

"Well, enjoy the game, and we'll talk soon," he said.

Danai came back with fish and chips for her and a sausage sandwich for himself. Charlotte sighed in relief that Danai hadn't been there to offer up any additional shade toward the manufacturer that would have raised the alarm for Clive.

"Girl, they have so many options and . . ." Danai stopped when Charlotte didn't seem as thrilled by the food as he was. "What's good?"

"I'm stressing about this shoe and the manufacturer. Clive just came by." Charlotte twisted her mouth. Clive had asked her several times if things with James were going well. As brand manager for the team, Clive's job entailed monetizing brand placement at the stadium and for the players. It also involved uniforms, including incorporating the latest technology in sportswear to help the players be their best and approving brand placement on those uniforms. His job was big, and she didn't want to worry his strawberry-blond head with the minutiae of her manufacturing problems.

"He's here? Isn't he team national, not team Dublin Rovers?"

"Exactly. They're here to see Eoghan play."

"They?" Danai asked.

142

"Don't look now, but the bigwigs are up in the stands too." Charlotte tilted her head in that direction.

Danai side-eyed upward to catch a glimpse. "Shit's been real, but it just got really real. That James person is back tomorrow, right?"

"Yes, and I will be at the factory bright and early for answers and progress."

"You need backup?" Danai asked.

"No, I got this."

Danai crossed his fingers. "Here's hoping Eoghan looks comfortable and plays well."

Charlotte pressed her hands together in prayer.

The game started, and Charlotte watched her first football game in Ireland. The energy of the fans and the players electrified the place, and Charlotte cheered in excitement as well as to blend in.

Eoghan ran the ball with his teammates, his strong, agile body poetry on the pitch. Did he stand out because of his super athlete abilities or because she zeroed in on the same body that felt like home when it was wrapped around her? She reprimanded herself to focus on objectively watching the match and Eoghan's movements. On the outset his play was on par with the other players. She couldn't take her eyes off him even when she tried, and it spoke to his natural draw as a celebrity player. Eoghan tried for a goal and missed. From her view, it looked like he took it in stride.

Each time he tried for a goal after that, Charlotte held her breath and prayed for the ball to land inside the net. Unfortunately, Eoghan's consistent misses and the opposing goalkeeper's blocks echoed throughout the stadium. Eoghan fiddled with his boots.

"Uh-oh," Charlotte said. If she'd only guessed at the connection between Eoghan's confidence and his boots before, the link was now crystal clear.

His energized strategy on the field turned tentative, and again he kicked at his boots.

"That has nothing to do with his boots," Charlotte mumbled, wishing that she could beam confidence into him from the stands. However, she doubted that words of encouragement would matter. She'd seen video of him dominating the field, and compared to what she saw now, he struggled to evoke that player.

Charlotte bit her lip. This was what she'd feared. Eoghan had a shoe that was being customized to him like a body part, yet he still held back.

"Play, ya tart," someone rudely shouted behind them, but that was only one insult of many that floated around her.

She watched the rest of the game agonizing over the quick decline of Eoghan's performance. When Boyle took him out for the second half, Eoghan directed his frustration right at her shoe. Charlotte shrugged off the personal attack and reminded herself that there was an adjusted boot waiting for Eoghan and that all she could do was her best. The rest Eoghan had to figure out for himself.

Technically, Eoghan should have remained on the field, yet he split to the locker room. "I'm going to check in on him," she whispered to Danai before making her way down to see him. She heard him before she saw him. He seemed to be throwing his boots and other things around. She knocked on the door to the dressing rooms.

"Feck off," he shouted.

Charlotte entered tentatively in case something he threw headed her way. When she laid eyes on him, he was pacing as if caged with frustration.

"Hi," she said.

"These boots aren't working," he grumbled, his kit clinging to him and his hair dripping large droplets of sweat.

"How do they feel?" she asked, keeping her tone calm and neutral.

"Fine, I guess," he said.

"Okay," she said. "We have some minor tweaks coming from the fourth and final round, but the ones we're waiting on are mostly done. It's the most important version, but it's in manufacturing."

"All right," he said but must've noticed her hesitancy. "What're you not telling me?"

"Before you get too excited. They won't be ready for more than two weeks."

"More than two weeks?" he inquired. "But the campaign. The press coverage."

"Yes, I know—"

"Plus, I need it to play my best for the national team. Charlotte, this needs to be sorted, and—"

"I get it, Eoghan." She wrung her hands. She didn't need additional pressure about this, but she had ownership of this part, and it pissed her off that she'd somehow lost control over the process. "I'm as disrupted by this as you are, but I'll take care of it. I'm going in person again tomorrow morning to get to the bottom of it."

"Are you having trouble?" he asked, studying her.

His question threw her, and she struggled for a proper answer. "I can handle it."

He combed both hands through his hair this time. "Tweaks are coming, and now a tester version is weeks away?" he questioned, the accusation heavy. "This is my career. I'm out there with boots that are incomplete?"

She sighed. "Not incomplete, just slightly modified."

"And you don't think that makes a difference?" he asked.

She folded her lips to not say something to fan the flames, but he wasn't making it easy. "Eoghan? Your shoes are there to support you, but you have to play. They are not magical any more than I am."

"What are you saying?"

"You were great out there in the beginning, and then you just . . ." Charlotte decided it was too late to back out now. "You gave up. Like you lost all your confidence."

His face twisted with the truth, and the lack of confidence and pain played on his face. She thanked the heavens that she'd given him a gentle version of the truth. Still, she braced herself for his wrath.

145

"I . . ." Eoghan's whole body stiffened like a rubber band about to snap. "I dunno what to do about it."

The confession hit her in the stomach. She had seen many emotions since working with him, but now she could describe him with one word. *Lost.*

"Have you told anyone?" she asked him.

"You."

Yup, he was pissed, but somehow, she felt special that he was comfortable enough to tell her. "The good news is you know what part of the problem is. The bad news is it's not something that I or anyone can give you." She moved toward him and touched his arm. His muscles were rigid, and she didn't know how to help him.

"Take off your clothes," she said, surprised by her own words.

"What?" he asked.

She didn't repeat herself, because she knew damn well that he'd heard her the first time.

He didn't say another word, pulled his shirt off, and then started on his boots.

"Leave the cleats on."

Eoghan obliged and took his shorts off, leaving them in a pile on the floor with his jersey.

Charlotte didn't know why she'd asked him to take his clothes off. Yes, she loved seeing him naked, but he'd been vulnerable with her, something she knew firsthand wasn't an easy thing to be. As a lover, he was confident and giving. Perhaps she wanted him to feel that now when he had reached a low point.

"This what you want?" he asked.

"Yes." She moved slowly, not knowing what she'd do any more than he did. Anyone could come in at any moment, and the excitement of potentially being found aroused her. However, this moment centered on him. She ran her hand over his defined shoulder and down over his pectoral muscles, then washed it over each of his abs. By the time she got to his pelvis, his arousal waited for her, hard and stiff.

"Char," he called, his arms on her shoulders as if to hold himself up. Her fingers curved around his size, and she stroked him. "This is how strong I see you, Eoghan." She kissed his chest as her hand worked, and her fingers tangled through the slightly curled hair, framing him there. She pressed her body against him, and her hand slid up his back slowly, then down, even slower. She grazed his nipple with her teeth and sucked gently before licking down his sternum. His salty taste from his activity on the field turned her on further.

His breathing increased with every caress she delivered, and now his precome aided in keeping him slick for the task. "You're so much more than the boots on your feet." She increased her pressure on him, and he shuddered.

"Fuck, Char," he moaned. "What're you doing to me?"

"I want you to come," she said in his ear. "I want you to spill that confidence right in my hand."

She'd love nothing more than to have him inside her, but it wasn't about her. She'd rub one out in the ladies' room if she had to, but him letting go here like this with her was paramount.

"Char."

"Let go, Eoghy. Please." She moaned as his knee went between her legs, and she rubbed her swelling clit against him as best she could through her leggings. His arms wrapped around her, and he shouted his climax into her neck. He jerked as his hot arrival sputtered into her hand, and she used the sticky cum to continue to play with him.

There were cheers coming through to the locker room, and she hoped the Rovers were winning, but mostly, she hoped that Eoghan knew that despite his failings on the pitch, she was there for him.

She stepped away from him and kissed him deeply, stroking his face. When the kiss ended, she left him to clean up. She washed her hands in the showers behind them and then returned to Eoghan.

"Danai will be wondering where I am," she said.

"Charlotte. I shouldn't leave you like this," he said.

"You didn't leave me any kind of way. I wanted to do that," she said and bent down to get his shorts. "For you." She handed him his bottoms.

"I don't know what I should say. Than—"

She pressed her finger to his lips. "If you thank me, you'll insult me."

He pecked her lips. "Okay."

"I'm going to go." She left without another word.

As she walked back to the stands, the fog of desire lifted, and what had happened between her and Eoghan inspired a fear that tensed her thighs as she climbed the stairs to her seat. What had she done? She'd never been that selfless with a lover in her life, and with Eoghan it didn't feel like a chore or a manipulation. She swallowed hard. "What is happening?"

She swiped away the confusion because she still had a part to play. She had to get Eoghan's shoe and fast. For his sake she had to fix this.

Chapter 15

Charlotte navigated Sandyford Industrial Estate in Dún Laoghaire–Rathdown, which was no easy feat. When she'd first visited the place, it had reminded her of Co-op City in the Bronx. Both were clearly planned from above, but on street level they were mazes that took time to navigate. No matter how many times she'd been there, she still got lost. Sandyford overwhelmed her with the many businesses located on the property, yet like most of Dublin, it captured a modern style with a European flair. She loved that the buildings didn't take over the surrounding suburb.

No matter her appreciation for the convenience of the manufacturing company being in Dublin, it held her shoe captive. Charlotte wore a black suit, her patent leather power heels, and a long red trench coat. When she walked into the factory, she was armored for war. She was done getting the runaround. She had to take a stand and get things done or suffer the alternative: reaching out to Clive for assistance at the eleventh hour.

She stomped through the factory with the specs and a physical prototype of Eoghan's shoe in her briefcase and met a representative. "I'm here to see James Brennen. Please direct me to his office."

"Who are you?" the representative asked.

"Who are you?" Charlotte asked.

"Shaun's the name, madam," he said and reached for his name tag to show her.

"I've spoken to you on the phone, haven't I?"

"Ah, the American," Shaun said with a bit of a distasteful smack of his mouth.

Charlotte rubbernecked. "Is there a problem?"

"No, madam. I speak to loads of people," he said simply.

"Well, Shaun, I have a meeting with Mr. Brennen. Please alert him that Charlotte Bowman from Seam and Sole is here." She kept the details light because, though Shaun seemed to be the gatekeeper, James's relationship with the club made him the person she needed to communicate with. James worked with Clive and was who Charlotte's communication went to. That was, if he ever read her emails or messages.

Shaun perused a clipboard. "I don't have you on the list, so you can't go through."

Charlotte didn't understand the reason for the power play, and his answer wasn't good enough. "That answer is unacceptable. Let's get Mr. Brennen on the phone so we can resolve this before this becomes a problem for you."

Shaun frowned. "Sorry, madam?"

"If you let me through to Mr. Brennen, we can avoid a problem," Charlotte said.

"Like I said, you're not on the list, and Mr. Brennen is very busy. I can't just let you in. Make an appointment if you will, madam."

Charlotte's capped frustration seeped out of the bottle. "What is the problem, exactly? I'm a client of this company and work with your boss. All you need to do is call him."

"No problem at all, if you make an appointment," Shaun said. "Entitled American," he mumbled.

"What? Wait," she called as the representative walked away from her. Charlotte's anger boiled. The treatment seeped into her normally thick skin, but if he thought she would just fold, he was mistaken. She rounded a corner, where a door with a Do Not Enter sign above it begged her to go through. When she pressed the handle, she got a little jolt of victory when she found it was unlocked. Unfortunately, when she opened it, an alarm sounded.

"Shit," she said and went through anyway. A few steps in, she was stopped by Shaun and a security guard who seemed to come out of nowhere. Shaun physically blocked her.

"You can't be in here, madam. I told you you'd have to make an appointment. Now the authorities have to be involved."

"Like I said, if you speak to Mr. Brennen, I have the prototype and specs right here. Look at me. Do I really look like some random person off the streets? Plus, I know you know you've spoken to me," Charlotte said. "Clive Sullivan will hear about this."

"Who now?" Shaun said.

She didn't want to overreact. Even in another country, she second-guessed if her reactions as a woman would be expected, exploited, and used against her. Besides Garrett mistaking her for a groupie, she'd had pleasant interactions in Ireland. Shaun, however, had a thing with her being American, and there was nothing she could do about that, but regardless of her nationality, he needed to do his job and get her to his boss. She blinked at the rise of angry water coating her eyes, and though she still stood tall, internally her anxiety had her slumped over, staring at her shoes.

Come on, now. Head up! She readied herself to go full steam ahead.

"Charlotte?" She turned to find Eoghan making his way farther into the manufacturing plant.

"Eoghan?" She blinked to make sure she was actually seeing him. "What are you doing here?" Alongside him was Clive, the brand representative, one of the most powerful men on the national team's payroll and Charlotte's new buddy.

"Mr. Sullivan." Shaun's inflated power immediately deflated, no doubt at the sight of the dynamic duo.

In a blur of events, Clive asked her if she'd made any progress.

"I was trying to get this guy to get me to James's office, but apparently I have to make an appointment, and—"

"An appointment?" Clive cut her off. "All right, we're done playing games here. I got this, CB. No worries." Clive reddened and marched to the manufacturing office. His suited form was too refined for the industrial surroundings. Charlotte's eyes tracked him as he passed Shaun and security without so much as slowing down.

"Apologies," Shaun said, hurrying behind Clive, who now knocked hard on James's door with his knuckles.

Charlotte had remained cemented in place but now allowed Eoghan to usher her along. "Come on. This is your project."

She walked with him, almost in a trance, and caught up with Clive. By the time they got to James's office, Clive was speaking firmly. "This is our shoe you're holding up."

"More specifically, my boots," Eoghan said.

"O'Farrell?" James's eyes widened, and he rose to his feet.

"Don't bother to get up," Eoghan said.

James hovered in a squat above his chair and then sat in slow motion. "I don't know what happened. Of course we can have the cleats ready for you, Mr. O'Farrell. You'll have to have everything you need for your fixture against Portugal."

Charlotte was going to be sick from the divergent treatment. The already closed-in space of James's office and the comingled smells of leather, fumes from melted plastic, and warmed machinery and its fuel didn't help her nausea.

"Why didn't you make room in the schedule for Miss Bowman when she first sent over her specs?" Clive asked. "The official team seal is on it."

"I don't know how this missed our priority list." James glanced nervously at Charlotte.

"This should have been ready a week ago. There is a campaign around Eoghan and the release of this shoe. You were informed that Miss Bowman is our new designer who would be doing the signature shoe design for the entire team. We sent documents over in January. It's almost March. She and her assistant have been communicating regularly. We've had some minor hiccups in the past, but this is unacceptable."

"I see there are a few messages here," James said, scrambling. He must have found what he needed, because he pressed an intercom. "Shaun normally helps prioritize things. Is that who you spoke to?" the manager asked.

"Yes. He completely brushed me off when I arrived." Charlotte had told him who she was and the importance of the design, yet it was as if she'd spoken to bathroom tile.

"I thought she was just trying to get in and make trouble," Shaun said. "I'd never seen her before, and we haven't worked with an American woman before for cleats. How was I to know who she was?"

"You spoke to me on the phone." Charlotte narrowed her eyes at Shaun's bold-faced lie and right in front of her. He couldn't possibly believe that was a plausible excuse. Even now, he refused to take responsibility.

"You check, you dolt," James said. "We'll see if you have your job at the end of the day."

"I'm sure it was an honest mistake, right, Shaun?" Charlotte said, the sarcasm smothering her words like gravy on biscuits. However, the last thing she wanted was to be the cause of anyone losing their job. That her voice now had the weight of the young man's job in its grip was enough to teach him a lesson.

Eoghan grew taller than his six-foot-plus height. "I'm sure it wasn't, and I—"

Charlotte put a hand against his arm to calm him. She shook her head, silently begging him to not make a scene. She had her suspicions about Shaun and his prejudices. She hadn't seen many women in the back offices of either club. A Black woman with big hair personally delivering a prototype for a signature shoe for Eoghan O'Farrell might have seemed like a long shot to Shaun, especially since the bigger companies did things differently. Still, Shaun had taken things to an uncomfortable level when all he'd needed to do was connect her with James.

"I'll be handling this personally. It's top priority. I'll be your direct line from now on, Miss Bowman. You can count on it," James said. "I'm sorry for any misunderstandin'. It won't ever happen again. You'll have your boots within the week." He glared at Shaun, whose face turned tomato red as he chewed on his lip.

"And an apology to Miss Bowman, please," Clive insisted.

Shaun's attitude took on a less powerful tone, and his embarrassment and fear for his job shook his voice. "Apologies, Ms. Bowman."

She nodded.

"I don't want another problem, James. Charlotte and her assistant get class treatment and the highest priority. Another snafu or whatever bollocks this was, and we'll have to reconsider your contract next year."

Charlotte loved watching Clive in action. It reminded her of her early years with Seam and Sole, when she'd had to learn that she was the big boss, the back office, the C-suite. However, in a country where football was everything, not even in Charlotte's wildest dreams could she wield Clive's power. It was impressive.

"Clear," James said.

Outside the factory a car waited, and the three of them climbed in.

"Thank you for coming," Charlotte said, sinking into the soft black leather seat.

"I wish you would have come to me sooner, Charlotte," Clive said. "I'm sure you wanted to handle it on your own, but you're new to this system here, and with all business, sometimes throwing weight at the onset can make life loads easier."

"You're right. I'm sorry you felt things were serious enough that you had to come down here," she said. "How did you even know I was here?"

Clive looked at Eoghan.

"You told him?" Charlotte glared at Eoghan.

Eoghan knit his brows. "No, I—"

"Don't blame Eoghan," Clive insisted. "I caught him on his way out, asked about his boots, and decided to meet you here."

"Because you didn't think I could handle it?" Charlotte asked. She was happy there was a resolution, but she didn't want Clive to think she didn't have the cojones to do the job when she was trying to navigate the cultural landscape.

"Not at all, Charlotte. Please don't think that. Simply put, time is running out. The financial backing behind Eoghan is enough to move any of us to action. If he needs his boots, I can't let a needle head like Shaun get in the way."

Eoghan pinched the bridge of his nose. "She'll be mad at me now," he said.

"I'm not mad," she said. "I just wish it hadn't come to that." Charlotte was pretty sure she could have handled it if she'd gotten to James on her own, but she'd never know now. She had to admit that having Clive and Eoghan there to back her up had felt supportive.

"It's water under the bridge. James'll never make that mistake again. Nor will any of his people," Clive said.

Eoghan watched Charlotte like she was some sort of puzzle.

They arrived at the stadium, and when she and Eoghan were alone, he asked, "You okay? I never doubted your abilities, but I know how the politics are in those places. What happened back at the factory before we got there?"

She gave him the quick and dirty about how Shaun had treated her at the factory despite the emails and phone calls. "He just wouldn't do what I asked."

Baffled, Eoghan asked, "Why would he behave so unprofessionally?"

"Several reasons why this happened probably. I'm new to this country, and to be honest manufacturing here has been different than in the States. Also, I know when I'm being profiled and when it's used against me. If you and Clive hadn't shown up, I would have been given the runaround no matter how much I name-dropped. I hate to say it, but that's how it is sometimes. Today was one of those days."

"You're not in the States, Charlotte, and you're not on your own. If you need muscle, don't fear to bring it along. We Irish look for character. Football is everything to us. No matter who is working for us, these vendors honor the sport. If they don't believe you or think you're trying to reproduce a fake, they deserve the backlash because the information they've received is legitimate."

"That why you showed up today?" she asked.

He was quiet for a few minutes. "I showed up because I'll not let anyone take advantage of you. You can be mad at me for showing up, but the point is that we got movement on manufacturing of my boots."

"Is that all that matters?"

"You know it's not."

They were both quiet as he walked her to the conference room, where Danai no doubt waited for updates. Charlotte looked up and down the hall before she pulled Eoghan down and kissed his cheek. "Thank you for showing up."

He stopped her. "I have a few days off. Can I take you somewhere?"

"Somewhere?"

"I know you haven't seen much of the country. I'd like to show you," he said.

"You asking me on a date, Eoghan?"

"Call it whatever you like."

She smiled. "Okay. That would be nice."

"Good."

"Good," she said, and just like that, she and Eoghan had agreed to go on their very first date.

◆ ◆ ◆

A few days later, Charlotte returned to the factory to personally pick up Eoghan's shoe. Shaun greeted her, and he was the last person she wanted to see. He might have apologized, but people like him didn't change overnight.

"Miss Bowman. Good to see you again," Shaun said.

Charlotte peered behind her to see if there was another Miss Bowman on the premises, because this was not the Shaun she'd had the displeasure of communicating with for the past two months. "Oh, you're talking to me."

He smiled. "Please come right this way."

Charlotte followed him, glaring at the back of the man's head like he might be a body snatcher.

Shaun led her to a couch just outside James's office. "Please have a seat. James is just finishing up a meeting. May I take your coat?"

"No, thank you."

"Would you like tea or coffee? Water?" he asked.

"Bottled water if you have it."

"Sparkling okay?"

"That would be nice. Thank you." Charlotte had to stifle her laughter several times because the difference between her previous visits to the manufacturing company and this one was night and day.

A few minutes later, she was in James's office with Eoghan's shoe nicely boxed front and center on his desk.

"Miss Bowman." James greeted her like a long-lost relative.

"Hello, James."

"I hope Shaun has been taking care of you."

"Yes, thank you." Charlotte kept her comments simple. She wasn't about to celebrate either man for doing their job.

"Here is O'Farrell's third-round boots. I hope everything is to your liking."

Charlotte evaluated the boots. "Looks good."

"I'm sure you'll communicate to Clive that we delivered the shoe and that all is well," James said.

Charlotte didn't answer. "Thank you again. I'll be in touch with any changes."

"You can count on me, Miss Bowman."

When Charlotte left the building, the birds were singing, and the new buds of the coming spring had started to form on the trees. With Eoghan's boots tucked under her arm, she could only think, *Today is a good day.*

Chapter 16

Charlotte and Ayanna walked arm in arm into the drawing room at Shelbourne Hotel for afternoon tea. The event was a year later than originally planned, but Charlotte couldn't have been happier to spend the day with her best friend finally doing something they'd had on their to-do list in Ireland.

"This is absolutely gorgeous," Charlotte said of the lord mayor's lounge.

"It really is beautiful," Ayanna said.

The regal, sparkling crystal chandeliers above glimmered as sunlight poured into the room. A large centerpiece of flowers, one she recognized as the bells of Ireland and another pink flower, burst with color against the cream and sage-green furniture in the lavishly decorated space. A musician played a black grand piano at the far corner, and Charlotte couldn't wait for one of the many bottles of chilling champagne on the left side of the room to be popped in celebration of herself and Ayanna.

Once they were seated at their white-clothed table with place settings for high tea, Charlotte filled Ayanna in on her work issues and what had happened at the factory.

"How gallant," Ayanna said of Eoghan and Clive as she bit into a small tomato-and-feta-cheese sandwich. Her low curls and golden-brown skin popped against her off-the-shoulder lush white sweater. "Girl, you better let this man advocate for you."

Charlotte rolled her eyes and gripped the white porcelain handle of the pink camellia teapot. "It wasn't that deep," she said and plucked a whiskey-smoked-salmon-on-Guinness-bread sandwich off the four-tier serving tray at the center of their table.

"It sounds like it was. I'm glad you got the project moving. I know it must have been excruciating to have those two show up."

"Girl, you know how proud I am." Charlotte smoothed her gold satin blouse with black drawn plum blossoms and placed her napkin on her lap. "Seam and Sole is my company. I have forged a reputation, and I thought that me showing up personally would help move things along. I wasn't expecting that my project would be stalled. I have a lot more work to do." Charlotte's ego had taken a hit. Her company was successful in its own right, and she had international traction. Apparently, not enough.

"They know now." Ayanna sipped her tea with her pinkie up.

"You're so silly," Charlotte chuckled.

"You were supported, and though I know it's hard for you to accept help, Eoghan showed up to make sure that you never experience being brushed off again."

Charlotte thought about that day. "You should have seen them when I came the next time for Eoghan's shoe. You would have thought that I was in that scene from *Pretty Woman* when she is in the shops and the salespeople are pandering to her every need. Or better yet, like I was the queen of Zamunda from *Coming to America*," she said. "I got *the* treatment."

Ayanna laughed. "As you should. They won't make that mistake again. That's millions of dollars in business, and from what Shane told me, they have been thinking of changing manufacturing companies. This did not help their cause to stay relevant."

"NMP." In the past, she used to feel guilty and then had been like, Why? "I'm not the one who fucked up, so it's not my problem."

"Agreed," Ayanna said. "So tell me, when did this thing happen with you and Eoghan?"

Charlotte nearly choked on her gingerbread scone. "I don't know what you mean, sis."

"Bullshit. I saw the way you two were sharing fuck-me eyes at the bar. And what about the hospital?" Ayanna asked. "And don't think for a second that I didn't know that you two hooked up in New York."

"You knew?" Charlotte gulped her words. "Did Shane tell you? Because Eoghan probably blabbed to him and Pippin. He already said he was no good with secrets."

"Chill out," Ayanna said. "I've known you most of my life. I picked up on that from the jump. At the award ceremony, you two were the weirdest. Why you decided not to tell me is another thing."

"I didn't want it to mean anything more than a hookup, so I treated it like he was just another hookup in the rotation," Charlotte said. "Are you mad at me?"

A waiter in a stiff white shirt and black pants arrived with a swaddled champagne bottle in his hand. "Champagne, madam?"

"Yes," both Ayanna and Charlotte said at the same time, then broke into giggles.

"May I get you anything else?" The waiter poured them each a glass.

"No, thank you," Ayanna said.

"I'll be back to check on you in a bit. Enjoy," he said.

Ayanna shook her head. "It's cool watching you get attached. It's cute."

"Stop." Charlotte blushed. "It's temporary."

"Is it?" Ayanna asked.

"Yaya, you know I don't do relationships like that. I'm too selfish for that."

"Hmm . . . if you say so," Ayanna teased.

"Are you going to slag me the whole day?" Charlotte asked.

"Look at you, using your Irish slang." Ayanna placed both hands over her heart like a proud mama.

"You are so annoying," Charlotte said, but she couldn't help giggling at her friend.

"Remember when you hounded me about Shane? Welcome to payback," Ayanna said.

"That's different. You two are so cute together, and he is pretty awesome, especially to you."

"He is. He's not perfect, neither am I, and I'm convinced no relationship is, but we make each other happy," Ayanna said. "We do have to make a decision on where we want to be. I'm open to being here, and he is open to being in the States. It depends on where he ultimately gets a coaching job. Right now, he's still helping out with the Rovers and trying to learn from coaches. Sometimes it's on contract; sometimes it's volunteer. I admire him for that."

"You guys are so adorable," Charlotte said. "You two are so in love."

"I know you're anti about relationships, but you might change your tune," Ayanna said. "You know, it's okay to want love in your life."

Charlotte sputtered tea, scoffed, and sucked her teeth. "Love?"

"You're doing a lot, right now," Ayanna laughed.

"Well . . ."

Ayanna mimicked her.

Charlotte might be annoyed by how clearly her friend saw her, but she wouldn't give up this time with Yaya for anything.

"I really miss this. I'm so happy we're here together," Charlotte said. "This place is so beautiful. I'm glad we still had this to experience."

"Is it weird knowing that I came here with Eoghan for dinner back before I dated Shane?" Ayanna asked.

Ayanna might be her best friend, but Charlotte couldn't deny the bit of jealousy that popped up. "I'm going to be honest. Yes. That man whore has literally been through you and Jada."

"Poor thing struck out in the end with both of us, not because he's not great, but I fell in love with Shane, and Jada's a twentysomething."

"How about we try to keep that from coming up," Charlotte suggested.

Ayanna pretended to lock her mouth shut.

"If you stay, we can do a lot more things like this together. A few more trips and I'll be here more consistently."

"I see what you're trying to do," Charlotte said.

"It's true, though. It will be like a new adventure for us." Ayanna clapped her hands together. "How about you come by this weekend, and we can chill at the house, popcorn and a movie, or go shopping on Grafton Street, or take a long walk through Saint Stephen's Green and feed the birds on the pond?" she asked. "We can even go get twisted at the Guinness Storehouse or at Temple Bar."

"I can't this weekend," Charlotte said. "Eoghan is taking me to see the sights."

"Oh, really?" Ayanna asked, intrigued.

"Don't lose your head," Charlotte suggested, but she couldn't stop the heat from rouging her cheeks.

"Okay." Ayanna locked her lips again but danced in her seat.

"What am I going to do with you?" Charlotte shook her head and let her friend indulge in thoughts of a future that Charlotte herself was unsure about.

Chapter 17

On the ride to the north of Ireland, Charlotte couldn't believe the beauty that surrounded her. Ayanna had told her how beautiful and green Ireland was, especially the northern coast, but seeing the rich color and promise of spring pushing its way through the snow-covered lands in person was so picture perfect that Charlotte just stared out the window at the never-ending landscape.

"There is so much open land," she said to Eoghan. As they drove, they munched on blueberry muffins she'd made and coffee she'd picked up for them at the bar. "All the images I've seen online and in movies truly don't compare." She snuggled into the leather in the warm passenger seat. That Eoghan was driving was a surprise, given the fact that she'd always seen him taken around by Garrett.

"Do you always have a driver?" she asked.

"Not at all, but sometimes it makes sense, and sometimes I'm just lazy. I thought that it would be nice if it was just the two of us."

So he was doing something that he didn't normally do. Their trip took on another level of intimacy, and though part of her prepped for the freak-out, the other part of her surprisingly was okay with it and not ready to jump out of the car and roll to a stop.

"Where are we headed?" she asked.

"I'm taking you up to County Monaghan. I know you haven't been much out of Dublin, so I thought this would be a nice excursion for you," he said.

"Excursion, huh?"

"Yes. It's important for you to get out in the fine, fresh Ireland air to really understand our country," Eoghan said in his best and heaviest accent.

"What are we going to do there? Are we taking a tour? Are we stopping for lunch, because you know I have a stomach? Are we going hiking? I don't know County Monaghan. I didn't add it to my research when Yaya and I were going to take our trip together. What other towns are close?" She rolled out back-to-back questions.

"Wow. You're like a kid in the back seat, whining about the destination when we've only just left the car park. We'll be there soon."

The radio played low in the background, and the sound of the road whirring in the cabin from the wheels became steady white noise.

"I didn't see your father at the Rovers game the other day. I know he is pretty involved. He okay?" Charlotte asked.

Eoghan gripped the steering wheel a little tighter, then relaxed. "No, he wasn't there. It was a good thing. He and my ma were visiting family in Scotland."

"Seems like you two are close."

"Not as close as we could be. I'd say he's more involved. Too involved sometimes," Eoghan admitted.

"I understand." She stared out at the farm and the bales of hay that stretched to building height.

"I need to be more . . ." He stalled. "Assertive with him, but he's had this role in my life for so long that it's hard to break the tie."

Charlotte silently agreed but still asked, "What role is that?"

"Running my career like his own. He is a bit presumptuous in all my affairs," Eoghan said.

"I have no advice for you. Family is tough. I don't have the same issues with my family. I wish my mom took more advantage of her skills and knowledge. She's so smart."

"What does she do?"

"She's an art dealer. Used to be. She gets paid sometimes just to give her opinion on a piece. She could be so successful, but instead she chooses to be a homemaker and support my father's career. She might be doing more now, but I don't know."

"Is that why you became a business owner? To take more advantage of your skills?"

"I guess. I just don't want to leave anything on the table. The worst thing in life is regret."

"I can think of some worse things," Eoghan teased.

"Oh, shush." She smiled.

The radio station playing in the background had changed as they'd gotten farther from Dublin, and Eoghan turned off the static-laden folk tunes that played. She kind of liked it but would much rather focus on Eoghan and their pretty drive.

"Have you dated diversely before?" he asked, interrupting her thoughts.

She stared at him for several seconds. "Where did that question come from?"

"I dunno. It popped into my head. Do you mind me asking?"

"No. It was just surprising. Yes, I have dated diversely, but I haven't been serious with someone for ages," she admitted. "Dating a Black woman is different than dating other women, even for Black men."

"How d'you know? Have you dated other women?" he asked, a devilish smile on his face. "I mean, I wouldn't care if you did."

She swatted his shoulder. "Smart-ass."

"Oi, I'm driving." He laughed. "I need a delicate touch."

"I'm being serious," she said. "I see couples all the time, and I want to know how they do it. Our experiences are so different."

"Not all experiences. We share many," Eoghan said. "Ayanna and Shane did it. Are doing it. I admit it's not as common here as it is in America, but it happens often," he said. "I date different women."

"We already know that you date the spectrum. Yaya. Jada." She rubbed her face with both hands. "I've never been anyone's thirsty thirds."

"It was all light," he said and briefly looked at her. "I promise you that. So don't go losing your curls over it."

"I'm not," she said.

"You know, Charlotte, there are some things about your experiences as a Black woman that I'll never fully understand, no matter how hard I try, but I'll always listen. I'd hope whoever I'm with would extend me the same courtesy. If you're willing to learn and be open to really listening to your partner's experiences and opinions, that can only make a relationship better. Any relationship."

Eoghan continued to surprise her. He put his money where his mouth was when it came to being part of the solution. When she'd learned about his campaign to help women in business and diversity, she'd been floored at his stance, especially since he was so famous. His opinions couldn't be popular with everyone, yet he was still extremely popular and, dare she say, the golden boy for both teams he played on.

They drove in silence for a little bit before he started to point out the different highlights for her.

Eoghan took an exit. "This is the town of Dundalk," he said. "Big horse town."

Charlotte said, "There's the Jockeys Bar. It's the oldest bar in Dundalk. 1790s, I believe."

Eoghan jerked the car a bit. "You know your Irish landmarks."

"Well, I was the one who researched places to go for me and Ayanna for our trip here. It's on the list."

"Did you know that Beethoven wrote his Fifth Symphony about ten years later?" he asked.

"I did not know that, Mr. O'Farrell. Only that it was written in Vienna." Charlotte looked at the corner bar and restaurant that took up the entire block. "It's old-world charming."

"Yep. There's a bit of trivia for you. It's a landmark. Want to stop? We can have a drink." He took a long glance at the car clock, and she didn't want to ruin whatever he had planned for her with the detour, plus there was another reason she didn't want to stop.

"No, I'd much rather see the places you want to show me. Maybe if we have time, we can stop on our way back down?"

"Sound."

He pointed out the horse stadium and Saint Brigid's Shrine and Well. The sun beamed brightly and shone down on Castle Roche. Even in the winter, the remnants of the old castle's presence and history towered over the land.

"It's magnificent. Isn't it impressive how these structures are still standing?" she asked him rhetorically. "It's massive. I can imagine the war that destroyed it. That's morbid, right?"

"Sort of." He laughed. "The leaves are starting to show off now," he said. "A few more weeks, and there will be so much green it'll turn your eyes the shade."

She enjoyed his humor.

"You look nice, by the way," he said, "for an American."

She deadpanned to him. "What the hell is that supposed to mean?" She looked down at her blue skinny jeans, calf-high boots, and tweed jacket with purple and green accents. "I look cute."

"It just means that you're dressed appropriately for what I have in store for ya," he said.

"Thanks?"

He smiled. "We'll be arriving shortly."

"Arriving where?" She clapped her hands together for each syllable. Her antics only made him laugh more.

"Calm yourself. We're here."

They arrived in County Monaghan, and after Eoghan turned left, right, and around the bend, they ended up in Clones, which for Charlotte felt like they'd landed in the middle of the country, surrounded by plotted fields separated by trees and shrubs, some evergreen while others were still bare from the change of season. She didn't know what Eoghan had in mind, but he was up to something.

"We're taking a bike ride," he said. "We're taking the Kingfisher Trail."

"I can't remember the last time I've been on a bike that wasn't stationary and in the gym," she said. She looked at the trail. "Wait, is that our path?" She pointed at a narrow trail along the cliff edge.

"You're not scared, are ya?"

"Look here." She called him closer with her index finger. "Between me and Yaya, I'm the more adventurous one, but I also don't want to die." She pointed at some of the narrow trails high up on some of those hills she'd admired so much on their drive. "Do you see how close that is to the edge? Not to mention there are no guardrails. Now, seeing as I haven't been on a bike in a minute, you really think that me riding on some of these narrow-ass parts of this trail, where the bike could easily swerve off, is a good idea?"

"Course it is. See that rainbow there?" he asked, pointing to a rainbow that, in her current conundrum, she'd completely missed.

"Yeah," she said.

"There's gold at the end of it," he teased.

"You're bugging," she said.

"It's not that bad. That part is not very long. I'll be right there. If you start heading off the path, I'll go after ya."

"Comforting." She smirked. Not to be bested by her fear, she made her way over to the bikes. "Okay."

As they rode, Charlotte's heartbeat throbbed in her chest both from the danger to her right with cliffs and crashing waves and also from the absolutely stunning view from this height of the cliffs.

She wasn't as close to the edge as she'd originally thought, and there were other cyclists in the distance. They biked by lakes and through gnarly trees for about forty minutes, taking breaks to stroll through the towns. Even as far north as they were, Eoghan was recognized and stopped for photos or to sign autographs, while she took in the view. From the short houses made of stone to the churches with steeples reaching skyward, Charlotte found herself surrounded by the same comforting old-world charm she'd experienced in Dublin and in Dundalk.

Her legs throbbed from fatigue, and they stopped at a spot where they had a view of a castle covered in ivy. Leafless trees sprinkled the property, and Charlotte could only imagine how spectacular the fall leaves must be from her and Eoghan's current vantage point. Castles were always impressive and a throwback to a time of ladies and lace, carriages, gowns, and balls. However, the majesty of this tucked-away castle stood in superb shape compared to Castle Roche, which had been destroyed. The memory on her phone had to be near capacity with all the photos she'd snapped so far.

"What is that?" she asked.

"Ah, Castle Leslie," he answered. "It's on about a thousand acres. Built in the 1600s, I believe."

"It makes such a pretty picture from here. Like, better than any postcard. Do you see how many photos I've taken?"

He laughed with her. "Glad you like it, because that's where we'll be staying."

"Shut up." She gripped his arm. "No! Are you serious?"

"Yes." He was smirking with pride at pulling off the surprise. "Want to go take a look?"

"Eoghan? Of course I want to go take a look." She jumped back onto her bike. "Wait, how do we get out of here?"

His continued laughter spun around her like a gentle breeze. "Follow me before you lose yourself in the forest." She rode her bike, shaking with excitement as much as the bumps on the trail.

By the time they got to Castle Leslie, they'd started to lose the daylight, but the lighting indoors and out allowed her to take in the remarkable place. Charlotte had seen many of the castles of Northern Ireland on her computer during the time that she and Ayanna had been planning their trip to Ireland. However, when the car pulled up to Leslie, she immediately fell in love with the place.

"Wow," Charlotte said. "It's so well restored."

"The family has invested in restoration for over twenty years. It's a true gem," he said.

Charlotte liked nice things, but the luxury of the estate as soon as they entered to check in was beyond anything she could imagine. Large sculptured fireplaces, antique wood, and a library and adjoining rooms, all with historic stories, offered a glimpse into the past in a modern era.

"There will be lots to see in the morning, but let's settle in. I'm sure you'll want a wee something to eat," he said.

"Yes," she said, perusing a brochure of the estate.

"It's a pleasure to have you here, Mr. O'Farrell. We hope you enjoy your first stay here with us," one of the staff members said. "The West Wing is right this way."

Charlotte's eyes bulged out of her head. The West Wing was a two-story suite and the most extravagant part of the house, and Eoghan must have spared no expense in securing it for them.

She steadied her breathing and followed the blonde woman in a white shirt and black pants through to their location.

"Here you are," she said. "Let us know if you're in need of anything. You can take your supper here or in the dining room, if you like, but

I'll remind you that your massage in the Victorian Treatment Rooms is scheduled at half seven."

"Cheers," Eoghan said. "We'll decide and let you know."

The woman smiled at Charlotte. "Enjoy your stay, madam."

"I will. Thank you." Charlotte ran through the West Wing like she'd just closed on a house. In the living room, champagne chilled in a glass bucket filled with ice and two glasses sat on their own perch. This place was hers, at least for tonight. She traipsed through all the rooms until she found the master bedroom and collapsed back on the silky green embroidered comforter. The mattress formed to her even through the levels of bedding. A fire burned in the fireplace, and the wood crackled like it would in a snowed-in cabin. She looked up at the door leading outside.

"Eoghan, this suite has a balcony and a terrace," she called. She sat up on the bed and looked at him watching her shenanigans as he leaned against the doorframe. The fading light glowing on him made him even more handsome.

"You like it, then?" he asked.

She jumped out of the decadent bed and skipped over to him. She hugged him around his middle. "Like it? What the fuck, Eoghan? There aren't words to express how nice this is."

"I said I'd show you Ireland. This place is special." He wrapped his arms around her, and he didn't have to say anything else. He'd done this for her, and that, too, was special.

"Thank you," she said into his chest.

"I scheduled a massage for you. I thought you might like one after the bike ride, but it's up to you whether you want to or not."

"Can we eat first? I'm sure you're hungry too," she said.

He patted his stomach. "I'm always hungry. If you don't mind, it might be best for us to take supper here. It's more private," he said. "Also, I hear the dining rooms in these places are better seen in natural light. We'll have a better view of it at breakfast."

"Sounds good to me."

A night in a castle with Eoghan? What the hell kind of fairy tale had she walked into?

◆ ◆ ◆

Eoghan sat outside on the Juliet balcony while Charlotte had her massage in their private treatment room. He'd wanted to do this for her, impress her and make her feel special, but now as he waited for her, he second-guessed himself. Maybe this was too much, and he'd overwhelmed her. This was more than dinner at the Shelbourne—hell, it was more than a stay at the Shelbourne. She trusted him enough to come with him almost two hours away from Dublin and to stay the weekend with him here.

He'd made it no secret that he wanted her. When she'd gotten hurt that night at her apartment when they'd given in to their desires, it had made him more aware than ever that while he'd been focused on his boots to play, Charlotte had stolen his heart. The question was, Would she ever trust him with hers?

Charlotte came out onto the balcony, wrapped in a thick white robe and her tan suede Ugg boots. She carried two cups of tea and somehow maneuvered the door to bring them out with her. She handed one to him.

"I thought you might like this. Spring is coming, but there is still snow out there," she said.

"It's heated a bit."

"I can feel it. It's nice," she said, sounding like she had a natural high.

"How was your massage?" he asked, though judging by her soft face and drowsy eyes, it'd had the desired effect.

"Divine." She smiled and sipped her tea. "I booked one for both of us for tomorrow."

"Thought you'd enjoy that," he said. "And thank you for booking the massage. I could use one."

"There is nothing out there. It's freaky, right? I'm from the city, so though we love our nature trips, the nothingness always feels a bit like the beginnings of a horror flick." She yawned, and he knew she was tired from the day's activities.

"You should head to bed."

"I'm not tired. I'm relaxed. That bitch squeezed all the tension out of me. I want to pack her ass into my overnight bag and take her back to Dublin with us," Charlotte said, and he howled. She made him laugh so easily.

"Shhh," she said, chuckling. "You're echoing. There are other guests here."

"You're a laugh, Charlotte." He reached for her hand, and when she didn't pull away, he intertwined his fingers with hers. He stroked her hand with his thumb and enjoyed these minutes of just being close to her.

"I don't expect anything while we're staying here, Charlotte. I didn't invite you here for some kind of upscale booty call. I really just want you to enjoy yourself."

He meant every word. His dick might ache for her, but the last thing he'd ever want was for her to feel obliged to be with him.

"That's a shame, Eoghan." She tsked. "Because I'm ready to take this craic up to ninety."

His chest rumbled with laughter. "Up to ninety, eh?"

She stood up, maintaining their hand connection, and tugged on him to follow her inside. "All the way up."

Inside she leaned against the master bed and undid her robe, showing her naked body to him. She flopped out of her boots and scooted up onto the mattress. The view of every inch of her, from her big hair down to her neckline to the curve of her back to the crack of her arse as she crawled to the black headboard, nestling herself into the pillows.

He shed his clothes quickly, eager to touch and taste her. Once free of his garments, he reached for her, flipping her onto her back. He dived in between her thighs to deliver the ultimate kiss.

"Eoghy," she gasped, and her hands went to his head, where she wildly raked her fingers through his hair. He loved it when she called him that. Her unabashed, unfiltered, and absolutely ridiculous nickname for him. He caressed her thighs as she crossed her ankles to lock him to her. He gripped her hips with one hand while sliding his fingers inside, all the while torturing her clit with a suck here and a lick there. Each one designed to evoke a response.

She tore away from him, her body alive and frantic. He moved toward her, and she pressed him back against the pillows. Shaking with desire, she climbed over him and slid onto his throbbing dick. Up and down she went, fucking him like a punishment. Making him remember why she was in bed with him, why he couldn't resist her in New York or now when she'd come to Ireland. Her tits bounced as she rode him, and her hips swirled like his Ma's stand mixer. And when she reversed her movements, he thought he'd literally died and asked himself if there was a better place than heaven.

"You like how I fuck that dick?" she asked, her hot mouth hovering over his.

"Char, yes," he hissed. "Fuck yes."

"Who else can fuck you like this, Eoghan?" she taunted.

He shook his head, wild with lust. "Only you, love."

Her lips touched his, but when he went to solidify the kiss, she pulled away, but not before wetting her lips with her teasing tongue.

"Let me kiss you, Char."

"That's not what I want."

"Anything you want, I'd give to you."

She held the weight of one breast in her hand and offered him her nipple. She didn't need to instruct him further, and he sucked on her. He took her as deep into his mouth as would fit, his tongue circling her dark areola and taut nipple. Her whole body shuddered, and he could even feel as her insides clenched around his cock. She moaned, and her hands glided through his hair before gripping a handful and pulling him to her. He delivered pleasurable punishment of his own by sucking her hard only to then pinch her sensitive bud with his teeth.

"Yes, Eoghan. Just like that," she huffed and licked her lip. "Mmm-hmm. Like that."

He continued to alternate, taking her higher. Her hips chased toward the prize as much as his did. Gripping her hips, he tried to slow her down because he never wanted this moment between them to end. Charlotte had other plans. She pressed him firmly against the mattress, her hands pinning his arms. Her body rolled and undulated as she took him in as deep as he'd go in this position, claiming him all for herself. Her mouth covered his, wet and wanton. Her tongue mimicked her hips. He drank her in and then wrestled his hands out of her grip. His hands glided over the sides of her torso. Sweat covered them both, and the sheets under him were drenched from exercise.

"I'm going to come, Char," he mumbled. He didn't know who was panting more, him or her. What he did know was that if Charlotte had any doubt about who he wanted, surely he'd put any of her concerns to rest.

Charlotte let go first, and to watch her release the tension and shout in ecstasy was something he'd pay millions for. She was beyond beautiful, beyond free. She was fearless.

"Eoghy," she cried for him, then pulled his arms around her middle.

"Yes, baby," he said, squeezing her tight to him. He held her face and claimed her mouth with a long, hard, and deep kiss as she shivered and shook through her orgasm.

The pleasure of her arrival only intensified his, as he quickly came afterward, shouting into her mouth. Emotion washed over him. *Bollocks if I shed a tear 'cause of a ride.* Their kisses turned more tender than he'd ever experienced, and in an instant he vowed to do anything for Charlotte Bowman. He'd been hers long before today.

Chapter 18

The next morning Charlotte woke up wrapped in the warm cove of Eoghan's arms. Their cuddles and snuggles quickly turned into a heated session of lovemaking, and she loved every minute of it. They'd never spent a night together, and having him in bed with her startled her a bit. That angelic face, that strong body, and his manly scent lured her to him and evoked feelings that she'd never felt before. It scared her, but when he gave her that crooked morning smile, she melted into his arms like butter.

"Sleep well?" He yawned and hugged her tighter.

"Mmm. Best sleep I've had in a long time," she said. "I thought your snoring would keep me up, but it actually helps me sleep. Weird."

He hummed and rubbed his eyes. "Same with yours."

She scoffed and stuttered.

"What? You didn't know you snored?" he asked.

"Uh . . . I know I snore, but you didn't have to say it." She laughed.

"You're the only one who can comment on snoring, now?"

"No . . . but—"

He nuzzled her neck, and the sensation cut off any further protest. "I love your snoring. It's like a chain saw."

"Eoghan," she giggled.

"Okay, an idle chain saw."

"You're terrible." She caressed his face. "We should get up and see some stuff, no?"

"Stay awhile longer. The day isn't going anywhere. Let me enjoy you while I have you," he said, and his lips touched hers, and she returned his kiss.

"Okay, five more minutes," she said and rested her head against his.

"Not if I do things right," he said, and his hands stroked her sides and down to her butt, where he caressed and pulled her forward so their naked bodies touched in the most intimate of places.

"Let's see," she said, moving against him. "It feels pretty right already."

Soon they were enthralled in the insatiable fever again, and she seriously considered if she'd ever get enough of him.

Charlotte showered in the luxury of the black tile shower. As she bathed with the moisturizing handmade soap, the scents of lavender and French vanilla perfumed the steam and her skin. She peered out into the bathroom area next to the soaking tub, where Eoghan slipped into a pair of black boxer briefs. She vowed to get him in that tub for a bath later.

He knocked on the glass, and she cracked it open and scanned his chiseled body, which was like a sculpture at the Epic Museum.

"I need to work out," he announced, jumping into a pair of jogging pants.

"I wasn't enough?" she asked, wiping water from her eyes.

"Charlotte . . ." He smiled.

"Can I come? You can do your push-ups on top of me," she said, highlighting the benefits.

Eoghan looked like he was actually considering her proposal.

"Kidding," she said.

He stretched into a T-shirt. "I'll keep that one in my back pocket, eh?"

"No complaints here. I'm going to tour the castle."

"They're pretty booked up, so don't be too disappointed if you're unable to see some of the rooms."

Charlotte took that into consideration.

"You'll be all right, then?"

She concluded that he was much more adorable when he showed concern for her.

"Yeah. I'll meet up with you in a bit," she said and gave him a wet, long, and thorough kiss. "Miss me," she mumbled against his lips.

Fortunately, Charlotte had had the sense to toss a bag with a change of clothes into the car yesterday, and Eoghan had paid a man from the bike rental stand to drive it to the castle early this morning. Now she dressed in dark-blue jeans and a cream-colored cowl-neck sweater. She took a tour of the castle, enjoying the antiques, paintings, and heirlooms that decorated the corridors. The twenty-one rooms were all decorated differently, and though she wasn't able to go inside several of them, she was able to read about them. She particularly loved the copper bathtub in Papa Jack's Room and the stories about the Leslie family. Her favorite room was the Chinese Master Room, highlighted with calming kha-ki-print wallpaper and bright-red drapes and pillows. Bonus, it also had a copper soaking tub and a riveting view of the grounds.

"Who needs TV when you have these views."

"It is lovely, isn't it," a woman also touring the castle said to her.

"Each room is dramatically different from the others, and I want to stay and enjoy each one," Charlotte said.

"Next time I come, I'll make sure that it's during a time when I can see all the rooms," the woman said as they walked, taking in the warmth from the fire in the main hall.

"Yeah, that's a bummer, right? I'm glad they were able to keep them so well over the years so we can enjoy it."

Charlotte found out the woman, Catriona, a middle-aged woman with back-length curls and green eyes, was from Dingle and was taking time off with her family. Charlotte shared where she was from and that she owned her own company.

"We met a professional footballer here. He was very kind. I'm sure he wants his privacy, so we said hello, then let him be."

Charlotte was at a crossroads. Was she going to claim him or deny him? "You must mean Eoghan."

"That's the fellow," Catriona said.

"Yes, he's very kind, but he's trying to get away from work and relax like us all."

Charlotte watched the understanding spread across Catriona's face. "Brilliant."

What Charlotte loved was that as they continued the tour, Catriona didn't treat her any different than before she'd realized Charlotte was there with Eoghan.

Once the tour was over, Charlotte and Eoghan reconnected for brunch.

"How was the workout?"

"Good, but I'm starving, and I don't know which I need more: you or food," he said, and she blushed at his seriousness and intensity.

"Let's eat," she suggested, though she also suddenly felt torn between the options.

They decided to have brunch at Snaffles Restaurant. Charlotte, normally underwhelmed by award-winning restaurants, enjoyed the delicious spread of fresh fruit, yogurt parfaits, cereals, eggs, sliced meat, and various types of bread. She filled her plate with it all. Both she and Eoghan had been going at it pretty hard since last night, and with his workout and her tour, they were nearing hangry.

"Mmm," Eoghan said as he tore into blood sausage.

Charlotte had made herself a breakfast sandwich, and between the two of them, there was a lot more chewing than talking.

Once her blood sugar normalized, she finally asked, "Feeling better?"

"Yes. I'm ready to enjoy the day with you. Thank you for suggesting food. It wouldn't have been my choice, but it was the right one." He smiled.

Charlotte took note of the eyes on them, but it was too late. She'd claimed Eoghan and took the looks in stride, especially since he was the star player, and she was sure she'd barely be noticed.

They finished breakfast and headed outside to check out the activities.

"I still can't get over this place. Something about it has made it my favorite place overnight," she said, walking arm in arm with Eoghan through the manicured gardens, past the light-green metal benches along Glaslough Lake. When someone stopped him to say hello or wanted a picture, Charlotte obliged or stepped aside. This only touched the surface of Eoghan's celebrity. Over the past month, she'd seen women lose their shit when they saw him and the press bombard him with questions and snap photographs. So far, she'd been spared being swirled into the mix, but she knew that if she continued to hang out with Eoghan, it was only a matter of time before she showed up in the rags.

"Are you okay with the attention? It can be a bit much sometimes."

"I'm cool. I know who you are, boo."

He pulled her closer again. "Good."

"Look at that." She pointed to the lake, where there were a few people fishing. "I don't know why, but I like that you can go fishing at this castle."

"You haven't seen anything yet," Eoghan said. "Wait till we round the back side."

They rounded the bend, and a string of horses charged over the green pasture, which resembled the pitch that Eoghan played on.

"The equestrian curriculum here is outstanding," he said.

Charlotte loved horses and immediately led Eoghan to the stables, knowing that whatever time they spent here would be on the back of a horse. She skipped over to the horses and started baby talking. "Hi. Aren't you a pretty girl?" She reached to pet the pecan-colored horse with a patch in the middle of her large head, deep-brown eyes, and lashes for miles. She ran her hand over her head and over her soft nose. "Oh my goodness. Isn't she gorgeous, Eoghan?" She turned, expecting Eoghan to be right behind her, but he was a few feet away.

He didn't look as excited as she was at all. In fact, he wore the same face she'd seen when he ran out onto the pitch for practice or to play or when he'd first worn her cleats. Just beyond the stoic veil were hints of raw emotion. Fear.

"Come and pet her." She tested her theory.

"Pass."

"Have you never seen a horse up close before?"

"I have."

"She's so sweet, Eoghan. Come here," she encouraged. "You'd be amazed how soft and gentle she is." Charlotte left out the part about them sensing human fear and possibly freaking out, but she wanted him to push past his fear. "She's penned up, so she is not getting out, and they wouldn't have her out here to pet if they thought she'd bite."

"You're having a gas."

"It's okay to be scared," she said, and she meant it. The epiphany hit her like a sack of bricks falling off NYC scaffolding. Deadly hard.

"I'm not scared," he grumbled.

"I won't let anything happen to you. I'm good with horses," she said. "When I was younger, we took lessons in the Bronx. They had an equestrian program there. My mom took me, Yaya, and Jada, and we had a lot of fun. I don't know—I really connected with horses. So when I see them, they make me feel good."

"I've never ridden a horse." Eoghan's voice, now inches away, startled her, and her heart raced. Wembley, whose name was on the outside of the pen, nodded, and Eoghan stilled.

"It's okay, girl. The big Irishman snuck up on me," she said. Once everyone calmed down, she stroked the horse again. "Want to give it a try?" she asked Eoghan and offered her hand.

With trepidation, he took it. His hand was colder than normal, and she warmed it in hers for a few seconds. Together they stroked Wembley. Eoghan connected their bodies, and as they petted the horse, she leaned into his warm body. "See? This is not so bad." Her racing heart made her sound as if she'd just jogged around the stables.

"No." His heartbeat was against her back, making her aware that she wasn't the only one affected.

"She's lovely, isn't she?" someone said, interrupting her and Eoghan's moment with Wembley. Charlotte turned into Eoghan and around to see who was speaking. She found an athletic man dressed in khaki with black riding boots and a black velvet riding helmet. He made his way toward them. "Yer wantin' to take her out for a ride?"

"Yes," Charlotte said.

"Will I, yeah?" Eoghan said simultaneously. Translation? He definitely would not.

She smothered her face like the emoji.

The man's eyes widened on Eoghan. Naturally, as a member of the Irish national team, Eoghan would be continuously recognized. Luckily, this man kept it together. His eyes went back and forth between them. "I and another rider can take you both out. It's a novice trail with the opportunity for advanced riders to have a bit of fun."

She turned to Eoghan. "Can we? I really want us to go together, but if you don't want to, it's okay."

A heavy, loud sigh left Eoghan's chest, and she knew she was pushing him beyond his boundaries. If it were her first time riding a horse, she'd be shitting herself too.

"I'll go," was all he said.

"Let me know when you're ready. I'm Gael, by the way."

"Thank you, Gael," she said.

The horseman left to tend to a horse several stalls from Wembley's. Charlotte turned to Eoghan. "You're sure about this?"

"No," he said, "but sure I'll give it a lash for ya."

Charlotte beamed up at him.

"Don't look at me like I'm yer hero. If I fall and break my neck, you'll have to explain to Gaff," he said.

She scoffed. "You'll be fine. Do you think these people want that kind of publicity? We'll all make sure the only injury you suffer is a sore ass."

He moved in quick and close. "You kiss yer ma with that mouth?" She felt his breath on her lips.

She couldn't even speak, so she pecked his lips defiantly. At least that was the original plan, but she should have known better, as his soft mouth pressed against hers and opened. The aphrodisiac from the transfer of heat between them ignited what felt like an insatiable desire for him to taste her, touch her, and do all sorts of things to her skin and body.

"I'm going to take you on this bed of hay if you're not careful," he mumbled against her lips.

She bit his lower lip, pulling slightly and giving a hearty suck before letting it go. "I dare you." She really wanted him to.

He pulled back and evaluated her seriousness. "Okay." He lifted her up and headed toward one of the empty stalls.

"Eoghan! No!" She gripped his shoulders so as not to fall flat on her ass. "I was joking."

"No, you weren't."

"Okay, okay. I wasn't, but I . . . we can't," she said. "You have to put me down."

He finally put her down. "Next time you dare me, be better prepared."

Holding her tongue hurt, and she was heated, not only from the exhilaration of him following through but because she'd had to back down, and she never backed down. She was wet, her heart wouldn't settle, and she was breathless and weak from adrenaline.

"This is Greta. She'll be helping us out today," Gael said when he returned with the other rider. "Ready to get going?"

"Yes," both she and Eoghan said in sync.

"Great. Let's get you ready. Don't worry, Mr. O'Farrell, we'll take good care of you," the female rider said, her cheeks red with fandom.

After she and Eoghan donned their gear and explained their individual levels of expertise, Gael chose Wembley, an Arabian horse, for Charlotte and a Percheron horse for Eoghan.

"His name's Beast," Greta said, walking Eoghan's horse toward them.

Charlotte died inside with laughter. The name suited the intimidatingly large charcoal-colored animal.

"I'm not getting on that." Eoghan's stance was as firm as his words.

"And for you, Charlotte, we have Wembley. She's lovely," Gael said.

"She's beautiful." Charlotte easily climbed onto her horse and patted the horse's neck to connect with her animal.

Eoghan still hesitated in getting on his horse.

"Hey," Charlotte called to him. "I know he looks big, but you're getting him because draft horses are gentle giants. They have a great disposition," she said from her perch on the gorgeous animal.

"Your girlfriend is right. They are perfect for first timers," Gael said as he secured the saddle and adjusted the stirrups. "He'll take care of you."

Girlfriend? Charlotte side-eyed Eoghan, and when he didn't correct the rider, she didn't either. *What just happened?*

"Great," Eoghan said, scratching his chin.

"We are here with you every step of the way," Gael said supportively.

One thing Eoghan was good at was following directions, and despite his fear, his athletic body climbed onto Beast with fair ease. Atop the animal, however, Eoghan was as stiff as a board, but he still looked good.

Beast jolted forward, and Eoghan's upper half swung back. The fear on his face was palpable, and she could've sworn that he was about to jump off the horse and say, *Forget this,* but he didn't. He held the reins so tight his knuckles whitened as he continued moseying with the horse.

"Relax your hips," Greta said to him.

Charlotte knew firsthand his experience with moving those hips. He had fucked her senseless several times with his hip motion, one of the highlights of each session, but as he straddled Beast, he seemed to not know how to do it anymore.

He looked board stiff and unbalanced, and if he continued like this, he'd have more than sore legs and bottom. He'd need a full-body soak just to relieve the stress in his body.

Charlotte steered Wembley close to Beast and rode side by side. "Eoghan?"

He quickly looked at her and back ahead as if Beast would go rogue if he didn't keep his eyes forward.

"You have to move your hips, or you'll hurt yourself," she urged.

"I am moving my hips," he said between his teeth.

"It doesn't really look that way."

"Whatcha want me to do about it?"

"I want you to move your hips like you're fucking me." She stated the last part in a hushed whisper.

"You're taking the piss." He turned scarlet red and looked to the two riders, who, judging by their varying shades of red, had figured out what she'd tried to communicate to him.

"I'm serious." She laughed. "Relax and do it to the rhythm of the horse. Nice and easy." She demonstrated, not that she hadn't been doing it the whole time, but with his attention on his own horse situation, he definitely hadn't been watching her. "It's okay to look at me, Chief. Beast is a pro. He's not going anywhere without us."

Eoghan locked on her hips and within seconds mimicked her. She didn't mean to get aroused, but watching him move on such a grand horse turned her on.

"Good," came her hoarse reply as their hips moved in and out of sync depending on their individual horses.

"Well done, Mr. O'Farrell," Gael said, then began to sing a song she'd heard at the stadium. "We have O'Farrell . . . I'm a Northern Ireland fan myself, but it seems fitting for your success on oul Beast."

Charlotte shook herself out of her trance from Eoghan's hips and sang with Gael.

"Let's take it up to a trot," Greta said. They started a trot, and without prompting, Beast trotted, and Eoghan looked like a rag doll flailing his arms and reins on top of strong, big, and graceful Beast. They were two of a kind, with the exception of the graceful part—for Eoghan on a horse, anyway.

She laughed. "You got it," she yelled.

"Shut yer bake," he yelled back.

After a few tries, Eoghan mastered the trot.

Gael rode over to Charlotte. "Yer game to take it up a bit? A gallop over that ridge there and through the water."

"Oh yeah," Charlotte said.

Eoghan felt like a fool as he watched Charlotte ride off with Gael while he moseyed with Beast. Charlotte and the horseman rode fast up a hill and down until they hit the water, where they slowed. Greta gave him the play-by-play.

"The horses canter in the water. Gael and Charlotte have to be aware of their stirrups because they will float backward from the drag of the water where it's deepest," she said. "No need to worry. Charlotte looks like a very good rider."

Charlotte had surprised him again. This excursion had been to impress her. Little had he known, as he'd tracked her riding Wembley with expertise, that she would be the one impressing him. Again. He wanted to follow and ride with her, but even he had to surrender to his limits on occasion. He'd just come back from a leg injury. The last thing he needed to do was hurt himself.

"Can we try to go a little faster?" he asked Greta.

"I don't know if that's a good idea. Cantering on a horse is pretty impactful. The horse's gait is like a carousel, up and down, but faster and harder. A gallop is easier because it's more even, but you're not quite ready for either."

"Let's try it." He had to be an idiot, but the last image he wanted Charlotte to have of him was this baby, walking on horseback instead of riding.

"You're sure? I don't want—"

"I'm sure." He didn't want to hear the rest of it.

Greta gave him a few instructions. "You'll feel the horse change his speed: he'll hit the ground slower but harder. Try your best to move with the horse. Keep the reins fairly loose so he knows he can go. It'll be tense going in the beginning, but you'll get used to it."

What the fuck am I doing? He'd never been on a horse before, and now he was about to canter?

"Here we go," Greta said, and off they went. He had the trot down pat, but then it felt like Beast tripped, and then came the change. When the animal's hooves hit the ground, it was harder than Greta had promised, and though they were moving fast, the hooves hit the ground slower than at a trot, and he could have sworn that there were moments when Beast was actually flying.

Immediately he knew that this had been a bad idea. Each time the animal cantered, he thought he was going to bounce right out of the saddle. The ground was a blur, and as they went up the hill, he heard Greta yell, "Lean forward slightly and hold on!"

"Whoa! Whoa!" he said to Beast and pulled on the reins, but the horse was stronger than he was and pressed on. Greta hadn't been kidding when she'd told him to hold on. He held on for dear life. "Fuck!"

His first time riding had quickly gone from not so bad to minus craic. Just when he was sure he'd be thrown off the horse, he pulled the reins back, and Beast responded.

Charlotte galloped toward him. "Hey, are you okay?" Concern painted her face.

His heart was in his throat, and he was stunned by what had just happened. "Yeah," he said but was sure his face showed otherwise.

Charlotte didn't appear convinced, and he waited for her to reprimand him. "I can't believe you gave cantering a try. I hate that speed—that's why I like to go fast, because a gallop is like gliding on water. Bravo!"

"Yeah," was all he could muster.

"Ready to get off and back on the ground?" she asked.

"How'd you guess?"

She offered him a sympathetic look but didn't slag him. "Let's go," she said.

She was proud of him, and that mattered more to him than how silly he felt on the horse.

Eoghan groaned as the masseuse worked on his body. Charlotte next to him buzzed lightly.

"I think she's fallen asleep," he whispered to the masseuse.

At his voice she woke up. "I'm not sleeping."

The masseuse smiled at him.

"Relax, darling, we've both earned it," he said.

"Ugh, it's been a long time since I've been on a horse. I'm so sore," she said, and he remembered how she'd hobbled into the room like she'd aged fifty years overnight. They would have laughed much more if it, too, didn't hurt.

He was in professional athletic shape, but riding used different muscles, and he was in no better condition than Charlotte.

His phone chimed.

"Isn't this a no-phone zone," she said and lifted her head to face him before resting it back on the face pillow.

"I should have left it in the room."

"Shall I get it for you, Mr. O'Farrell?" the masseuse asked.

His phone chimed several more times. "Might be important," he said, taking it.

"Boooo," Charlotte taunted and nestled her head back in the round hole.

He read an all-player alert. His practice time had been moved earlier. Apparently, there was a mix-up with rugby. He had to get back to Dublin tonight to be able to make it.

"Everything okay?" Charlotte asked.

"Yeah," he said, put his phone on silent, and handed it back to the masseuse to put in his robe pocket. He didn't want to give Charlotte the bad news while she tried to relax. They planned to have an early dinner in town. He'd tell her then.

The two masseuses left them alone to relax in their private therapy room.

"I'm really proud of you for getting on a horse today," she said. "I know you were scared, but you tapped into your confidence and let go. You trusted that you would be okay and that you can be good at it after a little bit. It was really nice to see you do that."

"I wasn't scared," he said, getting up off the massage table and approaching her. He helped her naked body up to sitting, draping the heated blankets that covered her around her shoulders. He gripped her waist and settled in between her thighs. His not-too-soft dick was poised in position.

She chuckled. "Of course that would be what you focused on. Succeeding at something you're not good at had to feel good, no?" She hugged his waist.

"I invited you out on this trip to show you parts beyond Dublin, not get tricked into riding Beast."

"I can't believe that was his name." She giggled, and he felt it all over. "I didn't even get him, and I was scared for you," she said.

He dipped down to graze his lips along her jawline and nuzzled the soft skin just under her ear. "You were scared for me, were ya?" His smile tickled her neck, and she leaned into it as much as she scrunched her shoulder to get away.

She reached for his face. "More nervous," she said, echoing his explanation.

"There are ways to exorcise nervous energy. Certain activities to release all that's pent up," he said and sat on a chair and pulled her to sit on his lap.

"Hmm. We just had a massage." She tapped her chin. "What possible other activity could there be, I wonder."

He nuzzled his head into her chest as he stroked up and down her thigh. "This kind." He claimed her mouth, kissing her lovingly. Their blankets fell away from them as he lifted and carried her to their master bedroom. He'd wanted more chances to love her this way, but he'd savor this moment with her.

"The shower," she suggested.

"That didn't turn out too well for us last time, love."

"It's standing. I think we'll be okay." He couldn't say no to her even if he wanted to. He carried her to the bathroom and set her down outside the shower. She adjusted the water's temperature for them before they entered, and inside neither of them got cheated the rays of water, as the streams came from everywhere.

He took her against the tile, both of them gasping and groaning and so wrapped up with each other that time seemed to stand still just for them. Cleanup was easy in the shower, and as the sprays washed over them and he kissed her, he thought that nothing could be better than this.

◆ ◆ ◆

They drove into town for dinner in a private room at O'Sullivan's. They sat side by side instead of across from each other, which spoke of the closeness between them. As they enjoyed their meal, they talked about the day, scrolling through pictures they'd taken on their phones and laughing.

"You were absolutely regal on Wembley," he said. "I, on the other hand, looked like a toy being wagged by a three-year-old. A complete goon," he said, tugging on the back of her Afro.

"Stop. You were handsome up there," she complimented him.

His phone vibrated in his pocket again. Another round of texts in the players' chat.

He checked his messages to make sure he wasn't missing anything else that was important.

"What is it?" she asked.

He sighed. "Practice is earlier tomorrow. You and I were meant to leave in the morning, but . . . um . . ."

Her shoulders slumped, and he hated to disappoint her. "We have to go back tonight, don't we?"

He nodded. "I'm sorry, Char."

"It's okay. This was so magical. Of course I would have loved another night here with you, but this has been such a wonderful treat, Eoghan, and a really special surprise."

"Who knows, maybe we'll come back one day," he said.

Charlotte struggled to smile.

He noticed immediately, and instead of racking his brain to figure out what had rubbed her the wrong way, he asked. "Did I say something wrong?"

"No, not at all."

"Why do I feel like I did?"

"It's just that we don't know what the future holds. There's a big question mark there."

"Question mark, now? I thought things were looking pretty clear. At least from my side."

"Eoghan, let's not do this now, okay? This has been so nice. I don't want to argue. I'm only trying to be realistic," she said.

Where had he gone wrong? Hadn't he shown her how much he cared for her and what it could be like between them? She still had doubts?

He leaned back in his chair, his arm still around the back of hers. "What are you so afraid of, Char?"

"I'm not afraid of anything. I just know that my life is dynamic. It's how I got to be here. Getting too attached might be a bad idea. For both of us."

"It's too late," he said. "For both of us."

Charlotte focused on her food, but her fork simply swirled the potatoes of her colcannon through the silky short rib gravy on her plate. He kept his eyes on her movements, knowing in his heart that no matter how unaffected by their relationship she wanted to be, they'd passed the point of no return.

"Okay," he said. He didn't push. They had to head back, and that already had him in shitty spirits.

Neither of them appeared to have much of an appetite.

"We should get going," she said, and he agreed.

Back in the West Wing, she packed up while he settled the bill. When he came in the room, he found her on the balcony taking in the last of the sights from the castle.

"Ready?" he asked. He would have thought nothing of her unresponsiveness if sadness didn't dust Charlotte's face.

He touched her arm. "What is it, Char?"

She didn't answer but instead fell into him, her arms squeezing his torso as she buried her face in his chest. He kissed the top of her forehead and stroked her. He believed that she was as unattached as a dog to his own tail.

Chapter 19

Monday morning when Charlotte got to the stadium, Eoghan's fourth and final version shoes sat in a box on her desk. She sighed in relief. Though the previous third round had been tumultuous, manufacturing had been a dream ever since, and barring any complaints from Eoghan, this was his shoe. When she opened the box and saw the beautiful, functional design of her cleats for Eoghan, she sank into her seat. She'd get these down to Eoghan, and if there were no problems and they fit him well, she'd have the kit man order additional pairs.

"They're here," Danai cheered as he walked over, dressed casually in jeans and a white puff-sleeved cotton blouse.

"They look really good." Charlotte showed the cleats to him. Her idea was no longer a design with specs on paper—it was a real, physical final product.

"You did a really good job on these. The top office, back office, whatever, should be thrilled with these," Danai said. "Wait until they see the signature shoe designs."

"Yeah," Charlotte said. The arrival of the pair marked the end of her one-on-one work with Eoghan. She'd still work with him and the team on their signature shoes, but their personal project was complete. Charlotte's heart pulled in multiple directions at the thought of not seeing him regularly. There were so many questions. What did that mean for her and Eoghan? He felt like part of her, but still she flipped back and forth with what she wanted and needed. She had to figure this out before she got hurt.

"So how was your weekend away?" Danai asked, his tone heavy with implication.

"We had a really great time." Charlotte couldn't control the cheese on her face if she tried.

"Okay, romance. I see you," Danai said.

"It wasn't like that," Charlotte lied.

"You and I both know that it was exactly like that. He wined and dined you, didn't he?"

"Girl, he did." Charlotte gave in to her time with Eoghan in County Monaghan, which had been lifted from a page in a fairy tale.

"I knew it," Danai said and pulled up a chair for more tasty bits.

Charlotte kept her details short, since she'd spent most of Sunday night with Ayanna, exhausting herself trying to figure out how she'd let her feelings for Eoghan get so out of control. "But you know me. I have to keep it moving." Her words sounded flat.

"Yeah." Danai squinted at her as he savored a sip of coffee. "Free him up for some other gorgeous model to benefit from his romantic ways. You're right."

Charlotte hated when Danai read her. This time, however, Charlotte didn't take the bait. Instead, she dissected and stitched together all the different ways that her and Eoghan's relationship could work without her sacrificing her career and her life for him. When no clear solution presented itself, she defaulted to work. "We should run these down to him. This way, he'll be able to start practicing in them for his first INT game."

"You go ahead," Danai said. "I'm going to check these specs for the signature shoes, then head over to the factory. I love showing up there so everyone can run around like the busy little bees they should be."

Charlotte jogged down to the field level to find Dodger on the field.

"Are those them, miss?" Dodger asked.

"They are."

"Sound," he said. "Maybe now I won't have to chase down Eoghan's boots."

Charlotte laughed. "If he tosses these, he'll have to deal with me."

Eoghan saw her, and she flagged him over. As his agile body jogged over to her, her stomach fluttered, revealing just how much she'd missed him. They hadn't spoken since he'd dropped her off, since he'd had early practice on Monday. Only twelve hours might as well have been twelve days with how much her body, heart, and soul needed him.

"Hiya, Charlotte," he said, and she immediately realized the tenor in his greeting was less than joyful. She'd hoped he'd be happy to see her, especially with his final cleats under her arm.

"Hi. How's practice going?" she asked, hoping that a little small talk might loosen the tension between them.

"All right," he said. "What's up?"

"Oh." She swallowed. "I have your boots." She presented them to him. "You can start wearing them now during practice. If there are no issues with the fit, you'll be all set and just in time for your Portugal game this weekend."

Even though his eyes didn't brighten for her, she was glad that they came to life. The meaning of the shoes was more important than her design would ever be. If the magic of the boots she'd designed was to inject Eoghan with confidence to get past his hurdles, then she'd done her job.

He sat on the ground and tossed his old version. From Charlotte's peripheral vision, she saw Dodger throw up his hands. Charlotte bit back a laugh. Eoghan slid his feet easily into the shoes and then stood up.

"So? How do they feel?" she asked.

"Like they belong to me," he said, staring at her for a long time.

Charlotte's mouth parched. "Good," she croaked, then cleared her pipes. "I'm glad they feel good. Go try them out," she said, trying to infuse some energy into him.

He did, running across the field kicking random balls right from under his teammates, who either chased him or hollered their disapproval. He sprinted back to her. "The fit is great, Charlotte. Thank you."

"The journey had its hiccups here and there, but it was worth it. You're going to do great in these."

He nodded, and though it appeared their conversation was over, Eoghan lingered.

Charlotte couldn't take the strain between them anymore and finally asked, "Okay, what's the matter? You've been weird ever since I got out here."

"Nothing's wrong," he said. "I'm just trying to be ready for the match."

She didn't believe him for a second. "How *do* you feel about the game on Saturday?"

He tapped his toes in the grass, a move she'd come to realize he did to exorcise nervous energy. "I feel good, yeah." His words faded.

"Well, if you can tackle Beast, then you can tackle anything."

He broke into laughter with her. "Beast," he repeated.

She stroked his arm. "You got this," she said.

"Will you be there?" he asked, a desperate edge to his words.

"Yup. Right up there in the stands with Danai, Yaya, and Shane. I wouldn't miss it, Eoghan."

He inched closer to her. "Will you let me see you tonight?"

She summoned all the excuses as to why they shouldn't continue to pick up where they'd left off at Castle Leslie. None were good enough. "Yes. I want that, Eoghan."

Walsh cracked a whistle, and she wanted to tie the lanyard around the coach's neck for the interruption.

"I should get back." As he ran, he yelled back, "The shoe fits good. Order loads—indoor, turf, grass, the works."

Charlotte passed Dodger on her way out and gave him the thumbs-up.

◆ ◆ ◆

Eoghan tidied up his apartment even though his cleaning service had already dusted and cleaned. He didn't want Charlotte to think him a slob on her first visit to his apartment. He needed her to feel comfortable here. He had been restless since they'd left Castle Leslie. She popped into his mind at the most inconvenient times, like when there was a lull in conversation with the lads or when he ate a garden salad for lunch. He had no control over it. If all he did was hold her in his arms tonight, that would be fine by him, just so long as she was with him.

Charlotte, however, wasn't the only reason for his sleepless nights. He was playing his first match with the national team, and the pressure of his performance had him wound so tight that when she'd said hello to him on the field, he'd been unable to relax. His rival on the Portugal team, Martim Santos, would surely be looking for his weaknesses, and word had it that he didn't think Eoghan was a formidable player to worry about this weekend. That got under his skin.

His uniform, his boots, his endurance, and his skill. He'd checked all the boxes and had felt back in good form. Yet he was still so nervous that only moments before she'd given him his boots on the field, he'd chucked his guts in the dressing rooms, considering if he'd be able to prove the rumors false. He was sure that there'd be a repeat performance on game day.

Tonight, he'd make it up to her.

His doorbell rang, which was strange, since he wasn't expecting Charlotte for another half hour. He peered through the peephole. "No," he groaned when he saw Aida, his neighbor, and her son, Ross. Resting his head on the door, he said a silent prayer before opening the door.

"Hi, Eoghan."

"Hi, Aida," Eoghan said and then bent down to greet Ross, her short-brown-haired four-year-old. "What's happening, buds? You being good?"

"I'm all right, mate," Ross said, which made Eoghan smile.

"I am so sorry to bother you. I just have to run out really quick, and you're the only one home," she said. "Please, please, can you look after Ross for a short while. I'll be back as soon as I can."

Every so often Ross would come over and play video games with him to give his single mother a break. It wasn't often, but today the timing was shitty.

"I'd love to help you out, Aida, but I have company coming and—"

"I'm desperate." Aida squeezed her hands together in prayer. "Please," she sang.

"Please," Ross said, imitating his mother.

"All right. Be back as soon as you can. Please."

"I will, I promise. Thank you so much." *Shite!* How was he going to explain this to Charlotte? She'd likely be pissed off that she was wasting her time to watch him babysit his neighbor's kid.

"Get in here, Ross, and make yourself comfortable," Eoghan said.

"Here's his bag. There are plenty of snacks for him, books, iPad, his favorite blanket, and a change of clothes. You know, the usual."

Eoghan took the bag from her. "Got it."

"I owe you more than a cup of sugar," Aida said.

"Even more than that," Eoghan said.

Not more than fifteen minutes, and he received a call from the doorman that Charlotte had arrived.

"Send her up, please."

When Charlotte arrived, she smelled like heaven. "Hiya, Char."

"Hi," she said and greeted him with a quick and gentle kiss.

Her long white wool coat hung open to reveal part of her outfit, which stunned him like a Taser as well as set him ablaze. He took her coat, and not only was she dressed in a deadly black dress with the midriff completely cut out, but she also wore strappy high-heeled sandals even though it was Baltic out. He felt honored that she'd dressed up for him.

"Your place is not too far from mine." She stepped inside and waited for him before she moved farther inside. He absentmindedly hung up her coat, unsure if he was even hanging it on the rod, then quickly made his way to her and pulled her into his arms, squeezing her against the length of him and devouring her delicious mouth. His palms found the bare skin of her midriff, and he caressed the soft skin.

The toilet flushed, interrupting the play of how he wanted the events to unfold that danced in his head and reminding him of his houseguest.

Charlotte jumped out of his arms. "Someone's here?"

"I missed," Ross said.

Charlotte looked down at Ross, then back at him, then back at Ross, and she pointed at him. "Yours?"

"My neighbor's. She had to run out. Single mam. Ross and I normally hang out to give his ma a break."

"Hi, Ross," Charlotte said, crouching down. The slit on her black dress revealed the length of her thigh, which begged for Eoghan's hand and his mouth. "I'm Charlotte. How's it going?"

"I missed," Ross repeated, pretty torn up about it.

"The potty?" Charlotte asked.

He nodded.

"Are you wet?" she tenderly asked the four-year-old.

He nodded.

"It's okay. Let's go see what's up and get you all sorted out. And then maybe Eoghan can help you change your clothes." She took Ross's hand and led him to the bathroom.

"You don't have to, Char. I can do it. Your dress."

"I don't mind," she said.

Eoghan watched Charlotte walk off with Ross, wishing he'd missed, too, so Charlotte could take care of him, and then he followed them.

In his bathroom he leaned against the white-marbled, slate-gray-tiled walls while Charlotte parked her arse on the large white soaking tub and evaluated the scene by the toilet.

"It's not so bad, just a little spill," she said to Ross. "Good job on the aim, buddy! High five."

Ross sloppily slapped Charlotte's palm and relaxed a bit.

Charlotte craned her neck to Eoghan. "If you put a few cereal pieces like Cheerios or something like that in the toilet, it may help him aim better and make a fun game out of it for him."

"Mam does that," Ross said cheerfully.

Charlotte spun Ross and checked his navy-blue jogging suit. "He looks pretty dry to me, no need for a change of clothes." She smiled. Once Ross was settled on the couch with a juice box and *Veggie Tales* playing on the TV, Eoghan and Charlotte sat at the dining table.

"Wine?" he asked.

"Yes, please." She crossed her legs and, with one elbow resting on her knee and her chin in her palm, watched him like he was the only thing in the apartment.

"What?" he asked, placing two wineglasses on the table with a clink.

"Can't I just look at you?" She smirked.

"I see those eyes working," he said. "What're you thinking about?"

"Just how interesting the night has gone. I didn't expect to be here with you and Ross, or I might have, uh . . . dressed accordingly."

"I thought you'd be upset with him here."

"It was unexpected because I thought we'd be alone, but I love kids."

"Another new thing I learned about you tonight?"

She tapped her chin. "What was the first?" she asked.

"That you're not pretentious at all."

Her eyes moved as if she were figuring out a calculus equation. "Is that supposed to be a compliment, Mr. O'Farrell?"

"Yes." He slid the glass of wine toward her and sat opposite her at the oval table. "I thought you'd be raging with me and maybe even leave, especially when I saw you in this dress."

"You sound like that's been your experience." She sipped her wine.

"Over much less than a child being present," he said, taking a gulp of the cabernet franc.

The truth was that none of the women he'd dated would have been as easygoing with Ross's crashing of their party. He'd had a woman leave because he'd wanted to relax at the apartment after a game instead of going out. Yet Charlotte not only was easygoing but went out of her way to help Ross feel comfortable and take care of him without batting an eyelash.

"And here I thought you knew me better than that."

He absorbed how lovely she looked in his space with the backdrop of the lights from the Docklands twinkling behind her from the observation window that took up one side of his apartment. "You're like uncharted land, Charlotte," he said. "I never know what I'm going to find when I'm exploring you. It's always an adventure."

Her chest rose with air.

"Are you hungry?" he asked.

She licked her lips. "Starving."

He gripped the bottom of her chair with his hand and turned it roughly to face him.

Charlotte yelped, "Eoghan?" She looked around to check for Ross. She twisted back to Eoghan. Her body didn't close up but rather opened when he dragged the chair to him. He lifted one of her legs up on his.

"Come here, Char," he said, and when her hands came up to his face and her fingers gently traced his features, he closed his eyes and let her scent guide him to her lips.

It hadn't been long since he'd last tasted her, but it felt like forever had passed, like he'd been in perpetual drought and she was his first few drops of water.

"Char." His tongue wrestled with hers as he drank her into his body and the depths of his soul.

She scooted closer to him, her legs wide and beckoning him to what she wanted. He slid his hands over her naked midriff, teasing her as he made his way down. He flipped open the material of her dress, which the split made too easy, and when he touched her center, he nearly died when he found her pantyless.

His eyes bulged open. "You mean to tell me you've been walking around my apartment this accessible? You're mad."

"I told you," she said, panting. "I came prepared."

"Feck yeah, you did." He swallowed her mouth. He didn't think his craving for her could get any more potent, but in classic Charlotte form, she continued to surprise him.

He slid his fingers inside, toying with her, bringing her to the brink.

"You're going to come for me this way, Char," he mumbled against her neck, clouded by his passion. "Just. Like. This." As his desire for her increased, so did the tempo of his strokes and pressure on her swollen clit.

"Yes, Eoghy," she whispered, biting his shoulder to muffle her cries from Ross.

When her body jerked and she cried her climax into his chest, he didn't let up. He milked every bit of pleasure from her.

"I can't, Eoghy," she squealed breathlessly, and her hand went to the one of his that pleasured her core.

He withdrew his hand and kissed her cheeks, her eyelids, her neck, and finally her lips. "You all right?"

"Mmm . . . yeah." The fog lifted from her eyes, and she again checked for Ross. She turned back to Eoghan and looked down at his dick.

"Later."

"Eoghan." Her voice was laden with concern for his balls.

"I'll be okay, love. I just needed to touch you like this. I'd been hungry for you, Char." He reached for her.

"I'm hungry," Ross called.

Eoghan withdrew, and Charlotte snickered under her breath.

"All right, you," Eoghan sighed, then addressed Charlotte. "You want to eat food?" he specified.

Charlotte's laughter wouldn't quit. "Yes. Food."

He fed Ross a meal his mother had made of rice and chicken with applesauce for dessert, while he and Charlotte shared steamed clams for an appetizer and a lobster meal with potatoes gratin and roasted vegetables. For dessert the three of them shared a layered strawberry tart, which Ross loved.

"Ross, are you going to watch Eoghan play this weekend against Portugal?" Charlotte asked.

"Yes, madam. Me and Mam."

"So freaking cute," Charlotte mouthed to Eoghan. "Who do you think is going to win?" she asked Ross.

"Ireland for sure," Ross said, then started singing. "We have O'Farrell . . ."

"Even the kids sing for you, Eoghan," Charlotte said. "I think Ireland is going to win too. Eoghan is going to do great. It's been a long time since he's played. You think he's ready?"

Ross looked at him and gave him the most adorable, chocolate-covered, toothy smile he'd ever seen on the boy's face. "He is ready to win."

Charlotte's eyes met his. "I think so too. He's going to play great, and Ireland is going to win," she said, backing up Ross.

Eoghan's throat tightened, and if he swallowed, he might shed a tear at the confidence Charlotte breathed into him.

"Thanks, guys." His voice faltered.

Though watching *Frozen II* wasn't the entertainment he'd thought he'd be sharing with Charlotte, when Ross fell asleep on her lap, he forgot about the movie altogether and took in the maternal scene. Something in his chest ached and longed for her in a way that he knew he'd never identify, but he wanted to see her like this again with her own child. His stomach dropped like someone had just kicked him out of an airplane without a parachute. She nodded off, and he had enough sense to take a picture of her. The photo might be the only one he'd have of her angelic sleeping face if she decided to go back to America after her contract was done. His pulse raced and his heart seized.

A knock on the door sounded, and Charlotte woke up.

"It's the door." He stood and went to it. "No doubt it's Ross's mam."

True to his words, when Eoghan opened the door, Aida slipped in. "Thank you again." She looked over to Charlotte, who eased Ross off her lap and started to fold his blanket.

Aida's eyes bounced between him and Charlotte, and a big smile spread across her face. "I'll get his things and carry him out." Aida packed her son's overnight bag, and after she and Charlotte made quick, hushed introductions, Aida gathered Ross in her arms. Charlotte handed her the packed bag. "Nice to meet you," they both whispered to each other.

"He's sweet and so easy," Charlotte said.

"Yeah, he's a gem," Aida said. "Thank you for helping Eoghan."

"It was a pleasure."

Aida carried Ross to the door and thanked Eoghan again before leaving. Charlotte picked up the few things they'd enjoyed while watching the movie. Her tummy crinkled as she bent over. He moved over to her, his love for her undeniable.

He took her hand. "Leave it, love."

She did as he instructed, and as he tugged her to his bedroom to make love, she didn't resist.

Chapter 20

On game day, Charlotte woke up groggy and in a bad mood. She stubbed her toe that morning and spilled coffee on the T-shirt under her O'Farrell jersey and had to change her whole outfit. If she was the determining factor on whether Eoghan and the national team won their game against Portugal, she should stay home because bad luck had stained her today.

Shane, Ayanna, and Danai met her at her apartment, and they walked to the stadium. Charlotte felt like a full-on pedestrian, not going to the game from the offices at Aviva but trekking with the fans to the huge wavy structure that was a mecca for Irish soccer fans. Portugal was a big rival for the Irish team, and between the two sets of supporters, some of the taunts and chants were vicious and started way before they even got inside the stadium. The treat of working with the team was their seats, and Charlotte knew that she'd never spend the kind of money it would take to sit where they sat.

The thunderous cheers of the fans as the stadium filled up were deafening, and the game hadn't even started yet. Shane went to grab them some eats and water. They'd get beer during halftime.

"The Irish team fans have it out for Martim," Shane said.

"Who's that?" Charlotte asked.

"Martim Santos. He's the star player on the Portugal team. He and Eoghan normally go at it pretty hard on the field," Shane explained.

"And off the field?" Charlotte asked.

"No better. They're both great, but Portugal does come out the winners five to one, but we still give them a run of it."

Rival teams often did give each other a run for the win. Charlotte settled in for an exciting game.

"Oi, Shane."

Charlotte recognized the voice of Eoghan's father immediately from seats higher up than where they were.

"How's she cutting, Gaff?" Shane hollered back and also nodded to Eoghan's mom. "Grace."

"Good," Donal said.

"Tell Nadine to call me when she's back," Grace said.

"Will do, yeah," Shane said.

Ayanna waved. "Hello, Grace. Donal."

"Lovely to see you again, Ayanna," Grace said.

"Hello to you as well, shoe lady," Donal said.

Charlotte waved, surprised by the man's acknowledgment. "Hi."

"How's the form?" Donal said and jutted his head to Eoghan on the field.

"All right," Shane returned.

Charlotte could only imagine how nervous Eoghan's father must be for his son. This was his first game with the national team in almost a year. Donal might be pushy, but Charlotte could at least understand that familial connection.

The moment had finally arrived. The teams gathered on the field with the referee for the first touch. Charlotte cheered Eoghan and the team on. She'd been trying to encourage him all week, whether he'd been at her place or she at his. He was ready, and he'd been practicing in his cleats all week. She'd customized them like a body part. If anyone else wore that shoe, they'd have to go to a podiatrist to get their feet fixed. The rest was up to him.

Eoghan's muscles worked as he ran the ball down the pitch and kicked it over to his teammates. His lungs ached before reaching a level where his fitness and conditioning took over and all he had to focus on was the game. The fans cheered when his team got control of the ball and groaned in unison when the opposing team regained control. His job as an attacker on the team was to go after other players, shadow them, and keep them from scoring, especially one player in particular. Martim Santos. He was an excellent player, but his personality was shite. Known for being a troublemaker on and off the field. Eoghan looked forward to the games with him because Martim's skill helped elevate his, especially when the matches went into overtime. Even better if Ireland took the lead and ultimately won the match. Unfortunately, Portugal had bested them often in the past, but Eoghan believed that today, with everything working for him, Ireland would take that match and move their club up the standings.

Martim dribbled the ball with Eoghan on his heels, passing with his teammates until the ball had gone back to Martim for a goal, but Eoghan was there to spoil the goal, as was Pippin, who also braced, ready to deflect.

Back our way.

Eoghan didn't know when the energy shifted, but he played in the zone, his feet light and comfortable and his legs strong. He'd never understood being in the zone until he'd become a player, but he definitely knew when he wasn't. He hadn't felt the haze of the zone once since he'd come back to play—that was, until now. His movements were easy, his plays effortless, and as it came to Martim, Eoghan was white on rice. Everywhere.

"Get off my ass," Martim yelled in Portuguese at one point. That only expressed to Eoghan that he was doing something right, and he gloated inside.

Eoghan slapped hands with his teammates before they reset. The game continued, and his body dripped with sweat.

"Pass," Eoghan heard and sometimes yelled, many times a deflection to confuse the opposing players. He ran the ball hard and tried to steal it from another player. Their feet tangled, tripping them both up, but unlike the other player, it was Eoghan who fell.

The fans gasped like he was a fragile Fabergé egg that had just broken. He lay on his back for a second, squinting out of one eye. He checked in with his body. *All good!*

"Get up, Eoghy!"

He could have sworn he heard Charlotte, but he couldn't possibly through the tons of fans at the stadium, and there was no way she'd call him Eoghy in public.

He leaped up, and the roar in the stadium had to be heard from across the pond.

He and the team ran a wide flank play in an attempt to unbalance their opponents.

A pass to Patrick and a kick into the goal.

Cheers erupted as the Irish national team scored first. Patrick ran down the sidelines, and the stands vibrated with stomping feet like an earthquake. The screaming fans released puffy emerald-colored smoke that fogged over the stadium in patriotic flair.

Charlotte blew into her gloves to warm her fingers and bounced her feet as she sat and watched Eoghan brilliantly work the pitch. He ran players down, attacked them, and kicked the ball from right under them.

Charlotte screamed her throat hoarse, along with the other fifty thousand fans in the packed house.

"He looks good," Shane said as he watched Eoghan with her and Ayanna.

"He looks great," Charlotte corrected, and Shane chuckled. "I mean, his cleats look like they're working well for him," she added.

"Mmm-hmm," Danai said, decked out in team colors. He and Charlotte sported Irish-flag-inspired scarves around their necks in patriotic support.

Ayanna bumped her. "I'm so glad that this is the first game we get to watch together."

"Me too," Charlotte said, but though she enjoyed this moment with her friend, she kept her eye on the O'Farrell jersey on the field.

Charlotte bolted to her feet and her heart stopped beating in her chest when she saw Eoghan fall. She was numb to the brisk evening air.

"Please, please get up," she prayed quietly to herself. The panic in her heart gripped her so fearsomely that she was ready to jog down to the field.

"Come on, Eoghy!" Her voice cracked from trying to scream over the rest of the fans gasping and moaning at Eoghan on his back.

Then, just as quickly as he'd fallen, he was back on his feet and running with the team.

"Yeah," she screamed and jumped up and down like she'd won the Powerball.

"We have O'Farrell . . . ," the crowd sang for him, and Charlotte thought her chest would crack open with joy.

"Eoghy, huh?" Ayanna teased her out of earshot of everyone.

Charlotte covered her face with her hands. Her hopes that no one had heard her scream the endearment were utterly dashed. "Hush. You didn't hear that," she retorted.

"We all did, boo," Danai chimed in.

The game continued, and Eoghan, Lance, and Patrick moved together in a wide flank play. Eoghan passed the ball to Patrick, who scored, and Aviva went mad. Charlotte jumped up and down, her arms reaching for the sky. Like the fans in the stands who high-fived and hugged each other, she did the same with Shane, Ayanna, and Danai.

"He's playing well," Charlotte said.

"Walsh'll take him out soon," Shane said.

"What? Why? He's doing so well."

"He might have some swelling as his leg catches up with the other one from his injury. It's natural, but best to take him out and work him up to a full game," Ayanna said.

◆ ◆ ◆

Halftime came, and in the dressing rooms, the team bounced off the walls. They'd drawn first blood, and even better, Eoghan was playing his best. He finally felt one with the pitch and couldn't wait to get back out there.

"Great job, lads," Walsh said. "Keep up the good work. Eoghan, way to attack the ball. I'm going to take you out and—"

That was all Eoghan heard. He couldn't have heard Gaff correctly. He'd come so far to get back to this very moment, this very feeling. Likely Gaff had made a mistake, misspoken, and meant to address his comment to another player.

"What?" Eoghan asked.

"You're done for the day," Walsh said.

In the past, he hadn't been one to normally question his coaches, but he couldn't comprehend why Gaff had made this move. "If I'm playing well, then why are you taking me out?"

"Just a little precaution. Good job, lad."

Eoghan seethed even as his teammates patted his shoulders and back. He drank some water to cool down but nearly choked on it.

"It's all right, mate. Well done out there," Pippin said.

Eoghan punched a locker, ready to snap.

"Let's go," one of their teammates said, and they headed back on the field. Eoghan stomped to the players' box and watched the rest of the game.

◆ ◆ ◆

True to Shane's words, Walsh took Eoghan out of the game. Ayanna knew her stuff, and Charlotte trusted her that if Eoghan had to be taken out of the game, it was for his own good.

Charlotte recognized that tantrum walk Eoghan did to the players' box. She half expected him to blame her shoes, kick them off, and have Dodger run and go get them. She knew how much he'd wanted to play a full game and be as good as he'd been before the injury. She hugged herself, wishing she could give him a hug, pronounce herself his biggest fan, and tell him how great he'd done. But most of all she wanted to tell him that she was proud of him. However, Eoghan spent his first five minutes on the bench sullen and unmoving. That was, until Portugal scored. The disgruntled fans booed their discontentment loudly. Eoghan jumped up and waved his hands up and down to get the fans excited, willing them to help the team get the goal back.

"Come on," he yelled, even though it sounded like a faint call under the roaring attendees. The crowd got hyped, and as Charlotte watched the game, the Irish team scored and got the goal back. She almost covered her head at the real possibility of Aviva tumbling down over them from the deafening screams.

"Yes!" Charlotte high-fived Ayanna and Shane. She clutched her heart, exhilarated for Eoghan and the teammates she'd come to grow fond of.

"Come on, guys," she yelled, willing Eoghan and her team to a win.

The second half started out well, but then Portugal tied the score quickly. Eoghan cheered his team on as they got a point back. In the end Ireland won the game, but the win was bittersweet since Eoghan had spent the second half benched. He'd been in the zone, and Walsh had taken him out? He clenched his fists. He wanted to be out there and play against his rivals. Had he shown signs that he was fatiguing? His insecurity from childhood, when he'd gotten pulled out of games, resurfaced like yesterday.

The fans were happy, and that would have to be enough.

After an ice bath and massage, Eoghan showered and dressed. Walsh pulled him aside. "I know you're stiff about me taking you out, but you're not ready for a full game yet. Your leg was swelling. I'd asked Miles to keep an eye on it," Gaff said, referring to the assistant coach.

"You know I can play through it," Eoghan said.

"And I'll need you to, so take the pin out of your arse," his coach said.

"Thanks, Gaff," he said and left the dressing rooms. He almost forgot that his father would be waiting where he always did.

"Dad," Eoghan said.

"Good game, son."

"Thanks," Eoghan said tentatively.

"But the second half. Walsh should have left you in," Donal said. "You have to show him, son. You have to show him that you're ready to lead at the helm again."

"Gaff knows what he's doing, Da," Eoghan said. "There will be plenty more games."

"That's the attitude you have?"

"I don't want to wallow in it tonight. Walsh explained himself, and it's good. All right."

"Don't get soft, son."

"Soft?"

"Stand up for yourself with your playing time. You're the star."

Eoghan shook his head. He'd accepted his coach's decision because Walsh had taken him out to protect him. Yet here his father was unable to let it go. "The lads are waiting, Da."

"Right, well, me and your ma will see you for dinner at the next weekend?" his father stated more than asked.

"Yeah," Eoghan said. "See you then." His father had parked on the other side of the stadium for years to avoid the traffic. When he left, Eoghan welcomed the time alone and dragged his way out to meet his friends.

Outside, Shane waited with Ayanna, Charlotte, Danai, and Pippin, but Eoghan's eyes landed and remained on Charlotte.

"Good win," Charlotte cheered.

Shane slapped hands and bumped shoulders with him.

Ayanna studied his leg. "You had a little swelling, didn't you?" she asked.

"Yes," he admitted to his physio.

"Good, it's behaving normally. That'll pass as you stay in games longer," Ayanna said. "I'm sure that's why Walsh took you out."

"Doesn't mean I was happy about it," he said.

"Did he crack a locker?" Shane asked Pippin.

"Nah," Pippin said. "Just a bit of a punch."

"Let's go out for a bit of the craic," Shane said. "The rest of the lads are there already."

"Grand."

Charlotte inched over to him. "Everything okay?"

"Yeah," he said. He boldly took her hand in his. "Walk with me for a bit?" He relaxed when she didn't pull away. He wanted her more than he could stand, but right now he just needed to be close to her. He hadn't had her in his arms since Monday last.

"Of course," Charlotte said. "You're never this quiet. Say something. You're freaking me out."

"Will you come to dinner with me?" he asked.

"Sure," she said.

"At my parents' house at the next weekend?" He didn't qualify it or overexplain it. He wanted her with him, and though his family wasn't perfect and she had concerns about their relationship, he wanted her to know every part of him, good or bad. She didn't respond for a long time, and he thought that perhaps he'd made a mistake asking her.

"I don't know, Eoghan. That seems so . . . formal and so serious."

"It's dinner." He smiled, though they both knew the level he was asking her to jump. Though she didn't physically run, he sensed she wanted to.

"Okay, I'll come."

"Yeah?" Sure, he looked like a little boy who'd just gotten his first date.

"I said yes, didn't I?" She made a fist and pushed him, gently, center chest.

"Okay."

Chapter 21

Eoghan and Charlotte arrived at his parents' home in Limerick. During the season his folks frequented Dublin more, staying at their flat in the city, but Eoghan visited his childhood home several times a year on special occasions, like Easter, Christmas, and now bringing Charlotte to dinner.

"It's such a sweet house," Charlotte said as they pulled up to a brick house on a row with other yellow-and-brick houses, common for the developments in many neighborhoods. Their door was black with evergreen plants on either side and a door knocker that he'd made for his mam when he was seven. He had a lot of great memories of growing up with his family, Shane, and eventually Pippin, but the more his celebrity had grown, the more had his father's need to control him.

He entered the house with Charlotte, the savory scent of his mam's cooking hitting them as they made their way farther inside.

"Hello," Eoghan called.

"Here he is," his father said and gave him a pat.

"Where's Ma?" Eoghan asked his father.

"She's gone to collect the messages," his father returned. "Something important she forgot. Should be back any minute." He looked at Charlotte and gave her a nod. "Hello there."

Eoghan had hoped his father would give her a warmer greeting than a nod, but Eoghan told himself that his da would warm up in his own time.

Charlotte, on the other hand, opened her arms wide. "Mr. O'Farrell! So good to see you again."

Eoghan's eyes widened when Charlotte hugged his father, who stiffened in her arms. Eoghan snickered into his hand, knowing exactly Charlotte's purpose. Thankfully, she didn't torture oul Donal with a lengthy embrace.

"Yes, well, show her where to put her things," his father tossed at him and quickly found his way to the couch. "Maybe you can go ahead and get her a drink while you're at it."

The instructions were more than Eoghan had expected from his father, who thus far had only shown distaste for Charlotte's role with the team.

Eoghan took her things. "My ma's just gone to get groceries. Make yourself comfortable. I'll bring you something you like," he said to Charlotte, who mischievously eyed his father, who was watching a game on the telly. "I know that look well enough."

"What?" she asked, batting her eyelashes too sweetly at him to be taken at all seriously.

"Behave yourself."

She winked at him before refocusing her attention back on his father. "I got this." Charlotte marched over and sat on a love seat close to where his father was sitting. "Whatcha watching, Donal?"

"The match from Thursday."

"I missed that one. Any good?" Charlotte asked.

"It's all right."

Eoghan smothered his face with his hand, questioning why he'd brought Charlotte here to his parents' house for dinner. Of course, he knew why. He'd fallen hard for her, though he'd never foreseen a moment where he brought any of the women he'd dated, with the exception of Eileen, to his parents' house. He'd convinced himself that he'd loved Eileen, but eventually, he'd been able to admit that infatuation had played a larger role in that relationship. Eileen chose him, and being in so deep, he took her from not just any bloke or pal but his friend. His best friend Shane. He and Shane, with the help of their best friend Pippin, worked things out a year after the incident two years ago, and then when the dregs of that conflict reappeared when they were in America for four months together last year, they cleared the rest of the toxic air.

Eoghan falling in love with a good, Catholic, Irish girl had been his ma's dream. But the dream of Eileen quickly had turned into one of the hellish nightmares that Poe had written about. Now he was with Charlotte. Not white, not Irish, and not Catholic, yet here he was bringing her to dinner. *Throwing her into the den.* At his childhood home with his parents. *Populated with lions.* What was his endgame?

Eoghan brought Charlotte a beer, and as he handed it to her, he heard a commotion coming through the front door. It was his mother returning from her shopping. Eoghan went to help, and his father stayed put, his eyes focused on the television. Charlotte put her beer down and stood up and made her way over to them.

"There's more in the car," Eoghan's mother said.

"I'll take these," Charlotte said and tried to take the groceries from him, but he shooed her away.

"Go on and relax, Char. We'll take care of it."

"Oul fella," his mother yelled to his father. "Get off yer arse and help me and your son with the messages." Her warning command always got both him and his father moving.

Used to his wife's barking, Donal dragged himself away from the TV, then revved up his actions when he saw his wife struggling with the bags she carried into the kitchen. One thing his father tried to be was ever gallant for his wife.

Despite Eoghan's suggestion, Charlotte helped with a bag or two. "I want to help."

"The cooking is done. I had to get one more thing but then went ahead and got groceries for the week, plus I wanted to make sure I

218

had a few extra things for your friend." His mother briefly looked at Charlotte, who smiled. "Dinner will be on the table in short order."

"Let me give you a quick tour of the house," Eoghan said and took Charlotte by the hand. "The house isn't terribly big, so this'll be quick." They walked down the corridor, where photographs of his family celebrating the holidays and Eoghan growing up lined the walls. "I'll show you my room," he said.

He took her inside his room, now the guest room, which contained many of his awards and trophies. Pictures of him and the MAKin' crew as they climbed the levels remained the best features in the room.

"Oh my gosh. You guys were so skinny back then," Charlotte cooed at his younger self. "So cute."

"Okay, okay."

"I love this one with you and your parents," she said.

"That was when I got accepted into the juniors for the Republic of Ireland. Big day." He reminisced about how excited he'd been. "Oul Donal couldn't have been prouder. It was the first day I'd ever seen him cry."

She hugged his waist and squeezed. "Thank you for showing me this," she said. "It's not every day a girl gets to be in the childhood bedroom of the most famous celebrity in the country."

He approached her and brought her body to his. "Exciting, isn't it." He fluttered his eyebrows for her before angling his head for a kiss. Her glossed lips were warm and inviting.

"I see where this is heading." She scooted around him. "Your parents are right downstairs, and your dad hates me. The last thing I want him to do is find us doing the nasty."

"I can't remember the last time I heard that term." He laughed. "First of all, my dad doesn't hate you. He's a hard man. You'll get used to it." As soon as he said the words, he heard how presumptuous they sounded.

"Supper's ready," his mother called, and he was relieved that he and Charlotte hadn't started something that would have been interrupted.

219

They gathered around the small dinner table, his father pouring wine and his mother pointing out the dishes for Charlotte.

"We have beef stew and corned beef, braised cabbage, and herbed mashed potatoes. There's plenty, so please help yourself. I also got a red-velvet cake for dessert from the bakery. I hear that in Harlem, it's a popular dessert."

Eoghan's heart melted at the thought his mother had put into making Charlotte feel welcome.

"Thank you for welcoming me for dinner. This is great, Grace. Red velvet is quite popular in the States. I appreciate the thought. It's one of my favorites." Charlotte smiled.

This was what he'd wanted to see happen with her and his family. They ate and drank with light small talk for the first half of dinner, and Eoghan loved the interest his mother took in Charlotte's upbringing and New York.

"Harlem is world known. The Harlem Renaissance," his mother said, her eyes bright. "When we visit the States, we pass through to see the Apollo Theater and the murals. The restaurants are amazing. Have you seen much of our country?"

"I've seen a few places in Dublin and the north of Ireland as well. County Monaghan," she said. "Eoghan took me to see Castle Leslie."

His mother dropped her fork and stared at him. He felt the heat on his face and probably looked like he did at the end of an intense game, minus the sweat dripping from his face, clothes, and hair.

Charlotte, ever sharp, noticed the exchange between him and his ma. "Is something wrong?"

Grace cleared her throat. "No. That's lovely, Charlotte. The north is the gem of the country for sure."

They continued to eat, and Eoghan settled into the meal, happily swallowing spoonfuls of his beef stew, but he was sure his mother would find him with questions later.

"So," Eoghan's father said. "You've worked your way up from doing Eoghan's cleats to doing ones for the whole team, eh?"

"Da," Eoghan said. Charlotte hadn't fully picked up on the intention of his question, but there was definitely one.

"What? It's ambitious, don't you think?"

"Yeah, it is. When the top of the organization approached me, I couldn't say no," Charlotte responded.

"And his boots?" his father asked her.

Eoghan interjected, answering in Charlotte's stead. "I'm wearing the boots game after game."

"How's that going for you?" His father scratched his brow with his thumb and sat up with his elbows on the table, and Eoghan wondered what lecture he was about to hear. "You're slow, tripping over yourself out there like you're in the juniors again."

Eoghan went into himself like he normally did with his father. He wanted to speak his mind but also stay respectful. It was a constant struggle, and there were times he'd just succumb to his father.

"That's not very fair," Charlotte tried to mumble, but it came out at standard volume for inside voices.

"Football isn't fair, deary," Donal said.

"Actually"—Charlotte held up a finger—"it's quite fair. I mean, there are plenty of rules, some of which I'm still figuring out and others that are just trash."

"Football means a lot to us, especially this family. I'm not sure how much you know about it."

"I respect that, but it doesn't take a football expert to understand when a grown man is being criticized for doing his best."

"You keep talking like you know my son better'n I," his father said.

"Not at all, Donal, but I know him very well, just in a different way," she said. Everyone at the table paused what they were doing. He could only imagine their interpretation of Charlotte's words.

She looked around the table. "Oh! Not like that." She giggled nervously. "I'm, well, not only . . . what I mean to say is, business-wise and working with him on something so personal as a customized shoe has allowed me to get to know him in a different way. Eoghan's such a wonderful man. I'm just saying that you can learn about that side of him too."

Grace jumped in. "Like what?"

"I keep telling you, we know him just fine," Donal said.

"Do you know that he loves horses?" Charlotte asked.

"Charlotte," Eoghan warned.

"Of course I do," Donal said.

"I actually don't, Da."

His father crimsoned, and his body twisted and rocked in his seat. "So now we're being tricked?"

His ma shushed his father, which Eoghan hadn't heard in a long time.

"Charlotte." Grace encouraged her to continue, curiosity in her gaze.

"Yes, you're right," Charlotte said. "That was unfair of me. I'm sorry. But I'm just trying to point out that there are things you can still learn about Eoghan."

"Just who do you think you are, coming in here, disrupting what we have?"

"Don't, Da," Eoghan said. "Don't speak to her like that."

"You're okay with her tricking us, then, to prove her little point."

"Her methods, no." He side-eyed Charlotte. "But she didn't mean any harm."

"You agree with her over your own father?" his father said, and Eoghan saw the hurt through the anger.

"Da, calm down. We can talk about this," Eoghan said.

Charlotte cleared her throat to speak. "I have a tendency to be too honest sometimes, Donal, and protect those I lo . . . I care about." Her lids fluttered, and she held her stomach.

"You all right?" Eoghan whispered, thinking Charlotte was about to hurl her guts.

"I didn't mean to—I only wanted to defend Eoghan," she said.

"I don't believe a word of it," Donal said. His father stood and left the table.

"Best to stop talking now, dear," Grace suggested to Charlotte. "Like you mentioned, my son has hair on his chest. He can speak up for himself."

"And when have I been able to do that, Mam," Eoghan said, wondering when it had all gone so south. "My whole career, once I'd been identified as talented to the point where they wanted to put me on the track, Da has been inserting himself."

"What was he to do? Let a child run his own career?" his mother asked.

"No, but as a man he never helped me take control and be a man about business. Most of that I learned from my agent."

"He just wanted to be close to you and part of things."

"I know, but he's taken over to the point where he's blowing up because I chose a boot without him."

His mother's face softened. She knew all too well about what Eoghan spoke of. "You have to find a way to make him understand, son. There are better ways to go about it than ruining his supper."

"I'll help you clean up, Grace." Charlotte exchanged glances with his mother, and whatever was shared between them, he stayed out of it.

What the fuck had she been thinking, agreeing to coming here? Charlotte found herself doing a lot of things she didn't think she'd do as it related to Eoghan, and many of them felt out of control and led by emotions that overrode her common sense. If she'd had her wits about her, she'd have declined his invitation when he'd asked her to come.

Thank you, but no thanks. Instead, her overwhelming need to protect Eoghan and stand with him had taken precedence. Now here she was, at the dinner table in the middle of an argument with a family that wasn't hers. Didn't Eoghan know that she was too bullish to be trusted to keep her mouth shut? He should have known better. What had he been thinking? She'd fallen into a trap and was petrified that, like her mom, she'd started making decisions with him in mind, yet the thought of being without him made her feel empty, lost.

Eoghan had gone to find his father, and Charlotte stacked plates on the counter and brought serving dishes with food into the kitchen. She genuinely wanted to help Grace clean up, but she needed to do her penance as well. She really had a problem and couldn't help but speak her mind.

"Will Donal be okay?" Charlotte asked, putting plates into the dishwasher.

"He'll be fine," Grace said as she put a pot in the sink to soak.

"My goal wasn't to disrupt dinner," Charlotte said hesitantly. "I'm not trying to replace anyone or pretend that I know Eoghan better than his family. I just . . ." She didn't know how to say what she meant without further irritating Grace.

"You care about him."

"Yes," Charlotte said simply. "He's a friend, and well, I've met a few bullies in my time . . ."

Grace put the food in more manageable containers for the refrigerator. "Donal is a bully for sure, but he loves his son."

"I don't doubt that."

"But?" Grace asked. "You've something to say, then say it."

Grace sounded just like her son. "I think he micromanages Eoghan and inserts himself when Eoghan can and should advocate for himself." Charlotte braced herself for Grace's wrath, which never came.

"You're right in some respects. I've asked him to ease off on occasion, but I think that it would be best that Eoghan asserts himself with his da."

"Because we're women?" Charlotte asked.

"A pinch perhaps, but he's waiting for Eoghan to show him and tell him what he wants. Donal's a private man and would have preferred to deal with something like this as a family affair."

"I overstepped," Charlotte said. "I'm sorry for that too. Please convey my feelings to him. I really was looking forward to getting to know you both more, but . . ."

"You have. This is our family. We're loving, brutish, opinionated, and dysfunctional like any other family," Grace said. "You were protecting your man."

"We aren't . . . I . . . um. I'm . . . we're actually . . ."

"Are ya or aren't you with Eoghan?"

"We haven't said anything official about it—"

"Yer face says you are."

"Whew. It's warm in here, isn't it?" Charlotte examined the silver handles of the brown cabinets above the black-and-stainless-steel stove in the updated kitchen. The pop of yellow from the stand mixer drew her eyes, helping her to avoid Grace's.

"He took you to Castle Leslie," Grace said. "I think you are. Even if you're not aware of it as yet."

Charlotte felt her brows knit. "What does Castle Leslie have to do with anything?"

Grace tilted her head. "Surely Eoghan has told you that if he ever found the person he wanted to spend his life with, he'd take her to Castle Leslie. He wants to get married there."

Charlotte's jaw locked, and her teeth ground with the pressure. She wasn't sure if she was still breathing, but by the dryness in her eyes, they were bulging.

"Sit down, dear, you look like you're about to fall over," Grace said and slid a circular stool directly under Charlotte's seat. "I'm assuming this is news?"

Charlotte nodded blankly, unable to recall when she'd actually sat down. The savory fragrances of the meal that had made her stomach growl earlier now nauseated her flipping stomach. She shouldn't have been surprised by what Grace had revealed. She and Eoghan had become intertwined in each other's lives. Why would the blossoming feelings between them be one sided?

Charlotte wanted to believe that she didn't care what his parents thought, but she remembered Yaya telling her about Grace's dig about Ayanna not being Irish in the traditional sense, and Eoghan had also not so gently alluded to the fact that his mother also wanted this girl to be Catholic. Charlotte, to her dismay, had to admit that she cared what Grace and Donal thought about her.

"How do you feel about that?"

"You seem nice enough, Charlotte, but I can't change what I've always wanted for my son. I do want him to be happy. That is what matters most to a mother, but I don't pretend to have modern values. It's not so easy to abandon or bury a dream that I've always had for his future."

"Understood."

What the hell did I expect? Grace and Donal's blessing? No, but she hadn't expected Grace to tell her what Castle Leslie meant to Eoghan only to knock her down with the fact that she wasn't good enough for him.

"Well, it looks like we're all done in here," Charlotte said, sliding off the stool, the stress in her body concentrated in her thighs as she stood. "I should get back to Eoghan." She started to make her way toward the living room and Eoghan.

"Thanks for your help," Grace said. "And for coming."

"My pleasure." Charlotte nodded. What was she supposed to say? *Thanks for telling me that I'll never be good enough for your son?*

"Let's go find the boys," Grace said and put one hand on Charlotte's shoulder and carried a container of food in the other.

Charlotte didn't expect the gesture and was comforted by it.

Charlotte and Grace found Donal and Eoghan deep in conversation in the corridor between the living and dining rooms. They stopped abruptly when they saw her and Grace approach. Eoghan offered her a tight smile, and Donal, with hands on his hips, nodded. Grace guided her to the living room.

Charlotte didn't know what to make of the situation, but she hoped that Donal hadn't mowed Eoghan down and had given him a chance to speak his mind.

"They'll be done soon," Grace assured her and handed her the container of food. "This is for you and Eoghan."

"Oh." Charlotte took the glass container with the blue lid.

"We'll be in the city for Eoghan's game in two weeks. Do you think we can meet for tea or lunch?" Grace said.

"Yes," Charlotte said, surprised by both Grace's suggestion and her own response.

"Ready to go?" Eoghan asked her.

"Yeah." Charlotte recognized the abrupt exit. They had to get back to Dublin, but they could have stayed a little longer for Eoghan to spend more time with his family.

Charlotte reviewed the events of the evening as Eoghan drove her back to her place. The darkness outside threatened to blacken the thread of hope she still clung to within.

"I know you think tonight didn't go well—"

She oscillated her head to him. "Didn't go well? Eoghan, if dinner was a natural disaster, it'd be a tornado. You were there, right?"

The steering wheel creaked under the pressure of his grip. "I warned you that my folks were tough, but I guess experiencing them is altogether different." He sighed. "They're not bad people, just set in their ways."

"I'm glad that you stood up to your father. I didn't mean to start an argument."

"Then why did you say those things or ask my father those questions? You had to know that he'd be frustrated."

Charlotte didn't miss the accusatory tone in his voice. "You know me, Eoghan. I speak my mind ninety percent of the time. I apologized to your father because I really was sorry. You're blaming me for sticking up for you?"

"No."

"Yes, you are," she said plainly.

He combed his fingers through his hair. "All I wanted to do was have a good dinner and have them get to know you."

"And we had a delicious dinner that your mom prepared, and they got to know me, whether they liked me or not."

"I'm sorry, this isn't the way I planned for this to go."

"Me either."

They drove the roadways back to her apartment in silence until they reached the entrance of her building.

"Do you want me to come up?" he asked.

That he expressed doubt squeezed her heart. "Let's talk tomorrow. It's been a long day, and you have early practice tomorrow." She wanted nothing more than his arms around her, but what was the endgame? His dad hated her influence in Eoghan's life, and his mother wanted Eoghan to be with a completely different person. Not only that, but Eoghan was a celebrity football player in Ireland. He had a life here. Charlotte had only come for an assignment, to fulfill a contract. Did she plan on staying after that contract was over? If she was honest and being real, the outlook was bleak.

"Umm, all right then," he said softly. "Till tomorrow."

He opened the door for her.

"Good night." He grabbed her hand. "We're all right, then?"

Her face couldn't quite crack a full smile. "Yeah, Eoghan. We're all right."

Upstairs in her apartment, she sat down and wondered if the words she'd spoken to him when they'd parted were true. He cared deeply for her, but would that be enough to overcome the many obstacles in their way? Her contract was ending, and she was free to return to the States and keep building Seam and Sole. Would she have the courage to let Eoghan go? Did she have to? Did she want to? Castle Leslie had taken on a completely different meaning, and she couldn't be sure if Eoghan bringing her there truly meant what his mom had said or if he'd taken her there so she could see the sights. Her heart told her it was the former.

She full-body sighed as she sat at her desk and checked her email. The one marked invitation couldn't possibly be real. Then she checked her phone messages and found she'd also gotten a voice mail from the executive assistant of the owner of the Portuguese national team. He wanted to meet with her.

Chapter 22

A few days later, Charlotte stepped out of the apartment, intrigued by what might happen to her next. She'd crossed all her t's and dotted her i's and was part of a campaign that would give her not only international visibility that couldn't be beaten but also an opportunity to take Seam and Sole to a level that would put her company in a class of its own.

She arrived in the seaside village of Dalkey at the house of the owner of the Portugal team, who she'd met briefly after the big game. Little had she known that she'd soon be in his home, a European-style mansion, to discuss business. The message from his assistant had been cryptic yet enticing enough to bloom her curiosity, and it was just the distraction she needed to help her cope with the disharmony between her and Eoghan when last they'd seen each other.

No matter what happened, she'd known she'd go even if just to find out what he wanted.

"Ms. Bowman. So glad you could make it." As far as silver foxes went, Conrad Mercury landed in her top five, along with Djimon Hounsou, Anderson Cooper, Idris Elba, and Daniel Dae Kim. He'd only said one line to her, and already she'd been exposed to his stealth persuasion.

"Mr. Mercury. It's nice to see you again."

"I hope you weren't too alarmed by the invite or our meeting place. I feel most comfortable tucked away here, and neither of us need have the press speculating."

"I'm okay. Thank you for being thoughtful. It would seem very strange for me to be meeting with the Irish national team's fiercest rival."

His friendly smile further disarmed her. "Please," he said as he offered her a seat at a table for four by a majestic bow window with a view of the pergolas, maintained lawns, and green bushes trimmed to perfection, as well as a small fountain and benches overlooking viewpoints of their own that she imagined burst with color in the spring and summer.

She took a seat. "How can I help you?"

"I love what you've done with the cleats for Ireland. I'd really like you to do something like that for our team. Your contract with that team is coming to an end, is it not?"

"How do you know that?" Charlotte asked.

He chuckled. "Owners talk. So do their staff, as do their players."

So much for privacy. "Oh, I see."

"They have their shoe, and you don't need to stay here in Ireland when you are free to go to Portugal."

He made the suggestion so nonchalantly that she just stared at him for a minute. This was not what she'd expected at all. He was offering her, for all intents and purposes, a job.

"So you're offering me a job?" She wanted to make sure that she was crystal clear what he was asking. Now that she'd spent so much time with Eoghan and the team, from top to bottom, she felt part of them. Loyalty started to gnaw at her, as well as the question of whether this was a good idea.

"Not only a job but a job with Portugal, my dear. One of the most successful teams in the league. A team that is known around the world tenfold to Ireland."

"You're serious?"

He gave her that elegant billion-dollar smile again that seemed to make everything feel like business as usual. This was big, huge, and something she could have only dreamed of months ago. Now, with her feet firmly in the football world with raving success, the offer sounded like a natural next step for her. Then why did she feel so off? It was only when she saw the image of Eoghan's crooked smile as he flopped around on Beast that she thought maybe this was something that wasn't the best for her. But how could she knowingly pass up a great opportunity when all she had wanted to do was make Seam and Sole more recognized, more valuable, more successful? *Cut the bullshit. You want to be more recognized, more valuable, and more successful.* Given the feelings that swarmed inside her, was that what she still wanted? Didn't she have that already? Had things changed? The guys in Ireland had become her adoptive family, had made her feel welcomed and most of all protected when she'd moved here. She thought of Pippin and Lance, Patrick, Clive, Ronin, and the lot of them. They recognized her talent and wanted her creative touch on their cleats. Management, too, which she knew wasn't always so keen to get into the low-level business of designs on shoes, had expressed their approval. How would they feel if she took a job with their rivals? She was a natural protector and advocate, and she still felt some loyalty to the men who'd become her friends.

The only reason for the dilemma swarming inside her was if she was considering saying yes to Conrad Mercury. "This is a big deal and something that I really need to think about. I have a good situation here and colleagues that I respect."

"Understandable," he said. "But again, your contract will soon be over. Perhaps you have something else lined up that I'm unaware of?"

She didn't.

He continued, "I will give you some time to think about it, but not too long. In two weeks, I'd like you to come to my country and meet with everyone. This way, you can get a better understanding of the greatness that you'd be a part of and tradition that spans over a century."

"So what was this?" She spun the glass of wine by the stem. "A prescreening?"

He leaned back his chair the way that one did when one was the king of one's castle and in charge. "I had to warm you up somehow. I've never met a woman who didn't appreciate the finer things when presented. Wine that you've barely touched, exceptional food, and being waited on because you're special. This is only the tip of the iceberg if you were to come and be a part of our team," he said. "Here is something else to consider. Whatever your compensation, we'll double it. Are you interested?"

She pondered what saying yes would mean. It meant making a commitment. A commitment to think about leaving Ireland, her new friends, and her new life, but most of all, it meant leaving Eoghan. Her stomach did flips.

"Are you all right, Ms. Bowman?" Conrad asked, getting up from his seat to aid her. "You look like you're going to be sick."

"No, I'm fine." She tried to shrug off the feelings rising inside her. "I haven't had much to eat."

With a wave of his hand, people appeared. "Let's move to the next course and bring Ms. Bowman some peppermint tea. Might that help, Charlotte?" He checked in with her.

"Yes. That would be great. Thank you," she said to both him and the butler taking the order. She remembered the time she and Ayanna had first arrived at Purchase House and she'd met Eoghan and Shane. She'd seen firsthand how the other half lived. That hadn't been her first exposure to the high life. It was all around her in New York and when she traveled. She'd get a taste of it here and there, even with Seam and Sole breaking a million dollars in revenue. Now she was being offered just that, a chance to step into that lifestyle by accepting a position with Portugal. She'd be a fool not to take this or at least consider it. So she made her choice.

"I'll consider it."

"Excellent. All your accommodations will be made, and someone will be in touch."

"Just like that, huh?" she asked.

"Just like that." Conrad smiled.

Was this how it happened behind the scenes? She was presented with an opportunity, and then just like that everything was done, and she was taken care of? There were times when she had thought about this, but this wasn't the same. She just didn't want to lose out on an opportunity like her mom had done so many times before. She wanted no regrets of missing things that could've made her great. So she would consider this opportunity seriously, even if it meant breaking hearts, including her own.

A demitasse cup and saucer, definitely fine china, were put down before her, and she traded her long-stemmed glass of wine for a cup of tea with peppermint-scented steam floating to her nose and calming her senses.

"Tell me, Charlotte, what brought you to Ireland in the first place? Why did you decide to leave New York, which is a hub for all things successful in business?"

"I wanted to regain full control of my company. It all came down to me and my investors wanting to take the business in different directions," she said, thinking back to months ago, when she'd felt backed into a corner in her own company. "We had different opinions, and the problems weren't easily rectified. I decided it was best to buy them out to take the company in the direction of my vision. Luckily an opportunity presented itself, and I was able to finally get a prototype of a cleat I'd been working on off the ground."

"The stars aligned."

"I guess you can say something like that."

"What else would you call it?" Conrad asked.

"Being prepared for an opportunity at the right time, which doesn't always happen." She blushed, listening to her own words. "The stars aligned."

He raised a mischievous eyebrow, as well as his glass, as if he understood her need to not be too easily figured out. She hated when she felt like she wasn't a hard worker and like she'd gotten her shit by luck. She worked too damn hard to let that slide. But even a man like Conrad Mercury saw that drive in her, or else she wouldn't be here.

Servers brought silver trays and covered dishes to the table, distributing them evenly in front of both her and Conrad. The fragrances of piping-hot meats and fresh, yeasty baked bread and the potency of the finest herbs and spices filled her nose.

The trays were uncovered, and her eyes feasted on the variety of food that had been brought out.

"Is all of this just for us two?" she asked.

"Of course. Only the finest for a prospect." Conrad again fanned away the hovering staff, picked up a silver slotted spoon, and served her. "Brisket?"

"Yes, please," she said.

He moved to the next dish, sweet potatoes smothered in a creamy sauce. "We didn't know exactly what you liked, so if there is something you don't want to eat, it's okay. The staff will take care of it and enjoy it later."

She nodded. "I appreciate the effort."

"Please help yourself." He handed her the plate he'd been meticulously organizing for her.

She handled a pair of silver claw tongs, taking several asparagus surrounded by baby onions and a sprig of rosemary. She placed them in the only empty space on her plate. The only time she didn't like seeing space on a plate was during Thanksgiving, when the sides of mashed potatoes, macaroni and cheese, collard greens, and green beans filled up her plate.

"You have a quiet tenacity about you, Charlotte," Conrad said, serving himself.

"It's not always very quiet." She chuckled. She had a big personality, especially when next to someone quieter and more introverted. She tried to be her genuine self, most of the time, which was sometimes loud and big and misinterpreted, but she'd long since put her middle school fears about showing who she really was away. She was celebrated by those she loved, who never asked her to constrain her big ideas, big personality, and big mouth. Did she have it perfectly down? No. Sometimes, she cared too much about representing her entire race and not leaving things worse for the next brown-skinned girl. There was always room for growth.

"Your drive is what got you here. In football, that's a quality worth possessing. Is it a wonder you fit in so nicely?"

She hadn't thought about it that way, but now that he mentioned it, she did seem like a great fit. She remembered being on the pitch with Eoghan, and even though she'd never coached or played or spent much time in the sport, working with him and the team felt natural. She had a lot to figure out, including the rules and the culture. She felt more and more at home. Now she tried to stuff her emotions down, the ones that would have her make decisions because of what others would think of her instead of what she needed to do for herself.

No. She couldn't come this far only to let things get twisted and manipulated by a false sense of loyalty to people she hadn't even known three months ago.

"Yes, I'll think about it and meet your team in Portugal, Conrad."

"I knew you'd make the right choice." Conrad raised his glass to her, and she returned the gesture. For someone who'd just landed a great job offer, she didn't quite feel like celebrating.

Chapter 23

The crisp scent of freshly cut and leveled grass filled Eoghan's nose as he performed his drill. He needed Shane to practice with him. To push him. Normally, after he'd had a rough couple of days, a session with the lads would refocus his mind. He hadn't seen Charlotte since they'd had dinner. They both needed space, he guessed, but what would things look like on the other end of this? He had to admit that he could have done a better job of putting her at ease after the altercation between them and his parents. He had hoped that the more time they spent with Charlotte, the more they'd love her. That night, he'd wanted to hold her in his arms and let her know that he was with her. That he loved her. But the disharmony with his family at the dinner table had followed them like a storm cloud about to rain on the parade they'd enjoyed these past few months.

"Run the ball," Gaff yelled, then did a hand gesture to let them know, from the sidelines, what positions he wanted. Eoghan was pent up and loved the shoe that Charlotte had developed. He felt ready to play, and not just for the first half but for a full game. He had to admit that something was different. He felt lighter and more spirited. He hadn't lost any weight, but his muscles remembered this level of play, and he went for it. He was in the zone, cutting around guys with the ball and heading for Pippin. His mate was the best, but so was he, and at this moment he didn't care who guarded the goal—he'd make the point.

He could see the change in Pippin as he approached. More serious, ready to block him at any cost. *All right, mate. I'm coming for ya.* Right and left he went, still dodging his teammates, riding on the magical wind carrying him. He was close enough to go for it. With the might of the gods, he faked a kick one way but then quickly dodged. Pippin corrected his defense, but it didn't matter, because the ball slipped into the net, centimeters from his friend's hands.

Eoghan held up a hand in acknowledgment as he ran. He looked over at his coach, who nodded approvingly. He hadn't seen Gaffer do that since he'd been back. He didn't need the approval. His body and his bones told him that finally, after all the pain of recovery and the doubt of training and the confidence that had seemed to slip out of his hands like sand, finally he was truly and unequivocally back.

An hour later, he saw Danai catwalk on the sidelines of the field. No matter who you were, you couldn't take your eyes off the confidence. He wore a charcoal suit that was loose and flowing and a white wrap draped around his shoulders. Eoghan was certain that this was the perfect moment to say *werk*, like he'd heard both Charlotte and Danai use. Danai definitely strutted to his own fabulousness, and Eoghan couldn't help but smile.

"I mean, really," Lance complained, palming the dark-brown stubble on his shaved head. "Is it me, or does he confuse your sexuality every time he comes through with his glamour?"

Eoghan howled at Lance's joke, but he completely understood.

Pippin jogged over to them. "What's this? Conference now?"

"Lance is confused."

"About?" Pippin asked.

"Danai makes him wonder." Callum winked.

Pippin chuckled.

"You know what I mean, mate," Lance explained.

"He's too much woman for you," Callum, a short midfielder with pale skin and jet-black hair gelled and sculpted to perfection, said as he playfully pushed Lance's shoulder.

"It's not just me, then?" Lance said, relieved.

Lance would be waiting awhile for any admission.

"He reminds me of that cat. What's his name?" Callum tapped his forehead a few times. "That Black bloke that does the gala." Callum snapped his fingers, also several times.

"You mean the Met Gala?" Lance said.

"That's the one. What's that guy's name. He acts and sings—maybe he wrote a book."

"Port something or other?"

"Billy Porter," Eoghan said.

"Yeah. Right," Pippin confirmed.

"That's the one. Man, that dude's got some style," Callum said.

Lance shrugged.

Eoghan enjoyed it when Danai was around just for the sheer pleasure of his teammates' banter. But where was Charlotte? Evidence proved that she was avoiding him. She'd been acting weird, and the thing was that she didn't talk much about it, only spent less and less time with him. Sure, her contract was coming to an end, but was not seeing him so easy for her? He'd gone down the list of possible reasons, but nothing had happened past their usual annoyances, tiffs, and squabbles that was enough for her to distance herself from him. Perhaps Danai had some insight.

"Gentlemen," Danai greeted. "Hi, Lance," he teased.

Lance turned more scarlet than his workout had already made him. "Good day to ya." Then he was off to run laps.

"That boy is fine," Danai said. "I have a wee crush on him."

"He's a good lad," Callum announced.

"I come bearing gifts. Your final designs for your signature shoes are ready. Dodger did me a solid and put them in you all's lockers. Eoghan, we have your regular cleats for all surfaces: turf, grass, indoor, et cetera. Should you have any problems, please let me know. Visiting the manufacturer's is my new favorite pastime. I do need them back today, so if everything looks brilliant, then make sure you sign off and either drop them off or have someone send them to my 'office.'" Danai air quoted, and his cologne perfumed their immediate space with English oak and hazelnut. Charlotte and Danai didn't have an office, per se, but rather a large conference room where they worked.

"Quality," Callum said. A gust of wind from the south rolled through, testing Callum's gelled hair, and Eoghan swore the structure atop his head moved just a centimeter.

"Sound," Pippin said, slapping his gloves together.

"Nice one," Lance called from a distance.

"Clean ears, that one," Pippin said.

"Where's Charlotte?" Eoghan asked.

Danai's perfect visage softened. "She had a conflict, so she sent me instead. What? You're not happy to see me?" he asked.

"Always," Eoghan said. "Just asking."

"I'm sure she's just busy."

"You mean you don't know?" He couldn't help feeling that perhaps Danai was holding some information back.

"I do know, but I thought that perhaps it's less of a blow if I told you I don't know." Danai gave him a half smile that spoke of duty and loyalty to his boss.

Eoghan quickly checked on the color of the pitch. "It's just that I haven't seen a lot of her these past few days. I'm wondering if something is up that I should be aware of. Normally she'd come by herself to deliver this kind of news."

"Mmm-hmm. You're not wrong, but I try to stay out of grown folks' business," he said.

"Gotcha." He must have looked pitiful, because Danai took pity on him.

"You know what? She is probably going to fire me for this, but I like the trajectory of this international love story. You've shaken things up in a good way, so . . ." He leaned in. "You didn't hear it from me, but she has something goin' on. I think you should make her talk to you. I want to protect her, but I feel like if I do that in this situation, I'd actually be doing her a grand disservice."

"So there is something, then?"

"What did I just say? Stop being pedestrian and be the man she needs. I can't serve you on a silver platter. Do the work."

"I didn't think I was—"

"You were," Danai said.

"Umm . . . okay."

"I have somewhere to be. Toodles, darling," Danai said, and as quickly and glamorously as he'd swooped in, he swooped out.

After practice Eoghan headed to do the rest of his schedule for the day. He had a photo shoot for his sponsors. His agent was already there waiting for him and quickly mentioned the food that they'd prepared, knowing he'd be famished after hours of practice. The way his stomach growled, he would've been better off going out for a bite with the lads after practice instead of waiting to get to the photo shoot to eat. Food wasn't the only thing on his mind—he still wanted to know what was going on with Charlotte. Before he headed inside, he texted her.

Eoghan: Didn't see you with Danai today. Nothing's wrong, no?

Charlotte: All good. Busy with stuff I need to get done for New York.

His thumbs drafted several follow-up comments and questions before he settled on one.

Eoghan: Dinner later?

Charlotte: . . .

Her working response had him doubting the proposition because he had gotten used to seeing her regularly. He wanted to tease her, smell her, and be close to her like they'd done at her apartment, at Castle Leslie, and on their walks to the bar.

Charlotte: Pretty tied up for most of the day. Might be wiped later. Let you know?

His heart did a weird thump. Not the kind that he got when he was with her but a feeling that he'd never cared about in the past, when things in a relationship headed south. That he might be losing her.

Eoghan: Grand

Eoghan: Gran

Eoghan: Gra

Eoghan: Gr

Eoghan: G

Eoghan: . . .

He gave a thumbs-up emoji and pocketed his phone and walked over to the next station to be dressed.

The stylist displayed a clothing rod with an array of choices for him. He liked sophisticated brands with a street feel for his leisure wear. He admired how the stylist had put together the various thermals, jerseys, leggings, and footwear for him. Many designers wanted him to be an ambassador for their brands, but because he liked many different styles, he was happy displaying the clothes at an event or party but not so much being tied to one brand. He checked the mirror and nodded in approval at the way the white-and-black ensemble complemented his dark hair and skin that would be more usual for an Italian man than an Irishman. Happily, makeup was quick and light, with the artist applying just enough for the photo.

The active-soccer-wear brand was a sponsor, and he'd likely leave with loads of complimentary clothes. He eyed a jersey that he could see Charlotte cuddling up in during the evening with her glass of wine. He was often on trend, and currently, tracksuits—by designers from unknown to haute couture—were all the rage and his favorite go-to. He also worked out, ran, and practiced. Sometimes he'd have to be in uniform, but sometimes when he ran balls with Shane or Pippin, he dressed in whatever made him feel good. Naturally they all displayed brand names simply by nature of being some of the top footballers in Ireland and getting sent random wear.

"Let's set you up here, Eoghan," the photographer said before positioning him where she wanted and taking candids of him as he modeled to music by the Foo Fighters, one of his favorite bands. The songs put him in a better mood than the one he had walked in with. The mood where he worried about Charlotte. He allowed himself to be free and sometimes a little bit wild with his movements. All caught on camera. Since he'd returned from the States, his life had been much tamer than it used to be. He had attended a party or two but found them to be a complete bore after he'd had several drinks and made the rounds. That was when he'd shown the new leaf he'd turned and hung out more with the lads or at home, and he hadn't regretted the change ever since. If he had to go in the future, maybe Charlotte would like to go with him. His lips curled at the thought.

"Love the smile, Eoghan," the photographer said. Charlotte's effect on him was also caught on camera.

Eoghan tossed a football up in the air, smiling and angling as the lights flashed. The shoot was coming to a close, and he was glad to be done. They'd already gotten a million shots of him.

"This one would be great for the cover," the photographer said back to an assistant, who scribbled down notes as quickly as possible.

"Last one . . ." The photographer clicked several more times. "And that's a wrap. Thank you, Eoghan."

"Anytime," he said.

He was led to a table where T-shirts and footballs were stacked. Eoghan signed them for the fans while his agent networked in the distance. Eoghan continued to talk and chat with those around him, and then Martim Santos arrived at the shoot. Eoghan knew the schedules were compact, so while he finished up, Martim got ready.

"*Olá*, Eoghan," Martim said.

"Hiya." Eoghan kept it brief. Upbeat.

Martim did his usual grandstanding with the team. It worked for him, and his fans loved it, especially the ladies. He was a good-looking bloke, which was another reason why he'd been selected for the shoot. Like him.

In between takes Martim moseyed over to him. No good in his features. "I hear that one of your business partners is jumping ship to come work with us. Did you hear?"

Eoghan didn't want to bite, but he did. "Nope."

"Yeah, Charlotte Bowford or something. The shoe designer. She's coming to work for our team in Portugal. Thanks, mate. I hear you're the one who brought her here."

Eoghan seethed. "I think you're mistaken. And it's Bowman."

"I have it on good authority that your boot designer is about to sign a contract with us. Apparently, she had dinner with Conrad at his villa, and he offered her a sweet deal," he said. "I thought you two were close. Really close, if any of the rumors are true."

"Sure, you're very interested in the gossip instead of the truth." Eoghan was heated, not only because this guy brought doubt into his mind about Charlotte but also because if any part of it was true, then what was the status of the truth and loyalty between him and Charlotte?

"Doubt I have it wrong, but I'm sure you'll ask her."

"I plan to. Till then, feck off," Eoghan said.

A wicked smile plastered Martim's face as he fanned Eoghan off.

Eoghan had intended to give Charlotte her space. He knew from experience that crowding a woman who craved space only ended with an argument or a breakup. The last word bugged him. He couldn't deny that he'd claimed Charlotte as his, but when had it happened? Since when did he require that she talk to him if something was up and if she was considering a position with someone other than the national team, let alone a whole other country?

His confusion baffled him, but one thing was for sure: he'd get to the bottom of this.

Charlotte buttered her arms and legs as part of her bedtime ritual. As she rubbed the cream into her skin, she thought about the choices she was making and all the people who were involved. "Is This Love," a remake of Bob Marley's song by Corinne Bailey Rae, played softly in the background. Charlotte loved this album, and it stayed in her playlist rotation.

An ugly knock sounded on her door. She didn't know who that could possibly be at this hour. She looked through the peephole, and there was Eoghan, red faced and agitated. She opened the door, and the way he shifted from foot to foot confirmed that he had loads on his mind.

"Hey," she said.

"Can I come in?" he asked, his fitted jeans and gray hoodie making him look bigger than normal.

"Yes, of course," she said, letting him in.

He strode inside and paced as if energy might just explode through the top of his head or maybe even from his ears.

"When were you going to tell me about this new deal that you have with Portugal? I thought that things were going great here in Ireland for you, and now you're leaving? What was all this about, just some stepping-stone for you?"

"Wow. First of all, I don't even know how you heard about it, two, I haven't made a decision yet, and three, everything is a stepping-stone. Someone came to me with an offer, and I'm doing what any business-woman with an apparel company whose contract is up would do. I'm considering it. Seriously," she said.

"That you're considering it *is* the problem. This is how it is with you? You just make up your mind and go on without any consideration for all the people who open their hearts to you."

She hated the look on his face. That look of disappointment, like she owed him something. Like she should be making decisions based on his feelings or what was best for him. This was everything she'd wanted to avoid.

No, I need to do what is best for me.

"Listen, I think we need to have this conversation when we both cool down a bit."

"I'm cool as a cucumber, love," he said, clenching his fists.

"Eoghan, I know you care about me, and I care about you too."

"You're not leaving. That's the end of it," he blurted.

"Excuse me?" She crossed her arms, and attitude shifted her hips.

"You're not taking the offer."

A wicked chuckle escaped her. "First of all, that's not your decision. You know what? I don't have to explain myself to you. I'll do what I need to do in order to advance my business."

"So that's all this was to you? Some agreement? Just a contract? Once it's done, it's done. Cut all ties and move on."

"Whoa! Where do you get off judging me for anything I've done or a legitimate deal? Instead of conversing with me like you want a real compromise or resolution and telling me how you feel, you storm in here, commanding me, like you have any control over what I do. News flash: you don't," she said.

"Had I known that you'd ever truly consider leaving, I never would've . . ." He cut himself off so abruptly she felt like she got whiplash in the process.

"Never would've what?" she asked. She'd never seen him like this. His anger pissed her off, but the redness in his eyes shredded her heart. "Eoghan?"

"Do what you're going to do. Leave. At this point it doesn't matter. You go on and do it then."

"Eoghan?" Every bone in her body called to him, but he blew out of her apartment with not even so much as a glance back.

She tried to swallow the frog in her throat, but she couldn't, and it came out in fits that only an ugly cry could provide.

Chapter 24

Charlotte stuffed her Louis Vuitton weekender for her trip to Portugal. Each piece of clothing felt like a weight on her heart, pulling her down and deeper into despair. Ayanna was in town and had come by with takeout from an Indian place for dinner and to help Charlotte pack for her trip. Charlotte needed more than food and help with her luggage. She needed a magic wand to fix all the areas that had gotten fucked to high heaven in the last forty-eight hours.

"I can't believe it. You just got to Dublin, and now you're thinking about leaving for Portugal. I thought that you were considering staying here. I mean, I know we didn't have it all figured about how or where you'd stay in Ireland, but I thought we'd hooked you. Maybe if I were here more when you first arrived, you'd feel more like staying longer. I feel like you haven't given the place a chance."

"First of all, I'm going for a meeting. I'm only going to be gone a few days."

"But if things go well, you'll be coming back to pack it up."

"Yeah." Charlotte sighed. "And what are you talking about? I love it here." She picked up the scarf Yaya had bought for her last year during her first trip to Ireland. "I've had fun getting to know the place. The team, both the players and the businesspeople, have been amazing to me. I couldn't have asked for a better experience. I had many reasons for wanting to get out of New York, whether that was for a short time or a long time."

Ayanna gripped her by the shoulders and shook her. "Then why are you leaving?"

"Because I got a great offer that I'm trying to consider. You forget that my contract here is over. I'd usually have my next steps all lined up already. Thankfully Conrad Mercury offered me something that can help Seam and Sole."

"Is that the only reason you're leaving?"

"What other reason is there?"

"Is it because of Eoghan?"

"Fuck no," Charlotte blurted, though the jury was still out on whether or not that was true. "I mean . . . I have a chance to get paid double, do more challenging work, and live in one of the greatest cities in Europe. It has nothing to do with Eoghan."

"Maybe it should."

"Why? So I can make decisions for him instead of for me when he can change his mind on a dime about . . . whatever it is we're doing?" Charlotte remembered Eoghan's words. *Had I known that you'd ever truly consider leaving, I never would've . . .* "You know how flaky men are today. Their loyalty changes with the wind or whatever new ass they get a whiff of." Charlotte threw down the scarf she'd refolded several times in the last minute.

"Not even close," Ayanna said. "You care about him. I've seen you two together, and might I remind you that I was the first person to say that he could use someone like you? I was right, wasn't I?"

"Oh, please." Charlotte huffed.

"No, really. He's changed from the first person we met last year, but you have too. I know it's scary for you to admit your feelings for him, but it's worth it to try."

Charlotte's heart raced. "Can we leave him out of this? He's made it clear that he doesn't want to talk to me."

"Nope."

"Quit it already, Yaya," Charlotte said, gripping her hips. "Why aren't you happy for me?"

The battle of the hands on hips between them commenced when Ayanna mimicked the gesture. "Now, you know that I am happy for you. If this is what you really want, I'm thrilled."

"But?"

"You seem upset," Ayanna said.

"I'm not upset." Charlotte wiped the wetness that rimmed her eyes from the dryness in the apartment. At least that was what she told herself.

"You're always chasing success, Charlotte. Don't get me wrong—I think a bit of that is great. I'm the pot calling the kettle black, but you literally let it get in the way of everything. Our trip to Ireland last year, dropping your life in Harlem to come here, and now you are jetting off to Portugal to not only consider a new contract but one with the rivals of the team you've come to love."

Charlotte's body stiffened. "That's not fair, Yaya. I had to do all those things for Seam and Sole."

"Isn't working for yourself supposed to give you a life you want? One with time and freedom to actually enjoy it and the people in your life? I feel like you're straying further and further away from that, all because of this fear that you're going to miss something and regret it later."

"Exactly. I don't want to have regrets. Remember, I grew up with regretting every opportunity Mom passed up. I don't want to be that person."

"Did your mom regret it, though? She always seemed happy to me."

"I know she did." Charlotte's confidence wavered.

"Yes, but have you ever directly asked her if she did?" Ayanna persisted.

Charlotte hadn't. "In my recollection? No."

"I just . . . you know what? Never mind."

"Girl, if you don't speak up . . . ," Charlotte growled.

Yaya draped an arm around her shoulders. "I'm just saying that maybe you should talk to her. It might help; maybe it won't."

"You're so annoying," Charlotte said.

"Yes, but if I can't tell you the truth, then we've got problems," Ayanna said. "I only want you to be happy, and if I can help you through the sludge to get there, then I'm doing my duty as your bestie."

Charlotte plopped down on the bed. "I don't even know what I'm doing anymore." What was she doing? She'd never been so conflicted over a business deal in the past, and it made everything heavy, like moss over rocks in a foggy swamp.

"You either need food or a nap. Which one would you like? Either way I'm here for you," Ayanna said.

"I need both, but I have to finish packing, so leftover saag paneer and a samosa sound like a better idea," Charlotte said.

"Coming right up."

"I'll pour us some more wine," Charlotte said.

"Let's pop open some sparkling. I may not like the idea of you leaving, but we are still celebrating your opportunity. No matter what." Ayanna hugged her and then left to make her a plate.

"Oooh, you fancy," Charlotte called to her, and they shared a laugh. As she poured, she thought about Ayanna's words about Eoghan and about her mom. She'd tried to contact Eoghan because at a basic level, if he was anything to her, it was a friend, and she hoped they could keep that friendship no matter what she chose. However, he'd answered neither her text nor her calls, and that was destroying her inside.

"Here you go, madam." Ayanna started to hand her a plate of food, then stopped.

Charlotte could only imagine what her friend thought when she saw her silently weeping into her wineglass.

"Oh, Char." Ayanna put the plate down and, like any good friend, held her close and let her have her cry.

◆ ◆ ◆

That evening, Charlotte chewed her lip as she summoned the courage to call her mom in the States. Ayanna had provoked a few issues that Charlotte had been carrying around with her, and though she might need to work out her issues with a professional, at minimum she could approach her mom.

"Hey, Char," her mother sang when she greeted her.

"Hey, Mom. What are you up to?"

"You know, this and that on a Sunday. We just came back from brunch."

"At Hothouse Hotcakes?"

"Yes, you know how we love that place," her mom raved. "It was nice for us to head down to your neighborhood. It reminded us of brunch with you and the girls."

"Aww, that's sweet. I hope you sent the owner my regards."

"Girl, you know they're always asking about you." Her mother's laughter felt warm and loving like it had always done. "'How she doin' over there?' and 'When she coming back?'"

"That's kind of them."

"What are you up to, dear? You were telling me about the team last we spoke. You sounded like a little family. I'm so happy you have that, Char. It makes being in another country so much more inviting."

"Well, I actually got another offer in Portugal to work there with another team. If I take it, I'll be leaving in a month or so and moving there."

"Really?" her mom asked.

"You sound disappointed."

"It's just that you've only been there a little while, Char, and you sounded happy. And you talked about that one player in particular. That Eoghan fella. I thought things were going well for you."

Charlotte sighed.

"I know that sigh. Okay, tell me what's happening."

Charlotte told her mom about her offer and what it would mean. "I just don't want to miss out on an opportunity."

"I know. This is something that you often worry about," her mother said. "I don't know what me and your father did to make you worried about missing out on opportunities."

"You're joking, right?" Charlotte said.

"Explain your tone, young lady," her mother warned. "I can't see what we did but give you a loving home and exponential opportunities."

"You. You're the one who had the great talent, and you just squandered it."

"Squandered it? Char, that couldn't be further from the truth."

"You were always saying no to these great opportunities. You raised a smart kid and exposed me to so much. Of course I knew when people were calling for your expert opinion and when you declined full-time opportunities. Mom, you are so well known in your industry. Didn't you want more? Did you feel you missed out? Because I did and took on those feelings because I wanted to see you be great instead of settling—"

"Let me cut you off there before you hurt yourself," her mother said. "You are so lucky you are across the way, because I'd snatch you up to let you know just how angry I am at you right now."

"I—"

"Shut it and listen to me closely. I never settled. I settled into the life I've dreamed about since I was a girl, which was to find true and deep love and have a family of my own. When I had you, I was so happy that I finally had a family of my own. That was where I wanted to put all my energy, love, and creativity because I wanted you to be great."

"But Mom—"

"Little girl," her mother said in that tone that shut Charlotte up even from her haven in Ireland. "I am not sorry for my life. The only thing I'm sorry for is the fact that you only saw what I was saying no to and not what I was saying yes to, which was you and your dad. That is my work, my passion. I'm a grown woman who knew what I was doing. These regrets you think I have are your own creations."

Charlotte didn't know what to say. She fixed her mouth to say something, but what could she say?

"I will admit that I was glad that before you were born I had a little bit of adventure. I loved being an art dealer and the lifestyle because it allowed me to use my mind in different ways, which was great, but if they wanted me to do full time or assignments that took me from you and your father, that was a hard no, and my choice, and I never wanted more than that."

"I'm sorry, Mom. I didn't know. I thought we were a burden to you and keeping you from a fabulous life," Charlotte said.

"I wanted you to live a fabulous life, but I thought that I'd given you an example of how happy life was at home too."

"I guess I felt like I had to live life like I thought you would have wanted to. I can't believe I got it so wrong, Mom. I've been so wrong." Charlotte sniffled into the phone.

"Listen to me, Char. You have to do what makes you happy. Life isn't perfect and is filled with right and wrong turns, but it's what you make of them. You can't try to do everything right because you don't want to have regrets. Regrets and mistakes are inevitable. It's how we learn and grow. You know this. Everything didn't go perfectly with Seam and Sole. You had investors, and that went great for a while. Then you wanted to do things differently, but your original decision to have investors wasn't wrong. Right?"

"Right."

"You could have sulked about it, but you pulled yourself up and worked to find a solution on how to take Seam and Sole where you wanted it to go. Now you're in Ireland working for the national team. That wouldn't have happened if everything went perfectly in Harlem."

"You're right, Mom."

"You don't have to live life for me. I'm Gucci, like you youngins say." Charlotte had to laugh at that. "Do me a favor, Mommy? Don't use that word like that again, 'kay?"

Her mom laughed. "Listen, if you really want this new contract, go for it, but if it's not the direction you want to go, then by all means, you're allowed to change your mind."

"Thanks, Mom, but I do feel like I owe it to myself to at least see what it's about. Old habits die hard, but I've heard you," Charlotte said.

"I'm just glad that you're happy."

"Happiness is a state that fluctuates, darling. It's not permanent. It's what sits in your heart that's important. Like how I love you and your father more than anything on this earth."

Charlotte wiped her tears. "Are you trying to make me cry?"

"In a world that doesn't always want you to be great, Char, that's all I've ever wanted for you."

"Okay, woman. Now I'm going to need you to stop before I bawl my eyes out and I'm nowhere near you for a hug."

Her mom laughed.

"Where's Dad?"

"He left the room as soon as he heard 'little girl.' He knows when I'm about to serve it up."

Charlotte laughed at that. "We know who's boss."

"And don't ever forget," her mother said.

"Thanks for always being real with me, Mom."

"Love you, baby."

"Love you too."

Charlotte hung up. She felt like something had lifted, however light, even though she had other problems that weighed on her. Her argument and parting with Eoghan, her trip to Portugal, and the looming decision that umbrellaed her from any joy or certainty. A few hours ago, she'd felt she'd made her commitment, but confusion seemed to swarm around her. She'd hurt Eoghan, but she'd hurt herself, too, and now on the eve of her parting, she wondered if taking the contract in Portugal, even if she wanted it, would ultimately be worth it.

◆ ◆ ◆

Eoghan hadn't felt much like going out on the lash, but he'd definitely thrown back a few beers in the luxury confines of his apartment as he'd handled the controller on his gaming system. Happy to drown himself in a fantasy world while listening to shite chatter from Pippin and Shane. Inviting the lads over to distract him from his sullen experience was worth all the gold at the end of the rainbow.

"Feck all. This game is the worst," Pippin said and swigged from his beer bottle. His white turtleneck sweater matched most of the neutral decor.

"Bollocks," Shane said, adjusting his black jeans as he sat back against the couch cushions. "You can't play for shite is what it is."

Eoghan was glad to have his friends around, but every now and again, Charlotte popped into his mind. Had she left for Portugal yet? How long was she staying? He loved her, and she wanted to leave him. She'd reached out to him, but what more was there to say?

"Eoghan?" Shane nudged him.

"What?"

"For the fucking fifth time, yer up, mate," Pippin said, smacking his forehead.

"Where's your head, man?" Shane asked.

"Up Charlotte's arse." Pippin howled.

Eoghan threw a beer bottle at him.

Both Shane and Pippin ducked.

"You could've injured me," Pippin yelled, then took a more philosophical approach. "This must be serious."

Eoghan grabbed the controller without a word, and as he side-eyed his friends, he saw them exchanging looks.

Shane turned off the game, and a screen saver of an underwater scene played. "You're going to make yourself sick if you stay bottled up."

"Or injure your best mate with a fucking beer bottle. That'll be a nice one to tell Boyle or Walsh," Pippin said.

"Sorry," Eoghan said, the words sounding dopey and pathetic.

"What a terrible state." Shane shook his head at Pippin, who agreed. "So what was yer plan if we hadn't come by? Sulk in here on your own, drink yourself until you got banjaxed, all because you're avoiding talking to her?"

"Sounds about right," Eoghan said.

"How's that working out for you?" Pippin asked.

"It'll work out just fine if you turn the telly back on and let us play the game," Eoghan said.

"Why don't you just talk to her? Tell her how you feel," Shane suggested.

"What're you talking about?" Eoghan asked as if he didn't already know how his friends had figured him out and come by to support him.

"Eoghan."

"Feck all," he said. He went for another beer.

"I thought I'd seen it all when Shane was falling apart at the seams last year, but you're all mangled up over Charlotte, and she's only going away for a few days," Pippin said.

"And what if it's not a few days? What if she goes for good?" The thought alone made him want to bust out of his skin like something otherworldly.

"You won't talk to her, but it's clear the thought of her even leaving is fucking you up royally," Shane said, and Pippin was in bits.

Eoghan sank onto the L-shaped part of the couch. "I don't want her to go."

"Did you tell her that?" Shane asked. "Sure look, it's something that she might like to know, along with your other feelings."

Pippin nodded. "The eejit is correct."

Shane elbowed Pippin, and the two wrestled for a spell. Laughing like a pair of hyenas.

"She's like me in a lot of ways," Pippin said. "I miss the lads when I'm gone, but when other teams want me to play for them, whether it's in Spain or Nigeria, if the deal feels right, I'm going for it. It's nothing personal, and I've been able to keep my friendships."

"What's your point, Pip," Shane asked.

"One thing I always do is come back home," Pippin said.

Pippin's status normally trended toward good humor, but it was no wonder that he and Shane often found clarity when chatting over a beer.

"Well said, Pip," Shane said. "The question is, Did Eoghan give her a good enough reason to come back?"

"Seriously, though, mate. You need to express yourself. Charlotte's a gem. Just like Ayanna, and . . . wait a minute. Is there another one? For me?" Pippin asked.

"Ayanna has a sister."

"The uni brat? Same one that snogged Eoghan? Feeeeeeccck no," Pippin said. "I'll take my chances with Channing."

Both Eoghan and Shane groaned.

"Look, man," Shane said. "Charlotte is lovely and fit and all those things, but mostly she's funny, honest, has a good heart, and makes you happy."

"Get out!" Eoghan had reached his breaking point. The lads were meant to come over and distract him, not give him love advice.

"I think you overdid it," Pippin said to Shane.

"It's because he knows I'm right," Shane said, getting his coat, grabbing Pippin's, and throwing it to him.

"Sending us out into the cold, are you? What a friend," Pippin said.
"Talk to her," Shane said before Eoghan pushed them both out of his flat. He heard their complaints through the door. They were right. He hadn't told Charlotte how he felt, but that was because when things had looked serious between them, she'd freaked and pulled back. Eoghan felt in no better position than before his friends had come.

That night in his bedroom, Eoghan flicked one of two light switches, and a lamp by the bedside glowed onto the charcoal duvet, white sheets, and pillows. Naked, he slid under the covers. He held the sheets and charcoal duvet between his knees, picturing Charlotte there with him. As his cock grew rigid, he rubbed out the anger, the hurt, and the indecision, all while looking through the skylight trio on the slanted ceiling overhead. He knew that Charlotte was the only one he wanted to love.

Chapter 25

Charlotte stood in queue for a coffee at Dublin International Airport.

"An Irish coffee, please," she said. In Dublin she'd stopped asking for an Irish coffee because all coffee for the most part was just coffee. She smiled at the changes the place had made in her in just a short amount of time. Picking up fresh fruit at the market, hanging out with the team at the Paddy Bath, and eating an Irish breakfast on the weekend.

She tried not to doubt her choices. She owed it to herself to go and take the better offer. The one that offered her more money, more visibility, a longer contract. But Ireland and the boys had grown on her and meant more to her than she'd ever imagined. Now she was leaving them. When she'd come to Dublin, she'd thought that Ayanna would be the only reason for her to make a transition here, but she'd forged her own way, made inroads, showed them what she could do, and they'd taken her in. Now she betrayed them for coin.

She released a big sigh and welcomed the first sips of coffee. She needed to stay alert for her flight, when what she really wanted to do was close her eyes and forget about what she was doing. Winning shouldn't feel this shitty. What did that say about her? Had she lost her touch, gotten soft, opened her heart?

The image of Eoghan's face when she'd said what she had still stuck, whether her eyes were open or closed.

The game with Liechtenstein played on the big screen as she sat down by the gate. "Great."

She didn't need any serendipitous signs right now. The guys were playing, and she would always root for them, but come hell or high water, she was going to get on the plane. If she didn't, what would that say about her? What would she be admitting to herself about being here? About how much Eoghan had come to mean to her?

"Fuck," she said under her breath. Things would be better if the airport was where she really wanted to be, but honestly, if she could bend time, she'd be at the stadium, too, cheering for a win.

"And O'Farrell is back on the pitch, dribbling the ball. He passes . . ."

Peering up at the screen, she saw Eoghan move effortlessly in his shoes, as did Pippin and Lance and the rest of the team. Eoghan's were special. She'd poured all her creativity into his footwear. The boots fit him like fingered socks, snug, as if they'd become a part of his anatomy. Close, the way she held him to her heart. She knew his feet better than anyone, including him. She knew he could perform in any boot, but she'd crafted the best shoe of her life working with him.

She settled into her seat and called Ayanna, who she'd promised to call before she boarded.

"Hey, girl. You ready to do this?" Ayanna asked.

"Yeah."

"Well, then why do you sound like your soufflé just sank? You're about to get on a plane and get wined and dined by the Portugal team. Even I can get excited about that, even if I don't want to see you leave Ireland."

"I don't know. I worked really hard with the team, and they're playing . . ."

"Oh, the FOMO is real. I know, all Shane is doing is grumbling about missing it while watching TV, and we're here for his interview," Ayanna laughed.

"Yeah . . ." Charlotte trailed off and crossed her legs. She blew on the steam from her coffee before taking a sip. "I guess I wasn't expecting that I would care as much. That wasn't part of the deal."

"Well, you have a good heart, Charlotte. Your ambition doesn't change that. You made some great friends here. One thing that I learned about the Irish is if you get into their heart, they'll cherish you and always welcome you back."

"Are you trying to make me feel better or worse?"

"Umm . . ."

"Yaya?"

"I'm just playing, girl. I'm wishing you luck for sure, but if they are flying you all the way there, then they really want you. You got this, boo."

"Thanks, friend."

A gasp came from the crowd on the screen and in the airport.

"Hang on, Yaya. Something is happening."

Passengers made their way toward the TV, and there was chatter about them. For a New Yorker, hearing gasps in the airport set off a bunch of alarms and flashbacks. Charlotte didn't know when she'd leaped to her feet, but she had, and she moved closer to the TV.

"What's happening?" Yaya asked.

"I don't know yet. I'm trying to find out," Charlotte said. She was only slightly relieved when there wasn't a special news report splashed across the screen and the soccer game still played. That was, until the announcer started to speak.

"Oh no . . . O'Farrell is down. This is disturbing, since he's only been back for a short while since his ACL injury and rehabilitation in America. Could this be another season-ending injury for him? Tough break. Really tough break. Let's listen in."

Charlotte wiggled her way closer to the screen through the crowd that had started to gather to watch the game. She wished that somehow the appliance would turn into a teleportation device. The players surrounded Eoghan, their backs to the activity of the trainers behind them. Her heart pounded, deafening any other information coming from the announcers.

"It's Eoghan," Charlotte choked into her earpiece. "Get up, Eoghan," she whispered.

"Charlotte? Shane says Eoghan is down."

"He's not getting up." Charlotte could hear the panic in her voice. Too much time had passed, and not knowing what Eoghan's status was made her nauseous. She felt for him and all the challenges he'd been through, the choices he'd made, the changes he'd made to be better. He'd been through so much. Being injured again was what he feared the most. And there he was on the ground alone. Was he breathing? Was he in terrible pain? The acid reflux from the Irish coffee told her that she wouldn't be okay until she knew the extent of his injuries.

"Yaya, I gotta go." Charlotte disconnected the call. She grabbed her overnight bag and fled from the airport, grabbed a taxi, and took it to Aviva Stadium.

The leveled stiff blades of grass prickled Eoghan's back like acupressure points. He'd gone down shadowing Lars, a defender on the Liechtenstein team. The fall had knocked the wind right out of him. Fear about his leg should have risen to the surface, but it didn't. If he wanted to play his best, he had to feel the fear and move past it. The game was dangerous. Players got hurt. Some even lost their careers, but not him and not today. Instead, he listened to the sound of the crowd as they rooted for him to be okay, some even praying. He embraced the emotion surrounding him as they sang.

"We have O'Farrell . . ."

"Rest time is over, you lazy hole." Pippin gripped his hand. "The fans are in bits for ya."

"I fucking love these boots," Eoghan said. He just wished that Charlotte were here to see him play.

"Stop flaffin' about. Leg it!" Pippin clapped his gloved hands hard and fast.

Eoghan jumped to his feet and shook his limbs to regain his circulation. The crowd roared and cheered. He'd never thought he'd be excited to get tripped up, banged around, and scuffed up. He knew he meant a lot to his teammates and the fans, and he wanted to play his best game and make them proud.

He felt back to his old self, better, as he ran the ball aggressively and used his speed, agility, and footwork to dart around players and stretch his body to pass the ball. There'd be a lot more scrapes, bumps, and bruises to come.

I'm back.

Charlotte had played a big role in quelling his neurosis and dependence on one element of his uniform to make him feel like he hadn't lost his talent and skill for football. His lack of confidence had been the illness that had tainted his play, and Charlotte had helped build him back up, one event at a time. She was gone. He should have stopped her. Should have told her he loved her. Would it have made a difference? In the end, she'd done what she had told him she would do. She'd confirmed who she was, and he couldn't fault her for that, only for breaking his heart.

Focus. He did what he could control at the moment: focus on the match and bring home the win for Ireland. He dribbled the ball up the middle. He passed the ball and stuck to the player who his instincts told him would get the ball. They knocked into each other, and the referee called it foul. They stopped the clock.

"Come on." Eoghan didn't believe that and wasn't happy with the decision, and he and several other players pleaded their case to no avail.

The opposing team got a free kick, and though one of their players made an attempt to score, Pippin was there, and again, Eoghan was after the ball on the pitch. Lars, who Eoghan ran down, was a great defender, but Eoghan outfoxed him and got the ball back. He dribbled, passed, received it again, and bicycle kicked it into the net. That was the game.

Aviva rocked with roaring cheers. He ran down the pitch into a knee slide, then leaped into the air just as his teammates grabbed him up, smacking his back and rubbing his sweaty head.

Damn, it felt good to be back.

"Be great if Charlotte were here to see her shoes do that," Pippin said.

Yeah, it would.

Ireland won the game one–nil.

Eoghan sat in the pressroom behind a long-clothed table, a microphone inches from his lips. There'd been a long line of players who'd come and gone from the room, but his Q&A was the one everyone had been waiting for.

"Eoghan, how does it feel to make the winning goal?"

"Eoghan, what are your thoughts about Portugal's draw with Russia?"

"Eoghan, how's the leg feeling?"

"Eoghan, has this season been different from last season?"

The press bombarded him with questions like they'd always done after the game. The last few times hadn't been anything he'd looked forward to, but today, the press was kind to him and, at least for a little while, celebrated the win with him. On his way to the dressing rooms to get his bag and head out, he met his father.

After their row at the house, his father had kept his distance, as had Eoghan. Eoghan's confidence had transcended football or dating swag—it had seeped into his most important relationship, the one with his father. He'd finally been able to not only speak his mind but penetrate through to his father because he had another important relationship to protect: the one with Charlotte. His father believed that he was choosing a foreigner over him, that Charlotte had turned his mind against him, but really, all she'd done was give him the confidence to say the things to his father he'd been holding in for years and advocate for himself.

"Didn't expect to see you here," Eoghan said.

"I come to all your games. You know that," his father said.

Eoghan nodded.

"When you went down this time . . ." His father hesitated. "Just making sure you're all right, boy."

For all his rough edges, his father vocalized his concern for him. Not for his career, not for his playing, not for his sponsors. Just for him.

"I'm all right, Da."

"Good. Yer ma wants you over for dinner on Sunday. We'll be here at the apartment to make it easier for ya," his father stated. "She'll be needin' to collect the messages," which was his father's way of asking if they could count on him to show up.

"Sure, I'll be there," he said.

"Great game." His father stretched out his hand to him.

"Thanks, Da." Eoghan took his hand, and his father pulled him into a brief hug. Eoghan choked on the emotion in his throat. He loved his father, even though he'd been a pain as well as a support.

"Love you, boy."

"Love you too, Da."

His father let him go as quickly as he'd hugged him. "Go on with the team, then."

Eoghan wiped the sweat from his face with his hand, sure a few tears had made it in there. He and his father would be okay, and the moment of mutual respect confirmed it.

Eoghan made his way to the loud dressing room elevated with triumphant energy. They'd won against Liechtenstein, and though there was still a way to go before securing their spot in the cup final, he and the team had shown that they were a competitive force to be reckoned with. With his mind and body in sync, there were no more weak links. Just one missing. Charlotte.

Chapter 26

Charlotte stood outside the dressing rooms, wringing her hands and pacing in her heels while she waited for Eoghan. She hadn't seen what had happened to him after he had fallen, but apparently, he was okay enough to finish the rest of the game. That hadn't stopped her from worrying her lip the entire car ride over to Aviva Stadium. She had that same feeling in her stomach as when she experienced bad turbulence. He had made his way into her skin, into her heart, and into her soul. She couldn't shake him. How could she ever have believed that she could leave Ireland—leave him—and be okay?

Eoghan strolled out of the dressing rooms, his hair wet and his clothes clinging to him. His slacks fit him perfectly, and he wore a loose-fitting shirt like he was getting ready to go out. He stopped in his tracks when he saw her, clearly not expecting her to be standing there in her suit with her overnight bag by her feet and purse hanging at her elbow. She loved how he smelled after a shower. His fresh scent and a hint of spice floated to her, licking her as if to remind her of what she'd lost. He recovered within seconds and dragged himself toward her as if pulled by the ear.

"What're you doing here? Thought you had a big job interview in Portugal."

She avoided getting pulled into the miserable disposition he displayed. Surely, she deserved a bit of standoffishness, but she was here for him because he was more important than some damn job in another country. Because here was where she wanted to be—with him.

"Are you all right?" she asked.

He ran his hands down his body. "Yep."

Under normal circumstances, this would be the moment when she gave as good as she got, but she'd come back. That meant something. Couldn't he see that? "I saw you fall, and you didn't get up right away," she said instead. She could feel the worry crinkling her face like it had done when she'd stood with her luggage, about to board the plane. Her chest tightened. "I was worried, Eoghan."

His stare bored into her for a long time, and she again questioned every action she'd taken in the last week. She'd damaged their relationship, broken his trust in her. Left him.

He'd just fixed his mouth to speak when a few players poured out of the dressing rooms.

"Charlotte! You've come back to us," Lance said, and he, Callum, and Patrick surrounded her. "We thought you were going to take the Portugal job. That'd be right shit, but we'd still love ya."

"No," she said firmly and glanced at Eoghan. "I thought that I should go after that job because I didn't want to regret not giving it a try, but my biggest mistake was leaving." Her eyes watered, and she sniffled.

"Okay, give her some space," Eoghan said to his teammates and steered her by the shoulders to someplace more private, which ended up being an en suite to the pressroom.

She leaned against a table and collected herself. Sniveling wouldn't make this any easier. She might have lost Eoghan because she'd been unwilling to course correct and admit that even entertaining the Portugal job wasn't right for her.

"You've come all this way. Have you something to say to me, then? 'Cause I have loads." His soft question made her look up at him instead of at her feet, and the hard glower on his face had softened with curiosity and a touch of concern.

"I'm sorry."

He shifted his stance as if uncomfortable with her words. "What for?"

"I have been doing this all my life, Eoghan. Going after offers and opportunities I thought would help me grow, make me better, seen, and respected for my work. I never wanted to have any regrets haunting me. I'm not good at sacrificing for a relationship."

"I'd never ask you to sacrifice anything for me, Charlotte."

"I know, but the thing is, as a kid, seeing my mom do it, I didn't realize that my mother wasn't saying no to being this great art dealer. She'd always wanted a family. That was her dream. She poured her life, energy, and creativity into me and my father. I've only been looking at it from one side. The side where her industry wanted her expertise, not the smile on her face when she cuddled up with my dad or did my hair or decorated for the holidays or cooked for us. I'd been scared this whole time and replaying this idea I had about her life in my head."

"And now?"

"It was only when I saw you fall and my stomach dropped to my toes that I realized that here was where I wanted to be. You're who I want."

"I messed up, too, Charlotte. I shouldn't have been so demanding. I should have talked to you better and . . . been happy for you and supported you and let you know that no matter what, I'd love you. I was just so . . ." He placed his hand on his heart. "I want you with me, darlin'. When you left, you took my heart with you."

She couldn't contain her emotions anymore. She was done. Her shoulders shook, and big mascara-inked droplets wet her face and Valentino shirt. "I love you." She stumbled to him, falling into his open arms, bawling into his chest. She locked her arms around his waist and sank into the warmth of his body that she'd thought she'd never feel again.

He kissed the top of her forehead. "I love you too, Char." His mouth found hers. "Always, love," he mumbled against her lips. Their kiss deepened, their tongues playing and wrestling with desperate strokes.

Eoghan brought her close to him. In this new light and in her acceptance of her love for him, his touch sparked fire within. Her worry and anxiety over him had created an adrenaline rush that crashed, and she felt drugged. Heat coursed through her, and she wanted him more than ever. She needed to be as close to him as possible. As her body felined along his limbs, she felt his rising desire against her lower abdomen. She needed him too.

"Jaysus, I'll get fined if we're caught, but I have to have you, Char," he said, his lips mushing hers. "I have to have you now." His hand traveled down her back and farther to her ass. His fingers curved across the underside of her ass to touch and lightly massage her pussy through her clothes.

She moaned. "I need you too, Eoghy," she said, her backside pushing against his exploring fingers. She shrugged out of her jacket and pulled up her skirt. Eoghan yanked down her blouse and with it her bra, and her breast popped out, close to his waiting mouth.

"Why do you always wear these damn things," he said, pinching the material of her tights from her thigh and in between gobbling her flesh and sucking on her nipple.

Her throaty laugh was wild with desire. "Well, see, I was going on a plane, and it gets cold—"

He bit her hardened nipple, cutting her off.

She leaped out of her tights and shoes. Partially free from the confines of her clothes, she quickly found her back on a long press table as Eoghan's strong arms lifted her and frantically put her in position to completely torture her.

She propped herself up on her elbow to see him pull his shirt out of his pants, and when he undid his pants, the clanking of his belt buckle delighted her as to what was to come.

"Please, Eoghy." She reached for his dick as it popped out of his pants. "Let me suck you," she begged. He stepped back, and she scrambled off the table and to her knees, where she swallowed him, sucking wildly and salivating for his taste. She moaned, and her pussy ached. She slid one hand between her legs, playing with herself as she throated him.

Eoghan huffed, close to arrival. She wanted him to come in her mouth, to taste his love for her and swallow him into her, but Eoghan withdrew and bent down to get her.

"I want you to come, Eoghan," she whined.

"I will, baby." He lovingly pulled her up and back onto the table. "Inside you. But not yet."

She reached for him, delirious from desire. Eoghan's head dipped down and disappeared between her thighs.

"Feck, Charlotte, you're absolutely gushing for me." He licked her slit and, with it, her slick arousal. His tongue fluttered over her clit, and his tantalizing sucking was soon accompanied by his expert fingers fucking.

"Eoghy. Fuck. I can't take it! Please. Send me over, baby!" Her legs locked him in.

"Your taste is lovely, sweetheart," he said. "Tell me how good it feels, love."

"Yes. You feel so good, Eoghy." She reached for his head.

"I'm going to fuck you to County Monaghan, Charlotte."

"Promise me," she demanded.

"I fucking promise."

"Now," she demanded.

"Condom," he mumbled against her pussy.

"Fuck! My bag." She pointed frantically. "I think there is one in my bag."

She heard him rummaging through her bag.

"Hurry up!" she half laughed, half cried. Straining her neck, she watched his perfect ass. "I need you."

"I'm coming," he growled. He returned to her and nestled between her legs, quickly and noisily unwrapping the condom and slipping it down his gorgeous dick. "I'm here, love," he said and sank into her. "Fuck, Charlotte, I'm here."

She dissolved into the table, weak from the glorious feel of him hitting every inch of her insides. She crunched up to grab him and dragged him on top of her.

He climbed on, slamming into her, humping her to a high she'd never experienced. This was what it felt like to love him completely.

"I love you with all of me, Eoghy," she panted, holding him with so much strength her arms hurt.

His eyes met hers, and his desire and love penetrated her so deeply that she couldn't control the tears that started to flow.

"You're everything to me, Charlotte. I love you with everything I have." His speed increased, hitting the spots that drove her wild.

"Eoghan," she whimpered, teetering on the edge of madness.

"Yes, Char. Come for me, my love!"

She shook and bucked against Eoghan, whose speed ramped up before he shouted his ecstasy into her mouth as they kissed, moaning, breathing, and drooling their love. He sank onto her and rested. She could barely breathe from his deadweight, and she wouldn't have it any other way.

"You all right?" he lifted enough to ask her, his arms framing her shoulders as one hand stroked over her forehead and down her cheek.

"Never better," she said in shallow breaths.

He climbed off the table and brought her up.

He tucked his shirt back in his pants.

"I ruined your shirt." She sniffled, smoothing his chest and the smudge stains from her tear-soaked mascara on his light-colored shirt.

"Yes, and you look like an absolute disaster." He laughed, stroking her cheek with his thumb and nuzzling his nose with hers. "But I love ya."

Epilogue

Easter

One thing that Charlotte had learned was that next to Saint Patrick's Day, Easter was the most popular holiday in Ireland. Between Eoghan, Shane, and Pippin, they gathered their family and friends for a big celebration at the house of Shane's parents, Nadine and Conor. In addition to celebrating the holiday, they celebrated the national team qualifying for World Cup. The excitement for the team, and of course the thrill that only a World Cup year could provide, had already filled the streets of the country, especially since Northern Ireland's national team also qualified.

Charlotte had long since stopped bringing up history about Northern Ireland and why there were two separate national teams, but Pippin had quietly told her to never ask that question in public. He, Eoghan, and Shane, as well as their parents, were helpful in sharing their knowledge with her. She still had so much to learn.

Danai scrolled through his phone.

"What are you looking at so hard?" Charlotte asked.

"I was trying to read a little bit about dual citizenship—that was until I spotted Jada on social wearing somebody's Romeo Hunte double-breasted black leather jacket."

"What?" Charlotte exclaimed and snatched Danai's phone. "No, she didn't."

"Yes, Mama, she did, and she is living in it," Danai enunciated.

"Wait till I see her." Charlotte had told Jada to stay away from her clothes when she'd let her stay in the Harlem apartment.

Pippin moseyed over at the commotion and looked at Danai's phone. "Who's that?" he asked.

"Jada. Ayanna's sister."

"Oh no, not that one," Pippin said. "She's a vile little thing, isn't she?"

"Yes, that one. And this one vile little thing is lucky she's in Harlem, or else I'd whup her little narrow behind," Charlotte said.

"I dunno what that means," Pippin said, "but it sounds painful." He moved on, nicking a slice of bread off the table.

"Are we ever going to eat? All this food looks so good," Danai said of the large table filled with all the Easter fixings. He munched on a creamed chocolate egg.

Charlotte could relate as she gawked at the spread of mussels in Irish cider, roast lamb with cabbage and peas, Irish creamed kale, both Irish soda bread and Guinness bread, and a lemon-marshmallow cake along with lots of Easter candies and chocolate on the dessert table. As she drooled, she felt a hand on her waist and turned to Eoghan. "Hey, Chief," she said, calling him by his public nickname, and pecked his lips.

"Leave some room. We're still to hit the pubs later on," Eoghan said.

"As in plural?" Charlotte asked.

"It's only fitting to make the rounds." Eoghan winked at her. "Anyway, my ma's looking for you. Something about a shoe of yours that Ayanna keeps going on about that she can run in," he said.

"Yes. I had Danai order a pair for her. I should go tell her when they'll be here."

Eoghan smiled at her.

"Now, don't go getting all weepy on me because me and your ma are friends now," Charlotte said.

He looked at her with those fuck-me eyes that she loved, and had they not been in a room full of their friends and family, she'd have been delighted to take him up on the offer his eyes were dishing out.

Charlotte was on her way to find Grace when she heard a piercing scream and knew immediately it was Ayanna. She and Eoghan locked eyes, and Charlotte led the way as they ran to see what the commotion was about.

"What was that?" they were asked as they followed the sound.

"Yaya is screaming." Charlotte didn't know if it was good or bad, but she sped to her friend with others in the house hot on her trail.

Outside, Charlotte spotted Ayanna and Shane a fair distance away. Whatever was wrong had caused her friend to scream louder than she'd ever heard. As Charlotte neared, she spotted Yaya with her arms anchored around Shane's neck and her legs locked around Shane's waist. They were embraced in a wicked kiss that made Charlotte blush. As Shane spun her friend, Charlotte noticed the evening sun reflecting off Ayanna's hand.

"No way!" Charlotte ran closer, as did Eoghan. They stopped a few feet away so that neither Ayanna nor Shane knocked them over. Ayanna jumped down off him and ran to her.

"He proposed to me!" Ayanna showed her a beautiful circular-cut diamond. The quality had to be at least VS2; Charlotte had memorized them when she'd requested a Tiffany catalog.

"You got sparkly. You're for real booed up now." Charlotte cheered, then turned to Shane, who beamed, his eyes red with emotion. Charlotte was over the moon that her favorite couple, with the exception of herself and Eoghan, had gotten engaged. Shane was so in love with her friend that Charlotte could only imagine what he'd said. By the tears flowing down Yaya's face, he'd done well. Charlotte smothered Yaya in a hug and gave Shane the thumbs-up behind her back. She watched as Eoghan hugged his friend.

"You know you're my maid of honor. Both you and Jada, of course."

"Of course. I'm not even mad at that," Charlotte said. "But you know Jada is going to sulk about it."

"We'll deal with her when she gets here."

"So you want to have the wedding here?" Charlotte said, imagining all the amazing locations that Ayanna could have the wedding.

Ayanna nodded.

"This is going to be bananas." Charlotte hugged her friend again.

As everyone traipsed back into the house, Eoghan held her hand to stop her from going in. She turned to him, and he pulled her into a kiss.

"What was that for?" she asked.

"To let you know how happy you make me, love," Eoghan said. He was such a sap when they were alone, which made the words even more special.

"I'm happy too"—Charlotte took a quick look around—"Eoghy."

He laughed, intertwined his fingers with hers, and brought her hand up and kissed it. She nuzzled her head against his and tilted her face up for a kiss, which Eoghan quickly obliged. Together they'd made it past the red flags and fear that had nearly stopped them finding the kind of joy in love they now shared. They sat down for dinner, and as Charlotte looked around at the table, she realized that the place didn't make a home. It was the people in her life, and they all just happened to be in Ireland. And that was fine by her.

ACKNOWLEDGMENTS

First and foremost, I thank God for His gifts and blessings.

I cannot express enough thanks to the wonderful and fabulous Sarah E. Younger for always giving me her best, no matter what. A heartfelt thank-you goes out to Maria Gomez for managing my books with respect, vision, and most of all, lots of fun, especially when choosing covers! Thank you to Andrea Hurst for again helping to hone the best book possible. And a big thank-you to Amazon Montlake and the extraordinary team for all your support throughout the process. You make the rest easy.

I couldn't have done any of this without the love and support of my family and friends who, during a difficult year, showed me such generosity and care. You've helped me find balance and acceptance, so that I may still live my dream. I'd be lost without you.

Last, but not least, you readers rock—thank you for receiving the Passion Players series with overwhelming excitement. I hope, whether in real life or through my books, that you are always surrounded by love and find your own happy endings.

ABOUT THE AUTHOR

Photo © 2021 Leah Yanachek Photography

JN Welsh is a native New Yorker. She writes juicy, soulful romances about strong, career-driven, multicultural heroines of color who are looking for love. Her punchy, entertaining dialogue and big-city stories are heartwarming, provocative, often humorous, and delicious. She's passionate about practicing mindfulness for body and spirit through a holistic approach to self-care, routines, and rituals. When she's not writing, she can be found being a good steward of the earth, dancing, streaming her favorite shows, baking, and looking for ways to bring joy to the people she loves.